學熱門關鍵字、和老外聊時事

What's up

之後
說什麼

最適合台灣大人的英文會話集

Contents

財金英文輕鬆學
Finance & Economics

政治英文面面觀
Politics

國際頭條這樣學
World Headlines

社會時事開口說
Society & Life

Contents

教育文化簡單聊

Education & Culture

影視運動談八卦

Entertainment & Sports

知識補充

Chapter
One

Finance &
Economics
財　　經
英文面面觀

從戰後初期，台灣經歷了進口替代時期、出口導向時期、十大建設黃金時期；領導人從蔣經國、李登輝、陳水扁到馬英九，各為台灣創立不同政治風氣；經濟狀況也從亞洲四小龍，到現在萎靡不振。台灣人拼死拼活也買不起一間台北市的小套房，卻還是只能看著政黨惡鬥、總統貪污、食安風暴、建商弊案每天不斷重播，比《大長今》重播次數還多。這樣的日子已經變成我們的生活、變成我們聊天的話題，學好這些英文，為自己開創更多的可能性，才可以在辦公室隨意說出 This mornig TSMC climbed ten percent, and United Micro Electronics advanced three percent.（今早台積電股價跳升了百分之十，而聯電漲了百分之三。）這種句子，說不定不經意被老闆聽到你英文這麼溜，派你跟廠商開會，年終獎金馬上多 3 個月唷！

Playing the Stock Market
反覆無常地雷股

trans-action 交易

transaction 指任一種「交易、買賣」；此字跟經常搞混的 trade 不同，trade 指公司對公司的「貿易、商業交易」。

新聞這樣說

Google's new mobile phone payment service, Android Pay, will not garner any transaction fees from credit card compa-nies, which may put pressure on competitor Apple to drop or lower its charges, the Wall Street Journal reported.

華爾街日報指出，Google 新推出的手機付費系統 Android Pay 將不會對信用卡公司收任何交易費用，而這可能會對其競爭對手 Apple 造成壓力，因而取消或降低收費。

內線交易 insider trading

形容詞 inside 加上名詞字尾 -er，變成了解機密情報、消息靈通的內幕人士。insider trading 指透過內幕人士操盤而進行牟利的交易。

新聞這樣說

Taiwan authorities are investigating possible insider trading linked to the planned $3.8 billion merger of MediaTek Inc. and MStar Semiconductor Inc., companies that produce 70 percent of the chips used in TVs.

聯發科技以及晨星半導體製造全台超過 70% 的電視晶片，其合併案金額高達 38 億，而台灣相關單位正在調查其中可能的內線交易。

漲價 price hike

hike 一般指登山遠足，口語上則可特指物價、稅率、薪資等猛然抬高、上漲的情況。

新聞這樣說

While everyone seems to be whining about how poor they have become, the island's national resources seems to be unfalteringly on the rise. Costs have gone up time after time this year, from gas prices to salad oil prices, toilet paper to sticky rice. This time the coming of the new year isn't welcoming in a new beginning but is instead welcoming in a new round of inflation.

大家都在喊窮的時候，民生物資卻不斷喊漲。今年連續好幾波的漲價，從汽油、沙拉油、衛生紙到糯米都漲。新的一年要迎接的不是新的開始，而是另一波全面的通膨。

股市大漲 stock market boom

boom 是爆炸的聲音，用來形容經濟時，則指「繁榮、景氣好」。 反之，「衰退、不景氣」英文則是 slump。

新聞這樣說

The lifting of the SARS-related travel warning to Taiwan, the gradual turn-around of the American stock market, and the revaluation of the New Taiwanese Dollar have all contributed to Taiwan's stock market boom. Investors finally have a reason to smile.

台灣解除 SARS 旅遊警戒、美股逐漸升溫、新台幣升值等消息，讓台股大漲。投資人終於笑得出來了！

投資人 investor

將動詞 invest「投資、入股」加上名詞字尾-or，就變成「出資者、投資人」的意思。

新聞這樣說

From 1988 to May this year, Taiwan businesses invested US$28.66 billion in Vietnam, making Taiwan the fourth largest foreign investor in the Southeast Asian country.

自 1988 年起至今年 5 月，台灣已在越南投資超過美金 286 億，讓台灣成為全東南亞第 4 大投資國家。

炒作（投機） speculate

speculate 為「揣測」的意思，投資市場上投機買賣也可用這個字。speculation 指的便是「投機買賣」。

新聞這樣說

China's stock regulator has launched a fresh probe into brokerages which are lending money to investors to speculate on stocks, amid concerns that the country's share markets are becoming over-leveraged and vulnerable to a crash which could strain the banking system.

中國股票專家正試著檢視新的一項嘗試，也就是出借手續費讓投資者炒作股票，因為他們擔心中國股市過多放貸，可能會造成崩盤。

泡沫化 bubble

常見用法有經濟泡沫化 economic bubble，房地產泡沫化 real estate bubble、股市泡沫化 stock market bubble 等。價格哄抬過高而導致泡沫化這樣的循環稱為 boom and bust cycle。

新聞這樣說

Tsinghua Unigroup Ltd (紫光集團) chairman Zhao Weiguo (趙偉國), who became a billionaire buying semiconductor companies, said the industry has entered a"serious bubble"in China.

以收購半導體公司致富的紫光集團總裁趙偉國表示，股市產業在中國已嚴重泡沫化。

com-pound interest

循環利息

compound 是「混合、合成」的意思，interest 是利息。循環利息以連本帶利方式計算利息。本金的英文則是 principal。

新聞這樣說

Credit cards are a part of daily life, appearing on TV and in Internet ads all the time. The beautiful ads make it seem as if the cash is coming from heaven, when in fact, paying late can land you into a hell of high compound interest.

信用卡已經變成日常生活的一部份，隨時隨地都會出現在電視、網路廣告中。美好的廣告讓人以為錢會從天上掉下來，但事實上，延遲還款就會讓你墜入高循環利息的地獄之中。

股票漲跌怎麼說

談股票最基本的字不外就是「漲」up 或「跌」down。如果你曾經聽過 CNN 財經新聞，主播們也常用 higher 跟 lower 這兩個字，例如「今天一開盤就上漲」，主播就會說：The stock opened higher. 如果是「收盤時下跌」則是 The stock closed lower。翻開晚報也常會看到股價「逐步上揚」或是「逐步走低」等詞彙，這時可以用 be trading higher / lower 或 be moving higher / lower 來表示。

主播報導股市時，為了力求變化性，他們會用到許多不同的動詞來形容漲跌，關於漲的動詞，最常用的有像 climb、gain、advance 或是 rise，如果是漲幅較大時，則可以用 surge、soar 或是 jump，讓人在使用上比較活潑有趣。下跌也有許多的選擇，例如 shed、slip、drop、fall、decline 及 dip，另外如果跌幅很大，則用 sink，正好跟 jump 相呼應。此外，遇到較大的跌幅，例如台灣股市一天之內跌了六百多點，這種崩盤式的下跌，你不能只用 slide 或是 drop 來形容，這樣子是無法盡情形容那種恨意的。此時可以用 plunge 和 plummet 表達才夠力。

示範對話 (MP3 02)

股票投資碰運氣

Dave: Did you get a year-end bonus, too?
妳也有拿到年終獎金嗎？

Anna: Sure did. Two months! They didn't [1]stiff the foreigners this time.
當然有。兩個月！他們這次沒有把外國人排除在外。

Dave: That's good. I felt bad for you last time. So what are you going to do with it?
那很好。上一次我為妳感到遺憾。那妳要怎麼用這筆錢？

Anna: I think I'm going to invest it in the stock market and get rich.
我想我要投入股市致富。

Dave: Are you sure you know what you're doing? Our markets are really [2]volatile.
妳真的行嗎？這裡的股市非常反覆無常。

Anna: Yes, I know. Prices [3]skyrocketing and then [4]plummeting.
對，我知道。股價爆漲然後又重跌。

Dave: You should be careful with your investments.
妳應該多留意妳的投資。

Anna: This is a bonus, so I'm willing to speculate with it.
這是獎金，所以我願意投機一下。

Dave: If you're going to just throw your money away, you might as well give it to me to invest.
如果妳要這樣灑錢，還不如交給我投資。

Anna: Where would you invest it?
你會投資在哪裡？

Dave: Probably traditional blue chips like Formosa Plastics and China Steel.
大概一些傳統績優股，像是台塑跟中鋼。

Anna: I think I want to ⁵⁾try my luck with ⁶⁾tech stocks.
我想我要買科技股碰碰運氣。

Dave: Those are the most volatile of all.
那是所有股票中最不穩的。

Anna: I know. I ⁷⁾lived through the ⁸⁾Internet bubble in the late 90s, remember?
我知道。我從九〇年代末期的網路泡沫存活下來了，記得嗎？

Dave: Yes, when everyone went crazy. No one was thinking long-term.
是啦，那時候大家都瘋了。那時沒人看好長期。

Anna: But isn't that true of Taiwanese investors ⁹⁾in general?
不過一般的台灣投資人不都是這樣嗎？

1. stiff (v.)（錢）少給、不給
2. volatile (a.) 不穩的，波動的
3. skyrocket (v.) 猛漲，突然高升
4. plummet (v.) 猛降
5. try one's luck (phr.) 某人要碰碰運氣
6. tech (a.) 高科技的，technology 的簡稱
7. live through (phr.) 活過
8. Internet (n.) 網際網路
9. in general (phr.) 一般來說

好用短句　(MP3 03)

看股市
你還可以說

· The stock market will go up tomorrow for sure.

明天股市肯定會向上攻堅。

· This morning *TSMC climbed ten percent, and United Micro Electronics advanced three percent.

早上台積電的股價跳升了百分之十，而聯電漲了百分之三。

· The Taiwan stock market was down across the board today.

今日台股全面下跌。

· News of the 9/11 attacks caused the stock market to collapse.

九一一攻擊事件造成股市崩盤。

· Lots of investors think the stock market is due for a correction.

許多投資者認為股市必須重新改正。

*TSMC「台灣積體電路製造股份有限公司」Taiwan Semiconductor Manufacturing Company 的縮寫

Where's my year-end bonus?!
年終獎金在哪裡？

報稅　file taxes

file 可當動詞「提出申請、訴訟」解釋。常見的 tax 有：income tax「所得稅」、sales tax「營業稅」、gift tax「贈與稅」等。

新聞這樣說

It's tax-filing season! Because of SARS, the Junior High School Basic Scholastic Subject Exam, the Golden Melody Awards, and various computer exhibitions have all been postponed. Alas, only tax filing goes on as usual.

報稅的季節又到啦！今年因為 SARS，國中學力測驗、金曲獎、電腦展都紛紛延期，只有報稅還是照常進行。

國民年金　national pension

pension 前加上 national「國家的」，特指國家發給勞工的補助津貼，是身為中華民國國民的「國民福利」national benefits 之一。

新聞這樣說

Sweet words just roll off the tongues of politicians when elections draw near. The DPP is promising national pension payments of NT$7,500 if the pan-greens win a majority, while the pan-blues are promising NT$15,000 if they win. With all this BS flying, it's no wonder that people complain that resisting the Japanese was easier than the campaign to win pensions will be.

選舉一到，政治人物再好聽的話都說得出口！民進黨提出只要泛綠過半，國民年金發放七千五百元，藍軍則提泛藍過半發放一萬五千元。藍綠雙方為了當選不惜亂開支票，難怪有人說，台灣人要領到國民年金比八年抗戰還難。

水電費　water and electricity bills

bill 可同時當名詞「帳單」及動詞「開帳單」解釋。電力除了 electricity，也可說 power。

新聞這樣說

The Ministry of Economic Affairs (MOEA) yesterday announced plans to raise electricity rates on all sectors by between 8 and 37 percent to reflect soaring energy costs and curb losses at state-run Taiwan Power Co.

經濟部昨日宣佈將全面調漲水電費 8 ％~37 ％以反映持續升高的能源消耗，並遏阻國營台電的損失。

尾牙 year-end dinner

year-end 兩個字加起來是「年終」的意思。現在的尾牙都伴隨許多抽獎、表演活動,因此也可稱作 year-end party。

新聞這樣說

Big-name companies have big-name year-end dinners. Hundreds of high-class cars and millions of company shares are raffled off to the employees, as big-name stars croon away and the media broadcasts live on-site. As the year ends, the only news is good news, and struggling companies are ignored.

知名企業的尾牙,動輒百萬名車、千萬股票大抽獎,要不就是知名藝人的勁歌熱舞,SNG 還實況轉播。每年尾牙,就是只見幾家歡樂,卻不見幾家愁的時刻。

加薪公務員 pay increase for civil servants

公務員的英文是 civil servant,civil 是「公民的」,而 servant 則是「獻身服務者」,兩字合起來便是「公僕」。也可說是 government employee「政府的員工」。

新聞這樣說

Even though the government is broke, civil servants are getting raises. Why? Unlike raises at normal companies, it's not because business has increased, or work performance has improved, or because workloads have gotten heavier. The only reason for their raise is that they haven't had one in three years.

雖然政府沒錢,但公務員確定要加薪了。加薪的理由跟一般民間企業不同,不是因為業績增加,不是因為表現優良,也不是因為責任變得更重。唯一的理由就是他們已經三年沒加薪了。

勞退新制 new retirement pension policy

新聞這樣說

The new retirement pension policy is about to be implemented, but nearly 70% of workers still don't understand it. And even more people are worried that employers will use it as an excuse to lower salaries or lay off workers. Actually, the new and old policies each have their own benefits. Regardless, unless the government can effectively supervise whether or not employers are lawfully implementing the policy, it won't make any difference how good the policy is.

新的勞工退休津貼制度即將施行,但卻有將近七成的勞工對新制仍然不了解,更多人擔心雇主會藉機變相減薪或裁員。新舊制其實各有好處,若是政府沒有確實監督雇主依法執行,即使這個政策再好也沒用。

pension 是員工在薪資以外,因年資、表現、受傷等原因,另可獲得的補助津貼、退休金。「發退休金」這個動詞也可用此字表示。

免稅 tax exemp-tion

免除履行某責任義務，獲得豁免權，英文可用 exempt 這個動詞；也可直接說 free from…、deliver from…。exemption 則是它的名詞。

新聞這樣說

Everyone says ROC taxes are high, but there are two kinds of citizens who used to be exempt from taxation—soldiers and teachers. But times changed, and the old reasons for their exemptions became irrelevant. In the interest of fairness and increased tax revenues, everyone who has an income now has to pay taxes.

大家都說中華民國萬萬稅，可是中華民國曾有兩種人不用繳稅——軍人跟老師。不過由於時代變遷，當初政府給予這兩種職業免稅待遇的原因已不再。為了符合公平並增加稅收，現在在台灣，除非你沒收入，否則大家都要繳稅。

擴大就業方案 policy to lower unemployment

employment 是「有工作、就業」的意思，前面加上代表相反的字首-un，就變成「失業」。lower 則是降低。要注意，英文習慣用「降低失業」來表達增加就業。

新聞這樣說

The recent policy to lower the unemployment rate in Taiwan isn't quite "alive and kicking." The first job offered to unemployed citizens is tomb sweeping for public cemeteries. Most unemployed citizens are reluctant to consider keeping the "homes of the dead" a great employment opportunity.

最近的擴大就業方案實施得並不怎麼順利。釋出給失業者的第一份工作是打掃公墓，但多數失業市民並不認為看管死者的住所是個很棒的工作機會。

尾牙兩樣情

年終尾牙或春酒是每位台灣上班族愛恨交織的日子，如果當天抽中最大獎就是辛苦一年的大確幸；若是什麼都沒抽到，還被逼著要準備表演節目，無奈只能下台後猛灌玫瑰紅，忘記剛剛發生的一切。在西方國家，尾牙、春酒是大多是以 annual party 的形式舉辦，或是直接以 Christmas party 為一年劃下句點。annual party 通常是員工共同分擔金額，或是大家都準備一道菜，一起吃個晚餐。酒水類當然是不會少，外國人也是會需要借由玫瑰紅來忘記老闆的一切，但差別是台上不太會有變裝唱跳的驚世同事們。

示範對話　(MP3 05)

年終小確幸

Merle: You sure are buying a lot. You get a big Chinese New Year
¹⁾bonus?
你買得還真多。年終獎金拿很多嗎？

Marvin: Just a little bit. How about you?
一點點而已。妳呢？

Merle: My company totally ²⁾ripped us all off this year. We only got
two thousand NT each.
我的公司今年騙了我們所有人。我們每人才拿到兩千元。

Marvin: I'm sorry to hear that. I guess that was since the ³⁾economy is
not doing so well?
我很遺憾聽到這種事。我想這都是因為經濟不景氣吧？

Merle: No, our company has a ⁴⁾moron for a ⁵⁾manager. We've been
⁶⁾on the verge of ⁷⁾bankruptcy for years.
不，是我們公司有個白痴經營者。我們瀕臨破產邊緣已經好久了。

Marvin: Have you ⁸⁾considered ⁹⁾switching jobs?
妳有想過要換工作嗎？

Merle: Of course I have, but good jobs aren't as easy to find as you might think.
當然想過，但是好工作沒有想像中好找。

Marvin: I guess you may have a husband and family to consider, too.
我想妳還得顧慮到老公跟家人。

Merle: [10]And then some. So, are you from the U.S.? Do companies there give year-end bonuses, too?
還不只咧。你是從美國來的？那邊的公司也會發年終獎金嗎？

Marvin: Some do, but I don't think it's as common as it is here. And we get them around Christmas, not Chinese New Year.
有些會，不過我不覺得像這邊這麼普遍。而且我們都是耶誕節那時領，不是農曆新年。

Merle: Of course. Which state are you from? I heard that if you live in Alaska, you get a thousand dollars every year.
當然。你來自哪一州？我聽說要是你住在阿拉斯加，每年都可以領一千美元。

Marvin: That must be because they have so much [11]oil money. I'm from [12]Pennsylvania, so I wouldn't know.
那一定是因為他們有很多石油收入。我來自賓州，所以我不知道。

Merle: With my company doing badly, maybe we should all just move to the [13]North Pole.
我們公司經營這麼差，也許我們全都該搬去北極算了。

Marvin: Do say hello to the polar bears for me, if you go.
如果妳去的話，幫我跟北極熊打聲招呼。

---

1. bonus (n.) 獎金，紅利。
2. rip off (v.) 欺騙，騙取
3. economy (n.) 經濟
4. moron (n.) 白痴，低能者
5. manager (n.) 經營者，經理。
6. on the verge of… 瀕臨…，即將…
7. bankruptcy (n.) 破產，倒閉
8. consider (v.) 考慮
9. switch (v.) 換。
10. And then some. 還有更多。
11. oil (n.) 這邊是指「石油」
12. Pennsylvania (n.) 賓夕凡尼亞州
13. North Pole 北極

好用短句 (MP3 06)

談年終獎金
你還可以說

· Some government-run businesses are giving out year-end bonuses of up to twenty months worth of pay.

有些國營事業的年終獎金高達二十個月的薪水。

· But most private companies are only giving one or two months worth.

但多數的私人公司卻只發一、二個月。

· And some don't give anything at all.

有些甚至根本不發。

· About forty percent of the working population thinks that one to two months pay is a reasonable bonus.

有四成左右的上班族認為要拿一至兩個月的年終獎金才算合理。

· Fifty percent say they'll think about switching jobs if their bonuses aren't sufficient.

如果獎金不夠，則有五成的上班族會考慮換工作。

· Bonuses are most important to the 26-30 year old demographic, two-thirds of whom say they'd leave over insufficient bonuses.

二十六至三十歲的人最在乎年終獎金，其中有三分之二會因為年終太少而離職。

Cross-Strait Service Trade Agreement
服貿事件

Hit! 話題單字 (MP3 07)

legality
合法性

也可說 legitimacy，指事件的合法性、正統性。口語用法是 legit。

新聞這樣說

Tainan residents fighting a running battle against the municipal government over plans to demolish their homes to make way for a railway project said they would appeal a court decision that sided with an environmental impact report's legality.

台南居民長期抗爭市政府徵收土地建造鐵路，並表示一定會上訴抗議其環保合法性。

契約 pact

雙方同意的協議，跟 agreement 同義但稍微正式的說法。更有拘束力的「合約」英文則是 contract。

新聞這樣說

The protesters moved in after ruling party lawmakers said a review of the pact by a joint committee was concluded. The protesters, who burst into the chamber late on Tuesday, say the agreement with China would hurt Taiwan's economy and leave it vulnerable to pressure from Beijing.

在執政黨立法委員宣布協議已經通過委員會審查、確立後，抗議者隨即湧入。抗議者在週二稍晚佔領議會，並聲明這件與中國的協定將傷害台灣經濟體，且讓北京更易對台灣施壓。

黑箱作業 black-box operation

指組織決議過程非透明化。另一個長得很像的英文 black operations，則指部隊的「秘密行動」。

新聞這樣說

No "black-box" operations were involved in negotiations over the cross-strait service trade agreement, a Taiwanese official told foreign officials on Wednesday during a briefing on the controversial pact.

在週三一場關於此備受爭議的協定的會議上，一名台灣官員向國際官員表示，兩岸服貿協議的協商過程中，絕無黑箱作業。

太陽花運動

Sunflower Student Movement

也稱為 318 學運，因兩天內送給在場學生打氣的 1300 朵太陽花而得名。此學運當時更以 Democracy at 4 am「凌晨四點的民主」為題，刊登於《紐約時報》週末廣告，向世界提出學運的民主訴求。

新聞這樣說

Sunflower Student Movement leader Lin Fei-fan and noted legal scholar K.C. Huang are among 22 people named in a lawsuit by the Taipei District Prosecutors Office for offences committed during the three-week occupation of Taiwan's parliament, which successfully blocked a controversial trade services pact with the mainland.

太陽花學運領導人林飛帆以及知名法律學者黃國昌在內的 22 人，將佔領立法院長達三週的罪行受台北地檢署起訴。此佔領行動成功擋下與中國倍受爭議的服貿協定。

立法院

Legislative Yuan

legitimacy「合法性」的形容詞 legislative，加上 Yuan，即為立法院。有時英文報導也會以 parliament「國會」來稱呼立法院。

新聞這樣說

Hung, who was vitriolic in her opposition to the Sunflower Movement's occupation of the Legislative Yuan, has also complained that controversial changes to school curricula, which present more China-centric material, are not going far enough.

立法院副院長洪秀柱除了立場鮮明的譴責太陽花學運霸佔立法院的行為，也批評備受爭議的新教綱（較偏向中國立場）不夠突破。

非政府組織機構

NGO

全稱為 non-governmental organization，不屬於任何政府或國家，是具社會政策導向的非營利組織（non-profit organization）。常見的有人權團體、環境或動物保護組織，以及社會福利團體等。

新聞這樣說

Two buildings constructed in Nepal with funds from the Taiwan chapter of an NGO will be inaugurated in late April, providing classrooms and dormitories for Nepalese orphans, according to the Taipei-based World League for Freedom and Democracy (WLFD).

根據臺北世界自由民主總會，兩座由非政府組織台灣分會出資的建築將在四月下旬開幕，提供尼泊爾孤兒教室、宿舍等設施。

爭議 controversy

指引起議論的事情。contro- 或 contra- 皆為表示「反對」的字首。形容詞是 controversial。

新聞這樣說

A China-based Taiwanese businesswoman raised controversy with her suggestion to KMT Chairman Eric Chu that, to ensure Taiwan's future, he should disregard other voices in Taiwan, and just focus on further cooperation between the KMT and the Chinese Communist Party.

一名中國台商的言論引起爭議，她告訴國民黨黨主席朱立倫，為了台灣未來好，應該要不顧台灣人民不同的意見，專注在國民黨和中國共產黨進一步的合作。

鼓吹 advocate

倡導、宣傳的意思。ad- 為字首「傾向、增加」，voc- 則是「呼叫」。

新聞這樣說

Analyst Bill Sharp of Hawaii-Pacific University said the DPP is walking a tightrope trying to keep both Washington and the mainland happy, not pull any surprises and not advocate independence.

夏威夷太平洋大學學者 Bill Sharp 表示，民進黨目前政策有如走鋼索般危險，一方面欲討好華府、一方面欲討好中國，且不主張獨立和一些出奇不意的立場聲明。

東西花朵學運

花朵革命：
又稱「色彩革命」，是指 20 世紀末期，在前蘇聯控制地區、中亞獨立國協、東歐地區陸續發展的和平爭取獨立、民主抗爭，由於在這一系列的民主運動命潮中，非政府組織、學生組織占有非常重要的角色，因此皆以顏色或花朵命名。

鬱金香革命：
2005 年中亞吉爾吉斯共和國的鬱金香革命，推翻了貪污且專制的前總統 Askar Akayev 的政權及其所有親戚的掌控。其名稱源自於被推翻的前總統一次公開談話，提到了吉爾吉斯不可能會發生「花朵革命」，示威者以及全球媒體便刻意以春天時節開滿吉爾吉斯山區的鬱金香，為此次革命命名。

茉莉革命：
2010 年，突尼西亞人民再也忍受不了總統 Zine El Abidine Ben Ali 政權造成的高失業率、通貨膨脹、貪污以及缺乏政治與言論自由的生活，加上水果攤販 Mohamed Bouazizi 因被貪污警察沒收水果及羞辱，憤而自焚身亡，以國花命民的茉莉花革命正式展開。

示範對話　　(MP3 08)

太陽花學運

Keith: What's the deal with all those students [1]occupying the legislature?
那些學生為什麼要佔領立法院啊?

Daisy: They're part of the Sunflower [2]Movement.
他們是太陽花學運的一部分。

Keith: The Sunflower Movement? What are they [3]protesting?
太陽花學運? 他們反對的是什麼?

Daisy: They're protesting against the cross-Strait service pact the government signed with China last year.
他們反對政府和中國去年簽定的兩岸服貿協定。

Keith: Is that some kind of free trade agreement?
那是一種自由貿易協定嗎?

Daisy: Yes. It's aimed at [4]liberalizing trade in services between China and Taiwan.
是啊,目的是為了讓中國和台灣之間的貿易服務自由化。

Keith: Isn't free trade a good thing?
自由貿易不是件好事嗎?

Daisy: There's actually a lot of controversy about it. It would be good for big Taiwanese companies that want access to the Chinese market. But it would be hard for small businesses here to compete with big companies from China.
這其實是件頗具爭議的事。對於大公司來說當然是有利於他們在中國市場的發展;但對於小公司而言,這將會讓他們難以和大陸公司競爭。

Keith: That makes sense. China's economy is so much bigger than Taiwan's.
說的也是,中國的經濟體比台灣大太多了。

Daisy: Yeah. There are other concerns too. Letting in Chinese media could be a [5]threat to freedom of speech, and Chinese telecom companies could be a national security risk.
是啊,還有其他考量啦。讓中國媒體進入台灣可能會威脅到言論自由,中國電信公司也可能造成國安風險。

Keith: So if the agreement was signed last year, why did it take so long for protests to start?
那既然去年就簽署好了,怎麼他們這麼久才開始抗議?

Daisy: Well, there was supposed to be a line-by-line review of the pact, but the KMT decided at the last minute that it should be put to a vote with no review.
本來應該要一項項條目的審核,但國民黨最後一刻決定不經過審核就投票。

Keith: I see. I guess that was the last straw.
原來如此,我想那真是壓倒駱駝的最後一根稻草了。

---

1. occupy (v.) 佔據　　2. movement (n.) 運動　　3. protest (v.) 抗議
4. liberalize (v.) 使自由化　　5. threat (n.) 威脅

好用短句　(MP3 09)

談服貿
你還可以說

- During the Sunflower Movement, students occupied the Legislative Yuan from March 18th to April 10, 2014.

太陽花學運期間，學生從 2014 年 3 月 18 日佔據立法院至 4 月 10 日。

- A group of protesters also briefly occupied the Executive Yuan on the night of March 23rd.

3 月 23 日當晚還有一部分的抗議者短暫佔據行政院。

- The movement was named the Sunflower Movement because protesters used sunflowers as a symbol of hope.

太陽花學運以抗爭者手中象徵希望的太陽花命名。

- Besides students, a number of civic groups and NGOs also participated in the movement.

除了學生，還有一些公民團體以及非政府組織參予這場抗爭。

- Protesters' main demand was that a law be passed to monitor all future cross-Strait agreements.

抗爭者主要訴求是希望通過一條能監督日後跨海峽協定的法案。

Gas Prices Going Through the Roof

油價漲翻天

可燃燒產生動能的物質，例如 gas「瓦斯、天然氣或汽油」及 diesel「柴油」。英式用法中常把 fuel 當動詞「加汽油」解釋，但美國人則會說 fill up the tank。

fuel

燃料

新聞這樣說

Many industry watchers attribute the high fuel costs to unique forces—chiefly California's clean-burning gasoline formula—that have isolated the market and kept it tightly balanced between supply and demand.

許多產業觀察家將高燃料費歸咎於加州乾淨燃燒能源將市場孤立，並且保持著緊密平衡的供需關係。

石油 petroleum

製作汽油（gas, gasoline）的原料，英式英語將汽油簡稱為 petrol，而美國人則說 gas。

新聞這樣說

Gas prices rose early this week on uncertainty over the Greek debt crisis and slumped mid-week as the U.S. released a surprise crude stockpile of 2.4 million barrels and the Organization of Petroleum Exporting Countries (OPEC) boosted production.

這周一開始油價因為希臘國債危機而上漲，隨後又因為美國發行了二千四百萬桶的儲存原油以及 OPEC 緊急增加的產量而下滑。

主食 staple

staple 意思廣泛，除了當主食、日常用品，也是我們常用的「訂書針」。訂書機的英文則是 stapler。

新聞這樣說

Argentina's government is extending its price control program aimed at curbing high inflation. The controls affect 476 supermarket items. They include staples like milk, bread and meat as well as other items like canned goods and cleaning products.

阿根廷政府決定為了處理通膨問題而將其價格掌控延伸至 476 種超市產品，包括牛奶、麵包、肉品等主食，以及罐頭和清潔用品。

通膨 inflation

動詞 inflate 原意為「充氣、膨脹」，衍生為「物價抬高、通貨膨脹」之意。相反字 deflation 則是「通貨緊縮」。

新聞這樣說

Cambodia experienced low inflation of around 1 percent over the last three months thanks to a decline in oil prices, according to the latest data from the National Institute of Statistics.

柬埔寨在過去 3 個月內經歷了 1% 的低通貨膨脹，其國家統計中心顯示原因為油價的下滑。

指標 index

指判別高低優劣的「指標」或書裡的「索引」等。手指頭的「食指」因常用來「指」東西，所以叫做 index finger。表達「指引、指示」的動詞則是 indicate，兩字意思不同。

新聞這樣說

The consumer price index (CPI) contracted 0.19 percent last month from a year earlier, dragged down by cheaper fuel prices and electricity rebates, though the food and entertainment industries were boosted by the Lunar New Year holiday, the Directorate-General of Budget, Accounting and Statistics said in a report yesterday.

行政院主計總處表示，消費者物價指數上個月因為下滑的油價以及電費而收縮 0.19%，但是食品以及娛樂產業則因為農曆年假而上漲。

煉油廠 refinery

此字從動詞 refine「提煉」而來，通常指提煉石油、金屬或糖的工廠。

新聞這樣說

The Taiwan Petroleum Workers' Union yesterday protested against state-run oil refiner CPC Corp, Taiwan's plan to shut down an oil refinery in Greater Kaohsiung's Nanzih District in 2015, calling on the company's new chief executive to undertake a thorough review of the policy.

台灣石油工會成員昨天向國營煉油廠中油提出抗議，主因為中油欲在 2015 年關閉高雄楠梓區的煉油廠，他們要求中油新總裁重新並全面評估這項決策。

consumer 消費者

由動詞 consume「花費、消耗」而來。除了百貨公司、購物中心外幾種常見消費去處的英文說法有 dollar store「一元商店」、strip mall「商店街」、thrift shop「二手店」等。

新聞這樣說

The Consumers' Foundation said a recent survey of grocery items sold at supermarkets found the prices of various items have increased over the past year, with the prices of eggs and toothpaste rising by about 7 percent.

消基會表示，根據最近一份調查，超市所販售的許多產品在過去一年都漲價了，雞蛋以及牙膏甚至漲價 7%。

manipulate

操縱

原指「用手精密操作」。字首 mani、man 或 manu 都是跟「手」有關，例如：manual「手冊」、manufacture「製造」、manicure「手部保養」等。

新聞這樣說

Jaime Court, president of Santa Monica advocacy group Consumer Watchdog, said that prices are artificially inflated. Refineries don't try to produce more gasoline to undercut their competitors, Court said. Instead, he alleged, they work together to limit refining capacity and manipulate the market.

聖塔莫妮卡的消費者看守員團體主席 Jaime Court 表示，物價是人為造成的通膨，煉油廠不試著製造更多油來和同業競爭，反而聯手控制煉油量以操弄市場。

美國加油這樣加

美國的加油站和台灣非常不同，幾乎全都是自助式的加油方式，常會讓習慣一開進加油車道就只要搖下車窗說：「98 加滿！」的台灣人手忙腳亂。通常現金付費會是較為直接的方式，但若是得選擇刷卡付費，首先，先把卡片插入插槽（通常在機器右上方），記得，請快速、準確地插到底，之後請選擇自己的卡是 credit card 或是 debit card，當螢幕顯示 remove nozzle 時，就可以將油槍插入汽車油孔了！

示範對話 (MP3 11)

油價漲不停

Liz: I'm sorry, sir. We need to stop for a minute to [1)]fill up the [2)]gas tank.
先生，對不起。我們得停一下車加油。

Tom: That's OK. Have gas prices here been crazy too?
沒關係。這裡的油價也很瘋狂嗎？

Liz: Yes, they have. Is gas cheaper in the States? [they stop at a gas station]
對，沒錯。美國的油價比較便宜嗎？（他們在加油站停下來）

Tom: Yes, but not by very much anymore.
有，但再也不會便宜到哪去了。

Liz: I thought everything was more expensive in the States.
我以為在美國每樣東西都比較貴。

Tom: Lots of things are, but our gas is the cheapest in the world.
很多東西都貴，但是我們汽油是世界上最便宜的。

Liz: Why is that?
怎麼會這樣？

Tom: Americans are really [3]dependent on cars, and raising gas taxes would be political [4]suicide.
美國人很依賴汽車，漲油價就等於政治自殺。

Liz: Actually, it's not just gas prices that have been rising here. Inflation is getting worse and worse.
其實，這裡不只油價漲，通膨也越來越嚴重。

Tom: The street food seems pretty cheap to me.
街上賣的小吃對我來說蠻便宜的。

Liz: Well, yeah, but even the price of staples like rice are going up.
呃，對啦，但甚至連米之類的主食都漲價了。

Tom: Are [5]salaries going up too?
薪水有跟著漲起來嗎？

Liz: Not yet, but people are [6]demanding pay increases.
還沒，但大家都在爭取加薪。

Tom: I [7]assume the government will take care of [8]civil servants.
我想政府會先照顧公務員。

Liz: Maybe, but it would be nice if our company [9]followed their lead.
也許吧，但如果我們公司也能夠跟進就好了。

Tom: They'll only raise salaries if profits go up.
只有利潤增加才會加薪吧。

Liz: Yep. Companies are the same everywhere.
是啊。哪裡的公司都一樣。

1. fill up (phr.) 加滿
2. gas tank (n.) 油箱
3. dependent (a.) 依靠的，依賴的
4. suicide (n.) 自殺性行為，自毀
5. salary (n.) 薪水
6. demand (v.) 要求，請求
7. assume (v.) 認為
8. civil servant (phr.) 公務員
9. follow sb.'s lead (phr.) 跟隨某人腳步

好用短句 (MP3 12)

聊油價
你還可以說

- Whenever a gas price increase is announced, long lines quickly appear at gas stations.

  每次宣布調漲油價,加油站就會大排長龍。

- Buying gas is interesting in Taiwan because you receive lots of stuff.

  在台灣加油很有趣,因為你會收到一大堆東西。

- Bottled water and tissue paper are the most common gifts.

  礦泉水和面紙是最常見的贈品。

- Usually, you just need to buy 100 NT worth of gas to get a gift.

  一般只要加滿一百元就可以拿到一份贈品。

- So a lot of car trunks are stuffed with tissue paper and water bottles.

  所以許多人後車廂都塞滿了面紙和瓶裝水。

- The most popular stations are the ones that give gas discount coupons.

  也有一些加油站會送加油的折價卷,這種加油站最受歡迎了。

Invasion of the Low-cost Airlines
廉價航空

旅行社 travel agency

agency 指代辦、代購、代理商品的機構，複數形是 agencies。在這類機構中工作的員工則稱為 agent。

新聞這樣說

Tourism Bureau Deputy Director-General Chang Shi-chung told the Chinese-language United Evening News yesterday that the bureau has recently completed drafting of related regulations that travel agencies need to follow if they wish to invite Chinese tourists to Taiwan for a luxury group tour.

觀光局副局長張錫聰昨天告訴聯合新聞晚報，觀光局正在擬訂一份相關法規，規範將來台灣旅行社處理大陸豪華旅遊團的相關事宜。

航線 route

route 可指如公車、飛機、郵差送信……等任何特定的路線。若把字尾再加上一個 r，router 就是電腦網路常見的「路由器」。

新聞這樣說

Southwest Airlines is adding more than a dozen nonstop connections to its U.S. route map. Some are entirely new routes while others mark the resumption of seasonal routes or the return of routes that Southwest had previously discontinued.

西南航空將在美國航線圖上增加超過 12 個直飛航班，有些為新航線、季節性航班以及一些先前停止通行的航線。

中繼站 hub

hub 指任何網絡型活動的「集散、轉運中心」，例如「運輸中心」transport hub、「金融中心」financial hub。hub 也是指各條網路線的「集線器」。

新聞這樣說

Japanese carrier All Nippon Airways (ANA) began flying from Houston Bush Intercontinental Airport on Friday, launching service to its Tokyo Narita hub. In addition to Tokyo, ANA's new route gives Houston passengers connecting options to dozens of cities in Japan and other Asian countries, including financial centers in China.

日本全日航周五開始從休士頓布希機場起航，並將成田機場做為中繼站。除了東京之外，全日航的新航線提供休士頓旅客更多的轉機點，有數個日本城市以及其他亞洲城市，包括中國經濟重鎮。

額外費 surcharge

surcharge 由字首 sur-（超越、在上方）加上 charge（收費）組合而成。可當名詞「額外費用」，也可當動詞用。

新聞這樣說

A headline on an airline website reads: "We're happy to announce that there will no longer be any fuel surcharge for all flights." Is this happy news coming from American, Delta or United? None of the above. The announcement is courtesy a low-cost Philippines-based carrier: Cebu Pacific.

一個航空公司網站的頭條寫道：「我們非常開心宣布，所有航班將不再徵收燃料額外費用」。這樣開心的新聞是來自於美國航空、達美航空還是聯合航空呢？其實都不是，而是一家菲律賓的低價航空——宿霧太平洋航空。

椅距 seat pitch

pitch 在這裡指傾斜的角度，seat 則是座位，合起來就是指飛機或巴士等前後座位所相隔的空間。座位椅子的寬度則是 seat width。

新聞這樣說

Azul began operating in December 2008, and its flights offer free LiveTV at every seat and generous legroom compared with many U.S. airlines-a seat pitch of 30 inches or more, two-by-two seating and no middle seats, according to Azul's website.

藍色巴西航空於 2008 年 12 月啟航，它提供每個座位 LiveTV 以及比起許多美國航空更加寬廣的雙腳活動空間，以及 30 吋左右的空間加上雙座位設計。

短程的 short-haul

haul 指「拖運距離」，加上 short 就是「短程運送的」，加上 long 便是「長途的」意思。

新聞這樣說

Airplanes that Korean Air is seeking to buy are models from the Airbus A320 family and Boeing's 737, both of which are short-haul, single-aisle jets. It will be the first time for Korean Air to order Airbus' short-haul passenger jet model.

韓國航空欲購買的機型為空中巴士 A320 以及波音 737 家族成員，兩者皆為短程、單一走道噴射機，這將會是韓國航空第一次購買空中巴士短程客機。

訂位 reservation

為 reserve 的名詞形，即事先安排以保留位子，如房位、機位或是餐廳座位等。中文的「機位」可以是飛機的班次，也能指飛機上的座位，而廉價航空在飛機上的座位不一定都開放選位，因此用英文表示可要講清楚才行。flight reservation 是班機的預定，而 seat reservation 才是座位的預定。

新聞這樣說

At Spirit Airlines, which touts low fares and adds lots of fees, only 63 percent of its revenue comes from fares. Southwest still lets customers check two bags or change a reservation for free; it gets 95 percent of revenue from the ticket price.

Spirit 航空以低票價但多項額外收費吸引旅客，其收入大約只有 63% 來自票價；然而；西南航空讓旅客免費更改訂位以及托運兩件行李，而其收入有 95% 來自其票價。

budget carrier
廉價航空

budget，是名詞也是動詞，指提撥的預算、成本。廉價航空的常見說法還有 low-cost / discount / no-frills（無附加服務的） carrier。carrier 是「運輸公司」，通常指船運或航運系統。

新聞這樣說

Taiwan's China Airlines and Singapore's Tiger Airways Holdings will set up a budget carrier as Taiwan's biggest airline by fleet looks to tap into Asia's low-cost aviation market. Tiger Taiwan will have registered capital of 2 billion Taiwan dollars ($67.5 million) and commence operations by the end of 2014, China Airlines said.

隨著台灣最大航空公司踏入亞洲廉價航空市場，台灣中華航空以及新加的虎航將會建立起一個廉價航空航線，華航表示台灣虎航已註冊 20 億成本並將在 2014 年底開通。

廉航二三事

談起廉價航空，大多數人都會有安全顧慮，但其實，廉價航空只是捨去了一些不必要的人事成本（如：空服員人數）以及一些消耗品的成本（如：免費餐點），以下就來介紹廉價航空的一些小知識，讓你可以安心省下旅費。大多數廉價航空和一般傳統航空的不同如下：

· 餐點及飲料通常須額外付費，可以和空服員拿菜單直接購買。

· 為了增加單機載客人數，多數廉航會壓縮走道、廁所等公用區域的空間，以增加機上座位，降低單張機票費用。

· 廉價航空的票價是浮動的，時常一小時前後的票價就不同，這並不是航空公司的行銷策略或欺騙消費者行為，而是和供需法則有關，所以貨比三家絕對是你購票前必須做的功課。

示範對話 (MP3 14)

廉價航空
搭不搭

CHEAP FLIGHTS

Cindy: Where are you [1]headed?
你要去哪裡？

Jerry: Singapore, on business.
新加坡，出差。

Cindy: Oh, wow. I have some family there, so I fly there a lot.
喔，哇。我有家人在那裡，所以我常飛那裡。

Jerry: Which airline do you like to take?
妳喜歡搭哪一家航空公司？

Cindy: Singapore Airlines, of course. It's the world's number one airline.
當然是新航。它是世界第一的航空公司。

Jerry: I've heard that too. But what about their prices?
我也聽說了，但價錢如何？

Cindy: Typical, but they've just started a no-frills, bargain route.
普通，不過它們剛開辦一條無機上服務的廉價航線。

Jerry: Like Southwest in the States?
就跟美國的西南航空一樣？

Cindy: I guess so. There's ²⁾minimal service. No food and limited ³⁾beverages.
我想是吧。它們的服務減到最低。沒有食物，飲料很少。

Jerry: I can ⁴⁾charge this flight to my company, so I think I want something a little more ⁵⁾cozy.
這一趟我可以跟公司報帳，所以我想我要搭舒適一點的。

Cindy: I don't blame you. I usually fly there for personal reasons, so I can't put it on an ⁶⁾expense account.
這也難怪。我通常飛那裡都是因為私人因素，所以不能報公帳。

Jerry: This is the first I've heard about no-frills routes in Asia.
這是我頭一次聽說亞洲有廉價航線。

Cindy: This is a new development. Qantas is doing it for their Taipei-Singapore routes, too.
這是新開發的產品。澳洲航空也推出台北到新加坡之間的廉價航線。

Jerry: That's not surprising, given the recent increases in ticket prices.
那沒什麼好驚訝的，因為最近票價一直上漲。

Cindy: Yes, ⁷⁾fuel prices have gone up, and airlines have had to struggle to stay ⁸⁾competitive.
對啊，油價上漲，航空公司得努力保持競爭力。

Jerry: Do you ⁹⁾foresee bargain airlines becoming more popular here?
妳覺得廉價航空在這裡會越來越普遍嗎？

Cindy: I think these two routes are being done on a trial basis, but I wouldn't be surprised if they become a future trend.
我認為這兩個航線還在試航階段，不過如果成為未來趨勢我也不會太意外。

---

1. head (v.) 前往
2. minimal (adj.) 最小的
3. beverage (n.) 飲料
4. charge (to) (v.) 記在…帳上
5. cozy (adj.)
6. expense account (n.)（薪水以外的）交際費、津貼
7. fuel (n.) 燃料
8. competitive (a.) 有競爭性的
9. foresee (v.) 預見，預知

好用短句

談廉價航空
你還可以說

- International airlines are introducing cheap, no-frills routes to Taiwan.

國際航空公司最近引進低價、無機上服務航線進入台灣。

- It's now cheaper to fly to Singapore than Kaohsiung from Taipei.

現在台北到新加坡的機票比到高雄還要便宜。

- Some people worry that these bargain flights are unsafe.

有人擔心這種廉價航線不安全。

- But the airlines promise that the airplanes they're using are all brand new.

不過航空公司保證都是採用全新飛機。

- The airlines have eliminated food and beverage service from these routes.

航空公司取消這些航線的餐點及飲料服務。

- Extra fees must be paid if you want food or beverages.

所有的飲料餐點都必須另外付費。

- Most cheap flights depart at inconvenient times.

低價航空起飛時間大多比較不方便。

- For short trips, these bargain tickets may be the most economical choice.

對於短程飛行來說，廉價機票會是最經濟實惠的選擇。

There's Still an Inheritance Tax?

蛤？還有遺產稅？

查帳 audit

審計、決算都可用這個字，audit 也可當動詞表示「審核帳款」。audit 在美式英文中另一個意思是「旁聽」。

新聞這樣說

Ko, a surgeon turned politician, said he was disgusted when the National Taxation Bureau audited his personal income taxes to see if he had reported income from speeches made in a few years prior to last year's Nov. 29 elections.

從外科醫師轉任政治人物的柯文哲表示，他對國稅局對其個人所得稅查帳以確認他有如實通報去年十一月選舉前幾年的演講費用一舉感到噁心。

納稅人 taxpayer

這是個常見複合字，由 tax（稅）+ payer（付款人）組合而成。稅額降低是 lower taxes，相反「增稅」則是 increase taxes。

新聞這樣說

U.S. government watchdogs warned the Internal Revenue Service (IRS) about security flaws in the federal tax collection agency's computer systems years before hackers stole the personal information of thousands of taxpayers from an IRS website.

在駭客侵入其電腦系統、竊取數千納稅人個人資料的前幾年，美國政府監督單位就警告過國稅局他們聯邦稅收系統電腦的安全漏洞。

逃稅 tax evasion

evasion 是「藉口逃脫、規避」的意思，與 escape 意思相近。動詞是 evade，後面可直接加上 Ving 或名詞，表示「逃避某事」

新聞這樣說

Independent Taipei mayoral candidate Ko Wen-je is under investigation for alleged tax evasion, the National Taxation Bureau of Taipei said yesterday, saying it had ordered several institutions to explain payments they made to Ko for giving speeches in the period between 2011 and last year.

國稅局表示，台北市長候選人柯文哲正在接受可能的逃稅案件調查，並要求許多單位解釋付給柯文哲在 2011 年時演講的費用細節。

白手起家 rags-to-riches

rags 是指破衫襤褸，衍生為相當貧苦之意；「穿著破衣」是 in rags。這個字是形容某人從穿破衣變有錢人、貧民致富的意思。

新聞這樣說

Li Ka-shing has an incredible rags-to-riches story. He was forced to drop out of school as a child to support his family, but today, he is one of the world's richest men.

李嘉誠被迫輟學幫助家裡的經濟狀況，而今日他是全世界首富之一，是一個不可思議白手起家而致富的故事。

避稅 tax avoidance

avoidance 由動詞 avoid「必免」延伸而來，「免於某事」要說 avoid of (doing) 某事。

新聞這樣說

Housing Reform Action Alliance spokeswoman Chiang Ying-hui said the ministry's property tax reform proposals have totally overlooked pre-sale house transactions and agricultural property sales. The ministry has yet to devise a measure to prevent potential tax avoidance by land developers, Chiang said.

房改盟發言人江穎慧表示，政府的稅收改革提案完全忽略了預售屋轉帳以及農業用地買賣，且尚待提出預防土地開發商避稅可能的方案。

繼承 inheritance

從動詞 inherit 而來，除了繼承，也有「遺傳」的意思，如「我遺傳了媽媽的藍眼睛」可說：I inherited my mother's blue eyes.

新聞這樣說

The number of property transfers for gift and inheritance reasons is likely to hit a new high this year as increasing holding costs drive people to pass on real estate to younger generations, analysts said.

分析師指出，今年贈予以及繼承財產案件應該會創新高，主要因為持有費用越來越高，讓許多人決定將財產傳承給年輕一代。

不動產 real estate

在 real estate 後加上 agent，就是不動產的經紀人。買房是人生大事，常見的住家不動產有 appartment「公寓」、condo「公寓大樓」、studio「套房」、town house「連棟透天厝」等。

新聞這樣說

According to the government's database, the volume of real estate trading nationwide plunged NT$1 trillion last year, which is indicative of the impact yielded by the government's "house-hitting" policy.

根據政府數據指出，去年房地產交易金額全國下滑一兆台幣，主因為政府打房政策。

國稅局

National Taxation Bureau

bureau 指國家機關的「局、司、署」等，有趣的是此字也是女生整理儀容用的梳妝台的意思。大家常聽到美國 FBI 全名即為 Federal Bureau of Investigation。taxation 不同於 tax「稅」，是專指「課徵稅務」。

新聞這樣說

Ko said that now that the elections were over, the National Taxation Bureau was "going overboard" in having his father go to the agency and explain the matter. "This goes beyond what any normal person can tolerate," Ko said, publicly asking the agency to explain its actions.

柯文哲表示現在選舉已結束，國稅局請他父親到相關單位解釋稅務問題的行為「太超過了」。柯文哲聲明：「這已經超過任何一般人所能容忍的」，並公開要求國稅局解釋其行為。

痛苦的繳稅月

對美國人來說，每年的 4 月是最痛苦的月份，因為美國人每年繳稅期限為 4 月 15 日，一旦遲繳或漏報，美國聯邦政府的國稅局（Internal Revenue Service）絕對讓你嘗到後果，輕則需繳交巨額罰款，重則關入聯邦監獄。留學生更需要特別注意，報稅紀錄絕對會是銀行貸款、工作面試、申請公民等重點評估指標之一。

示範對話　(MP3 17)

白手起家的
台灣首富

Joyce: Wow, it looks like you're taking every *Forbes* magazine you can find.
哇，你似乎在蒐羅每一本你找得到的《富比士》雜誌。

Kenny: They may be in the trash, but they're full of interesting info. Like this one on this year's world's richest people.
它們或許淪為垃圾，但裡面充滿有趣的資訊。好比這本報導今年世界上最有錢的人。

Joyce: [¹⁾*flipping through the pages*] Hey, isn't this Tsai Wan-lin? Didn't he ²⁾pass away recently?
（翻了翻內頁）嘿，這不是蔡萬霖嗎？他不是最近過世了？

Kenny: He did, and he ³⁾left behind almost 160 billion NT in property.
是啊，他身後留下將近一千六百億元台幣的財產。

Joyce: I bet the tax office is ⁴⁾having a field day. Just think how much inheritance tax will have to be paid!
我敢說稅務機關現在忙得不亦樂乎，想想要繳多大一筆遺產稅！

Kenny: Quite the opposite. Tsai managed his wealth really well, so it looks like there will only be…like a billion in tax.
正好相反。蔡萬霖把財富管理得非常好，所以看來只要繳十億元的稅。

Joyce: Oh great, just another example of how the rich can always figure out a way to stay wealthy. The same happens in the States all the time.
喔，真是太好了，又是一個有錢人總是知道如何保持富有的例子。這種事在美國天天上演。

Kenny: Maybe, but you know, he's a real rags-to-riches success story. He came to Taipei from Miaoli at the age of eight with like a hundred NT in his pocket.
或許吧，但妳知道嗎，他是個實實在在白手起家的故事。他八歲從苗栗到台北時，口袋裡只有大約一百元台幣。

Joyce: And went on to become Taiwan's richest man? That's hard to imagine.
然後爬上台灣首富的地位？真是不可思議。

Kenny: But it's true. He had businesses in banking, real estate, insurance, technology, and hospitals, 5)just to name a few.
但這是真實故事。他的事業橫跨銀行、不動產、保險、科技及醫院，這只是隨便舉幾樣來說。

Joyce: Sounds like you really 6)know your stuff about this guy.
聽來你真的很了解這個人。

Kenny: Well, he's my role model. When I'm as wealthy as he is, I'll be the "king of the world."
嗯，他是我的楷模。哪天我跟他一樣有錢，我就是「世界之王」了。

Joyce: But until then, I guess you need to 7)settle for being "king of magazine 8)recycling."
但在那之前，我看你得安分當個「雜誌回收之王」了。

---

1. flip (v.) 翻（頁）
2. pass away (phr.) 過世
3. leave behind (phr.) 遺留下
4. have a field day (phr.) 樂此不疲，盡情整人
5. just to name a few (phr.) 只是隨便舉幾個例子
6. (really) know one's stuff (phr.) 真的很了解（某件事）
7. settle (for) (v.) 安定下來，安份於
8. recycling (n.) 回收

好用短句 (MP3 18)

談遺產稅
你還可以說

· Overseas, inheritance tax has already become so outdated that it's mostly a historical term.

遺產稅在國外十分過時，幾乎已經是個歷史名詞。

· Even China has abolished its inheritance tax.

連中國大陸都已把遺產稅廢除。

· Inheritance tax isn't an issue that average people need to worry about.

身價不高的平民百姓不需擔心遺產稅。

· But multimillionaires, whose inheritance tax can reach astronomical figures, do everything they can to lower it.

對於遺產稅可達天文數字的富商豪門來說，則能節就節。

· One way to legally avoid inheritance tax is to put your wealth under your children and grandchildren's names.

把財產轉移到兒孫名下就是個合法的節遺產稅方法。

· According to inheritance tax laws, if one's wealth is over one hundred million NT, the inheritance tax is capped at fifty percent.

根據遺產稅法規定，財產超過一億，遺產稅率最高可達50%。

· It is said that the initial estimate of the inheritance tax for Taiwan's richest man, Tsai Wan-lin, is about a billion NT.

據說台灣首富蔡萬霖的遺產稅初步估計約十億台幣。

Politics
政　　　治
英文面面觀

從編輯還在讀幼稚園的時候就知道台灣大人有兩種：一種綠色、一種藍色。兩種大人常會在電視上打群架、罵髒話或是假哭，然後這兩種大人若是上新聞，後面都會經常出現一位怪叔叔，拿著紙板死盯著鏡頭，後來媽媽說這東西在台灣就叫做政治。

台灣曾是亞洲四小龍，現在變成吃個鍋貼只敢吃四Ｘ遊龍，生活品質每況愈下、經濟萎靡不振，最有爆點的國家大事從經濟成長、進出口產值飆高，變成台灣嬰兒都在喝毒奶粉、珍珠奶茶去糖去冰還是去不了整杯的農藥跟塑化劑。一切的一切，只因為政治惡鬥早已凌駕人民福祉。從兩種大人開始喜歡在立法院打架起，政治變成我們的生活，這樣的情況下，你必須知道自己的立場或想法是什麼，更需要知道這些新聞天天報導的字眼英文該怎麼說，或是該怎麼形容自己對於這些有毒食品的看法。

She's Deep Blue. What Are You?
她是深藍你是什麼？

exit poll
出口民調

exit 是出口的意思，加上民調 poll 就成了媒體在投票所出口訪問投票人的投票意願而集結成的民調。

新聞這樣說

Crafty people always find a way around everything. Even though the CEC prohibited pre-election polling, the media copied their counterparts in the U.S. and held exit polls. Are these "post-election polls" any more legal?

所謂「道高一尺，魔高一丈」，中選會禁止媒體「選前」公布民調數據，媒體就學美國來個出口民調。難道這些「選後公布的民調」就比較合法嗎？

公投
referendum

針對什麼議題進行公投是 hold a referendum on something，而公投法案的通過與否則使用 pass 和 defeat。

新聞這樣說

Is Taiwan really going to hold a referendum? When? What might the referendum include? Both the DPP and KMT are using referendums as a tool for winning the presidential election.

台灣到底要不要公投？何時舉辦公投？有哪些議題可以公投？公投這個理念，儼然成了兩黨拼總統大選的議題工具。

party chair
黨主席

party 除了派對的意思，另外指的就是政黨，而 chair 指的就是主席的意思（不分性別），女主席是 chairwoman，男主席是 chairman。

新聞這樣說

Taiwan's President Ma Ying-jeou resigned Wednesday as KMT party chair after surprisingly harsh local election losses, a signal the party plans to regroup for a tough 2016 presidential race.

國民黨黨主席馬英九在這次立委選舉藍營慘敗下辭去黨主席職位，此舉代表了國民黨為了迎戰 2016 年總統大選而做的人事大調動。

政治獻金 political donation

donation 指的是捐款或捐贈品,政治獻金通常指某財團或某人獻出支持政黨的金錢,也可以稱作 political contribution。

新聞這樣說

Former Tuntex group chairman Chen Yu-hao's open letter to a newspaper exposed how cross-Strait businessmen like to play both sides. But despite making large political donations, he's still Taiwan's most wanted fugitive.

前東帝士集團董事長陳由豪在報紙上刊登了公開信,揭露許多台商兩邊押寶的手腕。但即使他大捐政治獻金,最後還是逃不過成為台灣最大通緝犯的命運。

選舉民調 election poll

poll 這個單字指的是民調,加上了 election 就成了我們常說的選舉民調。

新聞這樣說

Election polls should be accurate and impartial, but political parties seem intent on exploiting them as elections tools. It's no wonder the Central Election Committee prohibited the release of poll results right before the election.

民調本應公正客觀,但各政黨似乎意圖利用民調做為選舉工具。難怪中選會要在選前禁止媒體公佈民調數據。

form the cabinet 組閣

form 是指組成、形成這個動作,加上 cabinet 這個原意為櫥櫃的單詞,就成了組閣。

新聞這樣說

Just because the legislative elections ended didn't mean Taiwan's political environment calmed down. It was soon time to form the cabinet, and political rumors flew like the smog over Taiwan.

即使立委選舉已經選完,並不代表台灣的政治紛亂就告一段落。很快的就是組閣時間,到時又是一陣流言蜚語要籠罩台灣了。

綠色台商 pro-green

pro- 為字首的字意指「對某種意識的傾向」。所以 pro-green 指的就是親綠的意思。

新聞這樣說

On the other side of the Strait, Taiwanese businessmen are afraid of being green. When the Chinese Communist Party labels a Taiwanese business pro-green, that business will have to deal with hostile treatment.

在大陸的台商,都怕被冠上綠色台商的稱號,因為一旦被大陸黨中央點名是綠色台商,下場可是不太樂觀。

forensic

刑事鑑識的 / 法醫學的

forensics 指的是任何有關刑事犯罪調查的科學項目。forensic 當作形容詞使用時，則代表「和法庭相關的」。

新聞這樣說

Forensic scientist Henry Lee came to Taiwan to investigate the shooting of President Chen. The results left one side happy and the other disappointed, but in a Taiwan split down the middle, is anyone surprised?

刑事鑑識專家李昌鈺來台協助調查陳總統槍擊案。鑑識結果讓一方高興、另一方失望，但在台灣這種藍綠分裂的時刻也不意外。

美國政黨派系

美國政治其實和台灣很像，都處於兩黨控制之下：共和黨（Republican Party）、民主黨（Democratic Party）這兩個美國最重要的政治支柱。共和黨主張：自由意識的經濟主義但保守的社會政策，如：反對墮胎、反對同性婚姻合法化，推崇信仰至上的行為基礎；在外交政策上則是支持反恐戰爭的新保守主義。民主黨則主張設立最低工資制度，並支持商業管制，及全國性的健保制度；社會議題上則大力支持平權法案、同性婚姻、合法且安全的避孕方案。對於反恐戰爭，許多民主黨員都稱入侵伊拉克是個錯誤。

示範對話 (MP3 20)

深藍深綠
吵不完

©1000 Words / Shutterstock.com

Lee: Sorry, Jessica is still in the shower. Can I make you some tea while you wait?
抱歉，潔西卡還在洗澡。你等的時候要我幫你泡杯茶嗎？

Tim: That would be lovely. I really like Taiwanese [1]oolong tea.
太好了。我很喜歡台灣的烏龍茶。

Lee: Great, because we have some [2]top-grade high mountain oolong. Have a seat.
讚，因為我們有一盒頂級高山烏龍。請坐。

Tim: Why are there boxes all over the place?
這裡怎麼到處都是箱子啊？

Lee: Oh. Our roommate is moving out.
喔。我們的室友要搬出去了。

Tim: Is she leaving Taiwan? Getting married?
她要離開台灣嗎？還是要結婚了？

Lee: No. She's moving back with her family. She got really upset with us about the election last night.
不。她要搬回她家。她昨天因為選舉的事，跟我們鬧得很不愉快。

Tim: You know what people say, "Never mix friends and politics."
所以有人說：「朋友跟政治別混為一談。」

Lee: No kidding. When she found out we voted for the 3)DPP, she totally 4)flipped.
的確。她發現我們投給民進黨的時候，突然就發飆了！

Tim: Is that really a good reason to move out?
那真的是搬出去的好理由嗎？

Lee: She's deep, deep blue. Her family is all 5)KMT.
她非常非常深藍。她家的人都是國民黨。

Tim: If she's deep blue, you're what? Light green? Ha-ha.
如果她是深藍，妳是什麼？淺綠嗎？哈哈。

Lee: Exactly. Anyway, it's fine. We were sick of her screaming at the TV all the time.
正是。反正，也好。我們也受不了她老是對著電視大呼小叫了。

Tim: So no big loss. Hopefully she's happier with her parents, right?
所以沒什麼大損失囉。希望她跟父母在一起會快樂一點，對吧？

Lee: Who knows? They are thinking about leaving Taiwan.
誰知道？他們正考慮離開台灣。

Tim: Just like I left the U.S when Bush got elected. Some things are the same everywhere.
就跟布希當選我就離開美國一樣。有些事到哪兒都不會變。

---

1. oolong tea (n.) 烏龍茶　　　　　　　2. top-grade (adj.) 頂級的
3. DPP (n.) Democratic Progressive Party 民進黨　　4. flip (v.) 突然生氣
5. KMT (n.) Koumintang 國民黨

好用短句 (MP3 21)

談藍綠
你還可以說

- Pan-blue refers to any of the people or parties that belong to or split off from the KMT.

  泛藍是指國民黨及由國民黨分裂出去的政黨。

- The pan-green are composed of the so-called pro-"localization" organizations.

  泛綠是由所謂「本土派」組成。

- Pan-blues are often resented for the "White Terror" period of the past, when a mainlander minority dominated the Taiwanese majority.

  泛藍時常因過去的白色恐怖遭到憤恨，那是由少數中國人統治多數台灣人的時期。

- The pan-greens are criticized for exploiting the 228 massacre to stir up ethnic tensions, provoking China, and advocating Taiwan independence.

  泛綠被指責不斷利用二二八挑起族群對立，並且不顧中國武力威脅，執意走向台獨。

- The south is seen as the stronghold of the pan-green.

  南部被認為是綠軍大本營。

- The pan-greens are called green because that's the color of the DPP flag.

  綠色是指民進黨旗的顏色。

- The pan-blues are so called because blue is the color of the KMT flag.

  泛藍的名稱源於國民黨黨旗是藍色的。

Who's Running For President ?

決戰美國 2016

re-elect

再選

re 開頭的英文單字都帶有重新、重複的概念，elect 是選舉的動詞，加上重新 re 的概念，就是再選。

新聞這樣說

Taiwan's president won re-election Saturday, paving the way for a continuation of the China-friendly policies that have delighted Beijing and Washington, and caused consternation among some in Taiwan worried about the durability of their de facto independence.

台灣總統於週六連任成功，也將持續讓北京以及華府都開心的親中政策；然而，這也讓一些台灣人擔憂獨立的現況能維持多久。

總統提名
presidential nomination

nominate 是「提名」的動詞，後面加上常見名詞字尾-tion，則指提名人選。若要特別說明提名的職位，則要加上介係詞 as，「nominate 某人 as 某職」。

新聞這樣說

In the midst of Taiwan's electoral insanity, U.S. Democratic Party voters determined their presidential candidate for the November election. Even though the local election is over, the media has yet another election to cover.

台灣選戰打得如火如荼之際，美國民主黨也決定了他們十一月大選的總統候選人。看來台灣選舉落幕之後，媒體還是會被選舉新聞占據。

民主運動份子
democracy activist

democracy 為民主的名詞，形容詞為 democratic（也是美國民主黨支持者的通稱），activist 意指運動份子、行動份子，常用在政治、環保、人權等議題中。

新聞這樣說

Hong Kong lawmaker and democracy activist Leung Kwok-hung was denied entry to Malaysia on Friday, the second time this week the country has stopped a Hong Kong democracy activist from entering.

香港立法委員以及民主運動分子梁國雄，於週五入境馬來西亞遭拒，這已經是這週馬國第二次拒絕讓香港民主運動分子入境。

初選 primary

primary 這個字本身指的是首要的、主要的，在美國大選中，黨內初選是最重要的一個步驟之一，它決定了能否取得黨內所有人的支持勝出，進而代表自己的政黨正式參選總統大選。

新聞這樣說

The 2016 Republican presidential primary contest may feature sixteen or more candidates. Fox News and CNN recently announced the criteria that will be used to select the candidates that will be included in, and, in Fox News' case, excluded from, the first two GOP presidential primary debates.

2016 美國總統大選共和黨初選可能出現超過 16 位參選人，Fox News 以及 CNN 最近宣佈資格標準將取決於頭兩場的共和黨初選辯論。

廢票 invalid ballot

invalid 法律上特指「無效的」，去掉 in- 字首，valid 則為「有效的」。

新聞這樣說

The One Million Invalid Ballot Alliance, originally overlooked by the media, became a center of attention after the election. But their message — switching one bad egg for another doesn't help anything — got lost in the shuffle.

原本被媒體忽略的「百萬廢票聯盟」，在選舉之後意外成為矚目焦點，但他們「爛蘋果輪替，民主牛步化」的抗議呼聲，似乎還是沒被注意到。

參議員 senator

senator 指的就是在 senate 參議院中工作的參議員，角色類似台灣的立法委員。

新聞這樣說

Senator John McCain on Sunday attacked the president for citing climate change as a threat to national security, suggesting that the Obama administration's focus on environmental issues was detracting from the fight against Islamic State militants in Iraq and Syria.

參議員 John McCain 周日抨擊總統歐巴馬的「全球氣候變遷是一個國安威脅」說法，並指責總統對於環保議題的重視已削弱其對抗伊斯蘭國伊拉克、敘利亞武裝戰爭的重視。

presidential inauguration 總統就職

presidential 是總統的形容詞，總統本身名詞為 president。inaugurate 就是開創、揭幕、就職的意思，名詞 inauguration。

新聞這樣說

The May 20th presidential inauguration ceremony had three records: the most heads of state and foreign dignitaries in attendance, the most attention paid to a speech by China and the U.S., and the first time a president was inaugurated after such a large vote recount.

本次五二〇總統就職典禮創下三個紀錄：來訪元首和外賓人數最多、就職演說內容最受美國和中國關注、首度經過大規模驗票背書後就任。

absentee ballot

不在籍投票

absentee 意指缺席的人，形容詞「缺席的」則是 absent 。ballot 指的是選票。

新聞這樣說

Voters would be able to register to vote and apply for an absentee ballot at the same time under a bill to be introduced in the City Council this week.

根據這周將進入市議會審核的法案，選民將可以登記並申請不在籍選票。

美國再創歷史？！

2016 年的美國總統大選有可能會是一場宛如 2008 年第一位非裔美國總統誕生的歷史性選舉，美國史上第一位女性總統有望在明年誕生。前第一夫人希拉蕊柯林頓在 2008 年雖然拱手將總統寶位讓給歐巴馬，但隨後她即任國會參議員，並於 2009 年辭去國會參議員職位，參選成為美國國務卿，成為美國史上政治成就最高的前第一

©patrimonio designs ltd / Shutterstock.com

夫人。擔任國務卿期間，盡責執行其身為美國外交最高指揮官任務，造訪全世界一百一十二國，飛行超過 956,733 英里，再度創下歷史記錄。夾帶超高人氣以及雄心壯志，希拉蕊將再戰 2016，企圖將其記錄再向前推進最大一步，創造美國女性參政最大勝利。

示範對話 (MP3 23)

總統大選 投給誰？

Steven: Hey, Holly. Are you gonna vote in the presidential election next year?
嘿，荷莉，妳明年總統大選會投票嗎？

Holly: Yeah. I've already [1]registered to receive my absentee ballot. How about you?
會啊，我已經註冊領取我的海外投票單了。你勒？

Steven: I'll be back in California next fall, so I can just go to my local [2] polling station. So are you voting Dem or GOP?
我明年秋天會回加州，我到時候直接去當地投票所投票就好了。所以，妳會投給民主黨還是共和黨啊？

Holly: I'm a [3]Democrat.
我是民主黨支持者。

Steven: So it looks like you'll be voting for Hillary. Eww.
所以看起來妳會投給希拉蕊囉？矮額～。

Holly: Ha-ha. You must be a Republican then.
哈哈，那我想你鐵定是共和黨支持者囉。

Steven: Actually, I'm a 4)Libertarian, so I'll be voting for Rand Paul in the primary. He's not very likely to win though, so I'll end up voting for whoever gets the Republican nomination.
其實我是自由人黨支持者，所以我在初選會投給 Rand Paul。他不太可能贏啦，所以我想最後我會投給共和黨的人選囉。

Holly: What's the Libertarian platform anyway?
所以自由人黨的立場是什麼呢？

Steven: Well, they say that Libertarians are more 5)liberal than Democrats on social issues and more conservative than Republicans on economic issues.
這個嘛，他們都說自由人黨在社會議題上比民主黨更開放，而在經濟議題上比共和黨保守。

Holly: So does that mean Libertarians are pro-choice?
所以自由人黨支持女性對於墮胎的自主選擇權？

Steven: Yep. And we also support same-sex marriage.
是的，我們也支持同性婚姻。

Holly: That's good. What about on the economic side?
不錯噢，那對於經濟議題的看法勒？

Steven: Like Republicans, Libertarians believe in reducing the 6)national debt and lowering taxes.
像共和黨一樣，我們相信應該減少國債並且降低納稅金額。

Holly: Who do you think will win the primary? Hasn't Jeb Bush announced his 7)candidacy?
那你覺得誰會贏得初選？ Jeb Bush 不是已經宣布參選了嗎？

Steven: Yeah. But I think the country's had enough Bushes—and Clintons—for a lifetime. But it's too early to tell who'll win the nomination at this point.
是啦，但我覺得美國已經受夠一輩子都在看布希家族，還有柯林頓家族在政壇打滾啦。不過現在要說誰會贏得提名真的還太早。

---

1. register (v.) 註冊
2. polling station (n.) 投票所
3. Democrat (n.) 民主黨員
4. Libertarian (n.) 自由黨員
5. liberal (adj.) 自由的、開放的
6. national debt (n.) 國債
7. candidacy (n.) 參選資格

好用短句　(MP3 24)

談美國總統大選
你還可以說

· Since President Obama has reached his term limit, he isn't eligible to participate in the 2016 presidential election.

歐巴馬總統將無法參與 2016 年總統大選，因為他已達到連任限制。

· So far, the frontrunner for the Democratic presidential nomination is Hillary Clinton, who served most recently as Secretary of State.

截至目前，民主黨聲望最高的參選人為前任國務卿希拉蕊柯林頓。

· Other major Democratic candidates include Martin O'Malley, former Governor of Maryland, and Bernie Sanders, a Senator from Vermont.

其他民主黨參選人包括前馬里蘭州長 Martin O'Malley 以及佛蒙特參議員 Bernie Sanders。

· On the Republican side, Jeb Bush, who last served as Governor of Florida, is considered the frontrunner.

共和黨方面則屬佛州州長 Jeb Bush 最有希望。

· But there are over a dozen Republican candidates, and the Republican primaries won't start until February 2016, so it's too early to say who will receive the nomination.

但共和黨參選人超過 12 位，而且初選要到 2016 年 2 月才會開始，所以現在說誰為成為候選人仍太早。

Politicians' Special Treatments
政客就愛耍特權

第一夫人 First Lady

總統周遭的一切都會被冠上「第一」稱號，所以總統的兒子就是 First Son，總統女兒 First Daughter，總統的家族 First Family。

新聞這樣說

The big distinction between the two Lady Chiangs this year was that one passed away at the beginning of the year and one at the end. While the people of Taiwan may have good and bad things to say about the husbands of the two, the two Mrs. Chiangs seem to be beyond reproach. At least the green and blue had one area in which there was no argument.

兩任蔣夫人分別在年初跟年底過世，雖然台灣對他們的丈夫褒貶不一，但對兩位夫人卻都是尊敬有加。藍綠雙方終於在某方面有了共識。

secret bank account 秘密帳戶

bank account 就是銀行戶頭，加上了 secret 秘密一詞，就成了政治人物必備的秘密海外賬戶囉。

新聞這樣說

In every election, Lee Teng-hui is always flashing his smile around, supporting one candidate or another. Every time the government investigates for fraud, his name always seems to pop up. Some people really never can retire.

每次選舉，總會看到李登輝笑容滿面、四處助選的身影。每次政府追查重大黑金弊案，也總會提到他的名字，真是老而不休的最佳例証。

家產 family wealth

wealth 是財富之意。若要描述一個人非常富有則需使用形容詞 wealthy，跟我們常說的 rich 意思一樣。

新聞這樣說

They don't care about the nation's future direction or what hope and happiness they could bring after being elected. Nah. The presidential candidates would rather just engage in mudslinging campaigns over family wealth. Candidates, please stop moaning about each other's family wealth and focus on regular people's lack of it!

候選人當選後，就不關心國家未來發展，或是如何為人民帶來希望與快樂。總統候選人之間盡打家產口水戰。請候選人們別管對方的家產了，看看沒多少家產的老百姓吧！

聯署　sign a petition

sign 這動詞除了簽名之外，還有簽署的意思。petition 指的是政治或法律約束的「請願」或是陳情書。

新聞這樣說

A group of DPP legislators signed a petition asking President Chen to think carefully about his choice for a vice presidential running mate. The same activists who fought fearlessly for democracy now fight fearlessly among themselves for political gain. Power corrupts, absolute power corrupts absolutely.

一群民進黨立委簽署了一份要求總統深思副手人選的連署。當年為了理想不怕死的同志，如今變成為了權位不惜內鬥的人。看來絕對的權利，果真帶來絕對的腐敗。

公器私用　misuse of government resources

misuse 是 miss（錯誤）和 use（使用）的複合字，指不當使用；government resources 是指政府資源。政治人物不當使用政府資源，即為濫用公權、公器私用之意。

新聞這樣說

From the Examination Yuan head to the First Lady's assistant, everyone who brushes with power seems to have a hard time resisting the temptation to exploit it. As much as bloodthirsty media and yapping party hacks generate popular antipathy, they still have nothing on high-level officials who feed like pigs at the taxpayer trough.

上至掌握全國公務員升遷的考試院長，下至幫第一夫人推輪椅的女侍，只要跟權勢沾上了邊，就很難不趁機占點便宜了。舐血的媒體、狗咬狗的反對黨緊咬這件事的猙獰表情雖然令人不耐，但那些占納稅人便宜的真高官、假權貴的嘴臉，才最令人討厭。

第一家庭　the First Family

與國家元首、總統家庭相關人物，都會被冠上「第一」的稱號，所以只要在英文加上字首大寫的 First 就是總統專屬的符號了，譬如總統的太太即為 First Lady。若總統為女性，其先生則稱 First Gentleman。

新聞這樣說

Every media outlet wants to be the first in ratings, so why not be obsessed with the first family, too? They report on everything from the prince's girlfriends to his brother-in law's Olympic doctor prospects, and from the princess's pregnancy to the First Lady's tax evasions. Ever since A-bian won his first presidential campaign, the First Family has become a sure ticket in the media's own ratings campaigns.

各大媒體老是在比收視「第一」，所以當然也不會放過「第一」家庭成員了。從王子交女友，到駙馬是否要當奧運隊醫，從公主懷孕，到第一夫人逃漏稅，台灣的第一家庭成員在總統選票開出的那一刻起，也等於被票選為媒體的票房保證。

arms purchases 軍購案

arm 除了指身體手臂部位外，也常當作軍火、槍彈解釋。此定義固定為複數 arms，也可以用形容詞 armed 說一個人身帶武器、槍支。purchase 是購買之意，動詞、名詞同形。

新聞這樣說

The high price of arms purchases is not only a reminder of how scary our bad friends are across the Taiwan Strait, but also how expensive our good friends are to keep.

軍購案預算的天文數字，除了反映出對岸那個壞朋友有多可怕外，也反映出美國這好朋友有多「可貴」。

Control Yuan 監察院

監察院功能在於行使彈劾權、糾舉權以及審計權，是掌控當權者行為的單位，所以用 control 這個字，加上 Yuan 這個台灣獨有的音譯字，就成了監察院。

新聞這樣說

"The power of control" is a unique feature of Taiwan's constitutional government. In order to carry out their supervisory and investigational duties and serve as citizen watchdogs of the government, Control Yuan members must be impartial and independent.

監察權是台灣獨步全球一種憲法權力。監察委員的地位必須超然獨立，才能公正地行使監督調查的權力，替人民監督政府。

最具影響力的第一夫人

Jacqueline Kennedy

賈桂琳甘迺迪夫人對於現在所見的白宮裝潢及美國當代時裝有相當大的貢獻。當時白宮裝修完工後，賈桂琳以一場電視轉播呈現了白宮巡禮，其獨特且優雅的時尚品味，也深深影響當代時尚潮流。

Rosalynn Carter

羅莎琳卡特夫人是其夫婿最親密的政治心腹之一，她以智慧及遠見，參與了多場國事會議。她更關注於精神疾病的議題，發揮身為第一夫人的影響力，投身於精神健康協會的榮譽主席一職。

Hillary Clinton

希拉蕊，這位美國政治史上最具影響力的第一夫人，是第一位直接指導政策走向的第一夫人。她對於全民健保、女性及孩童議題皆有深入參與，在柯林頓第二任總統期間，她更成為紐約參議員，並在 2008 年被推舉為總統候選人，雖最後敗給了歐巴馬，但其隨即受歐巴馬的邀約，成功選上美國國務卿一職。

示範對話 (MP3 26)

政客總愛惹事生非

Wen: Taiwanese news is pretty funny, huh.
台灣新聞很有趣，對吧？

Tim: It seems more 1)repetitive than anything else.
似乎比什麼都容易不斷重複。

Wen: Supermodels and computer shows, you mean?
你是指老是在報導超級名模和電腦展？

Tim: That, and why is the First Lady in the news again? More unbeliev-
ably good investments?
對呀，還有為什麼第一夫人又上新聞了？又有更多好到不可思議的投
資？

Wen: No. The 2)abuse of state resources.
不。這次是濫用國家資源。

Tim: She got her wheelchair 3)gold-plated?
她把輪椅拿去鍍金嗎？

Wen: That's funny. No, the First Family's housekeeper was using the
    4)chauffeur to run private 5)errands.
    真好笑。不，第一夫人的管家利用司機去打理她私人的雜事。

Tim: What's so surprising about that?
    那有什麼好大驚小怪的？

Wen: The chauffeur shouldn't be helping out with such 6)trivial non-
    state issues.
    那位司機不應該幫人做這麼無關國計民生的瑣事。

Tim: Yeah, but it seems like that kind of abuse is bound to happen.
    是啊，但這種事似乎注定就是會發生。

Wen: Politicians in your government also let resources get misused?
    你們政府的政治人物也讓資源被濫用？

Tim: Oh yeah. All the time. It's often worse where I come from.
    是啊。無時無刻。我的國家常常情況更糟。

Wen: You're from the U.S., right? I thought politics was less 7)corrupt
    there.
    你是來自美國，是吧？我以為那邊的政治比較不腐敗。

Tim: No. Our politicians are always getting in trouble, for everything
    from sex scandals to stealing.
    才不呢。我們的政治人物老是惹麻煩，從性醜聞到偷竊全都幹遍了。

Wen: Power corrupts, and absolute power corrupts absolutely.
    權力讓人腐化，絕對的權力讓人絕對的腐化。

Tim: That statement is sad but true.
    那種說法很悲哀，但千真萬確。

Wen: But if you can't beat 'em, join 'em, right? Maybe you should run for
    office?
    但是避免不了就乾脆同流合污，是吧？你或許應該去競選公職？

Tim: Maybe you should, too.
    或許妳也該去。

---

1. repetitive (a.) 反反覆覆的　　　　2. abuse (n.) 濫用
3. gold-plated (a.) 鍍金的　　　　　4. chauffeur (n.) （受僱用的）汽車司機
5. errand (n.) 差事　　　　　　　　6. trivial (adj.) 瑣碎的
7. corrupt (adj.) 腐敗的

好用短句 (MP3 27)

談政客耍特權
你還可以說

· When someone gets special treatment, it always makes others feel like things are unfair.

每當有人享有特殊待遇，就會讓其他人感到不公平。

· When someone with the right connections applies to the government for something, those people will have their requests satisfied first.

當有人向政府提出申請，有管道的人的申請就能被優先處理。

· This kind of behaviors isn't considered to be illegal.

這些行為都算不上違法。

· But if these people are misusing government resources, this is illegal.

但如果特權人士濫用公家的資源，就是違法的行為了。

· The assistant of former First Lady caused some eyebrows to raise when she paid the President's official chauffeur to help handle some household errands.

第一夫人的助理引發爭議，因為她付錢請總統官邸的司機幫忙家務。

· The problem stems from the fact that she also asked the chauffeur to water the plants and take care of household chores, both of which aren't jobs the chauffeur should be expected to handle.

問題就出在這位助理請那位司機澆花、做家事，這就不是那位司機應該做的了。

Taipei's New Mayor
柯 P 白色旋風

cam-paign for 站台

campaign 是動詞也是名詞，指「從事運動、活動」，為集合名詞，所以沒有複數。campaign for 後面接人或組織單位，就是「為某人站台」的意思。

新聞這樣說

At an election rally, the on-stage support of a key political player can be worth as much as the cheers of a hundred thousand people in the crowd. Politicians in both camps are lining up to support their leaders, and in this fiercely competitive presidential election, it's all or nothing for both sides.

選舉造勢場合，不只拼台下來了多少人，也拼台上到底來了哪些人。由總統大選這場超激烈的選戰可以看出不但人輸不起，陣仗更是輸不得。

大法官 Grand Justice

大法官是指最高法院的法官，一般法院的法官則稱作 judge。

新聞這樣說

As the highest organ of public opinion, the Legislative Yuan just keeps surprising everyone. The president has nominated a candidate for Grand Justice for approval by the Legislative Yuan, as the constitution requires. However, the Legislative Yuan still insists on nitpicking even the slightest problems.

身為全國地位最高的民意機構，立法院總是令人出乎意料。總統依照憲法規定提名大法官送立法院行使同意權，但立院諸公依然要在小問題上挑骨頭。

民意調查 public opinion polls

通常簡稱 poll，當名詞是指意見調查，也可當動詞「進行民意調查、投票」解釋。

新聞這樣說

Presidential candidates follow the polls for everything. The polls even include question about a variety of running mates for President Chen. This whole process is feeling more and more like the lottery, with people island-wide watching for numbers from the edge of their seats.

總統候選人做任何事都追隨著民調，甚至包括關於陳總統各種競選搭檔的問題。這整個競選過程越來越像樂透開獎，全台灣的民眾都引頸期盼著民調數字。

大選賭盤 election bets

經過投票的選舉英文叫 election，bet 當名詞是「賭注」之意。bet 口語也常引申作「極有可能發生的事、最有利的盤算」解釋，譬如 (a) good bet 是「極有可能的事」；safe bet 是「穩當的人事物」。

新聞這樣說

Are election betting markets useful as unofficial polls, or are they dangerous influences on the electoral process? With so much money on the line, gamblers on the recent election turned into a certain breed of election analyst, and it's no surprise they got so many interview requests from the media.

大選賭盤究竟是像非正式民調一樣有用，或是影響選情的黑手？近來選舉的賭金金額龐大，賭盤組頭儼然成了某種選情專家，難怪受到那麼多媒體的訪問。

televised debates 電視辯論

televised 是指以電視方式播送節目或訊息，也可以說 telecast。「播放，廣為散佈訊息」更常見的說法是 broadcast，此字則不限定在電視或電台廣播等播放方式。

新聞這樣說

Sick of hearing candidates idly boast of their achievements and attack each other separately, voters tuned in en masse to see them do it together during Taiwan's first-ever presidential debates.

選民厭倦了聽候選人各自宣揚功績、互相抹黑，轉而收看台灣首次總統辯論。

檢察官 prosecutor

檢察官為刑案偵查主導者，與被告處對立地位，等於案件的起訴者。一般案件的「原告」則稱為 plaintiff。

新聞這樣說

Taiwan's high court on Thursday upheld a ruling against the country's former top prosecutor for leaking confidential information to President Ma Ying-jeou about a controversial probe into influence peddling claims.

台灣高等法院於週四判定，前檢察總長黃世銘因將偵查內容洩密給總統馬英九有罪。

political advertisement 政黨廣告

advertisement 可簡稱 ad，參選公職（run for office）的候選人常在選前以廣告、競選活動宣導理念。

新聞這樣說

With the presidential election fast approaching, the media is busy reporting on political news, and politicians are busy trying to get their message through the media. In this age of mass media, it's hard to avoid having your emotions controlled by various methods of media manipulation.

總統選戰將至，媒體忙著播報選戰新聞，而各政黨也在媒體上搶登競選廣告。在現今傳媒當道的時代，選民很難不被各式選戰訊息左右情緒。

內閣 cabinet
改組 reshuffle

內閣制的行政系統中，若國會（parliament）對內閣（cabinet）不信任，可對其進行投票倒閣。shuffle 則指卡牌遊戲中「洗牌」這個動作，前面加上「再次」的字首 re-，就是「改組」的意思。

新聞這樣說

The current president has already seen quite a few "critical" department heads step down from their posts. So, he might as well do a cabinet reshuffling round. And the speed with which the president has chosen his new members has people wondering whether or not he was already prepared for this eventuality. While conspiracy theorists might be short-sighted, the lengths to which their creativity goes knows no bounds.

現任總統已經歷不少「重點」部會首長請辭，乾脆開始內閣改組。而他決定人選的決策速度，讓人懷疑其實他早有準備。陰謀論者的心眼或許很小，但想像力真是無遠弗屆啊。

美國第一場總統電視辯論

美國史上第一場總統大選電視辯論於 1960 年 9 月 26 日登場，這一場辯論會改變了政治、媒體以及電視歷史。9 月 26 日的清晨，甘迺迪還是一位默默無名的麻省參議員，他當晚要對上的是當時的副總統尼克森。在這晚之前，全國人民全靠收音機以及報紙認識他們的總統候選人，因此對甘迺迪相當陌生；而當時身為副總統的尼克森早是政界老鳥，論資歷、論民眾熟悉度，甘迺迪毫無贏面。然而當天晚上電視辯論結束後，許多人都說，甘迺迪已確定當選。這 60 分鐘裡，甘迺迪英俊、專業，舉手投足充滿肯定的自信；反觀尼克森蒼白、過瘦又滿身大汗。甘迺迪果不其然順利當選總統。從這一晚起，總統大選的策略及政治生態不再一樣，自我形象成為候選人最重要的一環，透過電視轉播時的所有肢體細節、言談語調都必須精密策劃。歐巴馬 2008 年第一次總統大選電視辯論時也正是因其表現出的沉穩、自信與專業，讓他兩次電視辯論都得到超過半數的支持，順利當選為美國第一位非裔美籍總統。

示範對話 (MP3 29)

反官僚，選柯 P 就對了

Kate: So what do you think of the new [1)]mayor?
所以你覺得新市長如何

Ron: Ko P? I'm a big fan. I voted for him.
柯 P 嗎？我是他粉絲耶！我有投給他。

Kate: What does the "P" stand for, anyway? [2)]Physician?
到底 P 是什麼意思啊？醫師嗎？

Ron: No—professor. He's a professor too.
不，是教授的意思，他也是個教授。

Kate: It seems like in Asia, lots of doctors and [3)]academics go into politics. I mean, he doesn't have any political experience, does he?
感覺起來在亞洲，好像很多醫生以及學者從政。我的意思是，他好像沒有任何從政經驗吧？

Ron: Well, he also has experience as an 4)administrator at Taiwan's top hospital. But I think political experience is 5)overrated. Would you trust a professional politician more?
他曾經在台北最大醫院有過一些行政經驗，但我覺得大家太過度重視從政經驗了，難道你比較相信職業政客嗎？

Kate: Good point. But hasn't he made a lot of 6)gaffes?
說的好，但難道他出糗得還不夠嗎？

Ron: Yeah. He talked about foreign brides being "7)imported," and joked about selling a watch that a British minister gave him for scrap.
對啊，他說過外籍新娘是「進口的」，又開玩笑說英國交通部長送的錶可以當垃圾賣掉。

Kate: But he's still really popular anyway, right?
但他還是很受歡迎吧？

Ron: Yeah. He has really high approval ratings. I think people like him because he knows how to cut through red tape and get things done.
對啊，他的支持度頗高，大概是因為他能夠突破官僚制度的牽制解決事情吧。

Kate: So has he?
所以他有解決什麼嗎？

Ron: Definitely. He's done lots of things to 8)streamline the 9)bureaucracy. He's also had 10)illegal rooftop structures torn down, and he's tackling corruption in public construction projects.
當然啊，他為了使公家體制行事順暢做了許多事，他拆了很多違建，也處理了很多公共建設弊案。

Kate: Wow. It sounds like voters made the right choice.
哇，聽起來選民們做了正確的選擇。

1. mayor (n.) 市長
2. physician (n.) 內科醫師
3. academic (n.) 學者
4. administrator (n.) 行政人員
5. overrated (adj.) 過度受重視的
6. gaffe (n.) 糗事
7. imported (adj.) 進口的
8. streamline (v.) 疏暢、使流線
9. bureaucracy (n.) 官僚體制
10. illegal (adj.) 違法的

好用短句 (MP3 30)

談柯文哲
你還可以說

- Ko Wen-je defeated KMT candidate Sean Lien in the November election, becoming the first non-KMT Taipei mayor since 1998.

柯文哲在 11 月市長選舉中，打敗候選人連勝文，成為自 1998 年以來第一位非國民黨籍台北市長。

- Running as an independent, Ko won support from voters for his non-partisan stance.

身為一位獨立候選人，柯文哲以他無黨籍身分贏得選民支持。

- Despite his many gaffes, Ko has maintained high public approval ratings.

雖然常常失言出糗，但仍然保持高公眾支持度。

- Some people believe his gaffes may be a result of Asperger's Syndrome.

有些人認為他失言行為的原因是亞斯伯格症。

- Ko has received praise for reducing bureaucracy and waste in the city government.

柯文哲也因他降低市政官僚制度及資源浪費而受到備受讚譽。

Democracy in Hong Kong
香港偽民主

指一國家的統治區域、版圖。若開頭 T 大寫，在美國則指不隸屬任一洲的領土，譬如印第安保留區、關島、水土保持區等。

terri-tory

領土

新聞這樣說

Hong Kong legislators have rejected a reform package that would have allowed direct elections for the territory's leader in 2017. The reforms were endorsed by the Chinese government, but many in Hong Kong are opposed to it.

香港立法委員拒絕了一項由中國指導的選舉改革配套，這項配套措施將讓香港在 2017 年能夠直選區域領導人；然而，許多香港民眾也反對此政策。

統一 unification

將數個國家統一為一個國家，動詞為 unify 或 unite。uni- 字首源自拉丁文，即 one 的意思。

新聞這樣說

The head of Taiwan's Nationalists reaffirmed the party's support for eventual unification with the mainland when he met Monday with Chinese President Xi Jinping as part of continuing rapprochement between the former bitter enemies.

台灣國民黨主席在週一和中國領導人習近平的會面中，再次提到該黨對兩岸終極統一的支持；而此次會面是兩敵對方持續尋求和解的一部分。

絕食 fasting

fast 當動詞用時指絕食或禁食，也可當名詞指絕食的這段時間。

新聞這樣說

Fasting can be used for protest, to wake up people to the reality of hunger, and, most recently, for entertainment! Magician David Blaine suspended himself above London's Thames River and went without food for a whopping forty-four days. Even Harry Potter couldn't pull this off.

絕食可以用來抗議、喚醒對飢餓問題的重視，也可以拿來表演！連續四十四天，魔術師大衛布萊恩在倫敦泰晤士河上方的絕食演出，大概連哈利波特都很難辦到。

公投
referendum

若公民對國家的法案、規章有意見，可有連署請願（initiative）的權利，並要求政府進行公民投票進行決議。

新聞這樣說

Wouldn't it be great if a threatened country could force its enemy to remove its weapons with a simple referendum? If the defensive referendum passes, we'll find out if this unlikely dream is possible.

如果世界上受威脅的國家，都可以透過公投來要求敵國撤除武器的話，那不是很好嗎？如果防衛性公投通過了，我們就可以得知這個幾乎不可能的夢想是否能成真。

正名
rectify

rectify 原意是矯正，同 adjust。台灣在國際上的正式名稱一直沒有定案，要替台灣正名，英文就是 rectify the name of Taiwan。

新聞這樣說

The people of Taiwan have been fighting for years about what to call this place. No matter what the opposing teams insist, there's no question about what China's government would call Taiwan: The People's Republic of China.

台灣人民多年來為了要叫什麼國名而爭論不休。但問大陸台灣正名之後是什麼？他們只會有一個答案：中華人民共和國。

驗票 recount

re- 是表「再次」的字首，加上 count（計算），就是再次計算票數的意思。

新聞這樣說

Lien Chan, the Nationalist candidate who lost the election to President Chen by less than a quarter of a percentage point of the vote, said in an interview that he wanted an immediate recount.

國民黨總統候選人連戰在以少於四分之一百分比的票數敗於陳水扁後，在一場訪談中要求立即驗票。

軍權 military power

military 指國家的軍力、軍隊。這字常跟 army 搞混，army 單純指軍人組成的陸地戰隊，兩者完全不同意思。

新聞這樣說

The former head of the Communist Party Jiang Zemin stepped down from his final post of power by giving military power to President Hu Jintao. As the world hoped that Hu will bring some new perspectives to Taiwan-China relations, Jiang Zemin reiterated that military action is still an option.

中共前國家主席江澤民日前交出他的最後一項職務，正式把軍權交給總理胡錦濤。當舉世寄望這位接班人對於兩岸關係有新見解時，江澤民卻在交接時重申，他從未，也不會承諾放棄對台灣動武。

take to the streets

走上街頭

因遭受不公的待遇表達強烈不滿，或想高調宣示某種意見的一種集體行動。想更明確說「上街抗議」，則可在片語後加上 to protest（抗議）。

新聞這樣說

After the handover of Hong Kong six years ago, this pearl of the East has not only failed to get brighter, but has even lost some of its luster. The economy is doing poorly and democracy seems farther away than ever. It's no wonder the Hong Kong's people, normally detached from politics, are taking to the streets.

香港回歸六年來，這顆東方之珠不但沒有越來越閃亮，反而越來越黯淡。經濟上百業衰退，政治上開民主倒車，無怪乎原本政治冷漠的香港人，也開始走上街頭了！

美國五月天事件

香港佔中事件，又稱雨傘革命，再度展現學生運動在爭取民主過程中的重要角色。除了台港兩地的雨傘革命、野百合學運、太陽花學運，美國史上發生過最大規模的學生運動則是著名的 May Day Protest「五月天事件」。當年，尼克森總統宣布入侵柬埔寨，引起國內反戰學生的抗議，並在 1970 年 5 月，國家安全保衛隊在俄亥俄州的肯特大學射殺了四名抗議學生，並造成九人受傷。事件一爆發引起超過四百五十所大學聯合罷課，並有四百名以上學生參與這場抗議。

示範對話　(MP3 32)

淺談香港

Wei: Have you been to Hong Kong before.?
你以前去過香港嗎？

Tim: I've been there many times over the years, starting in the seventies.
從七○年代開始的這些年，我去過很多次了。

Wei: Wow. Has it changed much.?
哇。它有改變很多嗎？

Tim: It's ¹⁾certainly much more ²⁾built-up than before. The ³⁾harbor used to be filled with ⁴⁾junks.
建設得的確比以前好多了。那座港口以前都堆廢棄物。

Wei: Now it's ⁵⁾cruise ships and new ⁶⁾high-rises, eh?
現在都堆滿了遊輪和新大樓，對吧？

Tim: Exactly. The city got so rich so quick in the eighties and nineties.
沒錯。這座城市在八○、九○年短短時間內變得極有錢。

Wei: But the economy's [7]collapsed in recent years. I think returning to China was bad for it.
但最近幾年就經濟蕭條了。我想回歸對香港而言並非好事。

Tim: I don't know, really. Most of Asia had trouble for a while in the late nineties.
這個我其實不太確定。大部分亞洲在九〇年代末那陣子都碰上了難題。

Wei: But Hong Kong's still not doing any better. And, they won't have [8]democracy [9]any time soon.
但是香港現在還是沒有比較好。而且他們短期內不會民主。

Tim: Very true. I can't believe that Tung Chee-hwa is still [10]in power.
那倒是真的。我不敢相信董建華還在執政。

Wei: You know, a lot of people in Taiwan look at Hong Kong to guess what [11]unification with China might be like.
你知道，台灣很多人在看著香港，猜想和大陸統一可能會變得怎樣。

Tim: So what's the [12]prognosis?
那麼預測結果如何呢？

Wei: Pretty [13]grim, don't you think? Less freedom, people on the streets protesting....
蠻糟糕的，你不認為嗎？不夠自由，街上人們抗議個不停……。

Tim: Yeah, they've had huge protests in the last year. I went last July, actually.
是啊，他們去年舉行龐大的抗議活動。我去年七月還參加了。

Wei: So has China [14]blacklisted you yet.?
那中國把你列入黑名單了嗎？

---

1. certainly (adv.) 無疑地　　2. built-up (a.) 建築林立的　　3. harbor (n.) 港灣
4. junk (n.) 廢棄物　　5. cruise ship (n.) 遊輪　　6. high-rise (n.) 高樓
7. collapse (v.) 崩潰　　8. democracy (n.) 民主　　9. any time soon 很快
10. in power 掌權　　11. unification (n.) 統一　　12. prognosis (n.) 預測
13. grim (a.) 可怕的　　14. blacklist (v.) 把…列入黑名單

好用短句 (MP3 33)

聊香港民主
你還可以說

- Although Hong Kong was a British colony for over 100 years, the government began democratic reforms before the handover to China in 1997.

雖然香港被英國殖民超過一百年，香港政府在 1997 年回歸中國前就已進行民主改革。

- After the handover, Hong Kong became a Special Administrative Region of China under the "one country, two systems" principle.

回歸中國後，香港在中國一國兩治政策下成為特別行政區。

- While Beijing promised that the territory's chief executive would be elected by universal suffrage in 2012, the date was later changed to 2017.

雖然北京政府曾保證在 2012 年會有行政首長普選，但隨後又延期至 2017 年。

- In July 2003, 500,000 joined a march against an authoritarian security law called Basic Law 23, which was shelved as a result.

在 2003 年 7 月，五十萬民眾遊行抗議一項名為「基本法 23 條」的政權安全法，隨後該法案被束之高閣。

- During the 2014 Umbrella Movement, hundreds of thousands of protesters occupied the city center for 10 weeks to protest proposed non-democratic changes to Hong Kong election laws.

2014 年的雨傘革命，成千上萬的香港人霸占中環超過 10 週，為了就是抗議香港先前提出的非民主性選舉法條。

Chapter Three

World
Headlines
國　　　際
頭條這樣學

了解國際新聞，並且進一步談論國際新聞絕對是你培養世界觀、踏出自己舒適圈的首要步驟。台灣新聞媒體因為收視率競爭、商業考量等原因讓人搖頭，內容不是充滿偏頗的報導就是聳動卻言不及義的標題，國際新聞永遠是篇幅最少、最精簡的。種種因素造成台灣自我邊緣化的危機。國際觀不代表絕對成功、不代表高人一等的優越感，也絕非自我膨脹的虛無假象，它單純代表另一種看世界的角度、另一種生活的態度以及更多自身成長的可能性。所以，多看看國際新聞、一邊學習一些常見的新聞用語，讓你下次用英文跟老外聊時事不會尼泊爾災後狀況講不出口，或是反恐行動在幹嘛都不懂。

MERS

MERS 風暴

---

treat-ment
治療

常見的搭配詞和用語包括：to seek treatment（尋求治療）、provide treatment（提供治療）、get/ receive/ undergo treatment（接受治療）、respond well to treatment（對治療反應良好）。

新聞這樣說

As Nepal has expressed hope that it can send some of its earthquake victims to Taiwan for medical treatment, President Ma Ying-jeou said Tuesday that "we are considering receiving them."

尼泊爾曾表達希望能送入一些地震受傷的病患來台灣治療，而總統馬英九在週四說「我們正在考慮接受」。

中東呼吸道症候群
MERS

原名為 Middle East Respiratory Syndrome，syndrome 為「症候群」，表示罹患（be infected with）某種疾病時，經常會同時出現的一系列症狀（symptom）。

新聞這樣說

South Korea is grappling with two battles: the virus itself and the public fear over MERS, one official declared. The nation has been struck by the largest outbreak of the Middle East Respiratory Syndrome outside Saudi Arabia, where the virus was discovered.

一位官員指出，南韓正在面對的棘手戰役有二：MERS 病毒本身以及大眾對其的恐慌。南韓現今正慘遭中東呼吸道症候群襲擊，是目前在其發源地沙烏地阿拉伯之外最大宗的疫情爆發。

醫療口罩
surgical mask

surgical 指「(外科)手術的」或「與(外科)手術相關的」，只能放在名詞前面，例如：surgical instruments（外科手術器械）。

新聞這樣說

Across Asia, surgical masks have lost their stigma to become an everyday sight in the street or on the subway, despite some experts believing they do little more than provide psychological reassurance against diseases such as MERS, which has already left 23 people dead in South Korea.

醫療口罩已去除汙名，在亞洲街道與地鐵上每日可見。不過某些專家卻相信醫療口罩對 MERS 這種已在南韓造成 23 人身亡的疾病來說，其作用不過是心安而已。

症狀 symptom

symptom of ~ 意指某疾病的病症。symptom 也有「徵兆」之意，但多是指壞事或問題的徵兆。

新聞這樣說

The ongoing avian influenza outbreak in poultry continues to persist. Although no bird-to-human transmission of H5N2, H5N8 or H5N3 has occurred, the CDC is monitoring everyone who has been exposed to the poultry farms where avian influenza outbreaks have occurred for influenza-like symptoms.

在家禽間傳染的禽流感疫情持續加溫，雖然目前沒有家禽傳染人類像 H5N2、H5N8、H5N3 等禽流感的案件，疾管署仍然監控著每一位曾與流感症狀爆發區域的家禽農場接觸過的民眾。

併發症 complication

complication 為可數名詞，有「混亂；複雜」之意。當作醫學名詞時，意指「併發症」，需以複數表示。

新聞這樣說

The Centers for Disease Control on Thursday reported the year's first severe complications arising from enterovirus infection and urged better personal hygiene to prevent the spread of the disease. A nine-month-old girl has been confirmed infected with coxsackievirus A2, the Centers said.

疾管署週四發布今年第一起因為腸道病毒引發嚴重併發症案例，一名 9 歲女童確認感染克沙奇病毒 A2，驅策民眾更加重視個人衛生習慣以避免病毒的散播。

散播 transmission

transmission 做「（疾病的）散播」解釋時，為不可數名詞，後面不可加 s。不過，若是指「（廣播、電視播送的）節目」時，則為可數名詞。

新聞這樣說

The Council of Agriculture's Bureau of Animal and Plant Health and Inspection Quarantine (BAPHIQ) released the newest set of data yesterday from samples submitted on Feb. 4 showing that the virus transmission rate among ducks is relatively low.

行政院農業委員會動植物防疫檢疫局昨天公布由 2 月 4 號送檢樣本統計出的數據，表示病毒在鴨子間相互散播的機率相對較小。

具傳染性的 contagious

當我們說 somebody is contagious，是指此人患有傳染性疾病。contagious 也可指人的感受、想法、態度或行為具感染力，例如：Her laughter was contagious. （她的笑富有感染力）

新聞這樣說

The Centers for Disease Control (CDC) this week reminded those who have traveled abroad in recent weeks to be alert for symptoms suggestive of contagious diseases within 14 days upon return and to inform doctors of their recent travel history if they seek medical attention.

疾管署這周提醒所有最近有出國的民眾，多加注意 14 天內是否出現傳染疾病病徵，並且就醫時一定要告知醫生近期旅遊史。

hygiene 為抽象名詞，泛指人為了健康，保持自身與環境清潔的一切作為。因此，個人衛生用品稱為 personal hygiene product，擁有良好的衛生習慣的說法則是 to have good personal hygiene。

hygiene

衛生

新聞這樣說

According to the CDC, 16 suspected cases of MERS infection have been reported this year, though all patients have tested negative for the MERS virus. Officials also said that hygiene measures such as hand washing before and after touching animals and avoiding contact with sick animals, should be followed.

疾管署指出，今年申報之 16 起疑似 MERS 案例，皆被診斷為陰性反應，相關專員表示，接觸動物前後洗手及避免接觸染病動物等衛生措施仍須持續進行。。

關於 MERS

中東呼吸道症候群和 SARS 一樣，屬於冠狀病毒，在 2012 年於沙烏地阿拉伯發現。症狀包含發燒、咳嗽、喘不過氣來等，確定染病案例的年齡層為 1 至 99 歲，也就是說任何人都有可能感染此疾病，死亡比例為 10 位患者中，會有 3～4 人身亡。死亡案例皆伴隨併發症，如肺癌以及腎臟衰竭。世界衛生組織考察團至韓國研究 MERS 疫情在韓國快速傳播的原因，發現其一重要因素是因首位病歷在感染後 5～7 天才就醫治療，而此期間病毒的傳染力最強所致。

示範對話 (MP3 35)

MERS 危機

David: Are you busy getting ready for your [1]business trip to Korea?
妳在忙著準備去韓國出差嗎?

Amy: No, it was cancelled. Haven't you heard about the MERS outbreak there?
沒啊,被取消了。你沒聽說那邊爆發 MERS 疫情嗎?

David: MERS? Is that like SARS?
MERS? 是像 SARS 嗎?

Amy: Yeah. It's caused by a similar [2]coronavirus. It stands for Middle East Respiratory Syndrome.
是啊,這也是相似的冠狀病毒引起的,全名是中東呼吸道症候群。

David: Does it come from [3]camels or something?
它是來自於駱駝之類的嗎?

Amy: Good guess! They think it spread from camels to humans, but it probably came from bats originally—just like the SARS virus. The first case was reported in Saudi Arabia in 2012.
猜得好! 他們認為 MERS 是由駱駝傳到人類身上的,不過最初應該是

85

跟 SARS 病毒一樣來自於蝙蝠，第一個病例在 2012 年發生在沙烏地阿拉伯。

David: So how did it spread to Korea?
那怎麼會傳到韓國呢？

Amy: A Korean businessman brought it back from a trip to the Middle East last month.
上個月一位韓國商人去中東出差時將它帶回來。

David: How contagious is it?
它傳染性很高嗎？

Amy: They say it's much less contagious than SARS, but the 4)mortality rate is a lot higher—30 to 40%. So far, there are a hundred and sixty-something cases in Korea.
他們說比 SARS 低很多，但是死亡率卻高很多，大約是 30 到 40%。目前為止，在韓國已經有 160 幾起病例。

David: That's a lot.
很多耶！

Amy: Yeah. That businessman visited a few different hospitals before he was diagnosed and 5)quarantined. By that time, he'd already infected a lot of people.
對啊，那位商人在被診斷出來並隔離前，去過幾家不同的醫院。這時就已經感染給很多人了。

David: What are the 6)authorities doing to contain the outbreak?
官方有實行什麼措施來控制疫情嗎?

Amy: All the patients and people who came into contact with them have been put in quarantine. There's no 7)vaccine or cure, so that's really all they can do.
所有病患以及他們接觸過的人都已被隔離，但因為目前並沒有疫苗或解藥，所以也只能做到這樣。

1. go on a business trip (phr.) 出差　　2. coronavirus (n.) 冠狀病毒
3. camel (n.) 駱駝　　　　　　　　　　4. mortality rate (n.) 死亡率
5. quarantine (v.) 隔離　　　　　　　　6. authority (n.) 官方
7. vaccine (n.) 疫苗

好用短句 (MP3 36)

談 MERS
你還可以說

- Symptoms of MERS may include fever, cough, diarrhea and shortness of breath.

MERS 症狀包括發燒、咳嗽、腹瀉以及呼吸急促。

- MERS is a severe pneumonia-like respiratory disease caused by a virus.

MERS 是一個由病毒所引起的類肺炎呼吸道疾病。

- The infection can be spread from person to person through respiratory secretions.

感染方式可以在人類之間以呼吸道分泌口沫傳染。

- To protect yourself from viruses like MERS, you should wash your hands frequently and avoid touching your face.

為了保護自己不被 MERS 這種病毒侵襲，你應該勤洗手且避免摸臉。

- Similar to SARS, there are no effective treatments for MERS.

如同 SARS，目前並無有效治療 MERS 的方式。

Counter-terrorism
反恐行動

Hit! 話題單字 (MP3 37)

behead
斬首

behead somebody 是指「將…斬首；砍下…的頭」，常以被動型態表示，例如：He was charged with treason and beheaded.（他被控叛國並遭斬首），同義字為 decapitate。

新聞這樣說

In a new propaganda video released Sunday by ISIS, the militant group claims to have beheaded over a dozen members of Egypt's Coptic Christian minority on a Libyan beach.

週日公佈新的 ISIS 宣傳影片中，激進團體聲稱已在利比亞海灘斬首超過 12 位埃及科普特基督徒少數族群。

IED 簡易爆炸裝置

全名是 improvised explosive device，是指利用現有或臨時材料所製成的炸彈（bomb），俗稱土製炸彈。動詞 improvise 意指「臨時製造」，當名詞也可指「爆炸物；炸藥」，improvised 是它的過去分詞，explosive 則指「會爆炸的」。

新聞這樣說

A small improvised explosive device exploded at a popular restaurant at Nairobi's airport, damaging a metal trash can and the ceiling but causing no injuries, a high-ranking security official said Friday. The IED caused little damage in the Thursday night explosion, and airport operations quickly returned to normal.

國安高層於週五指出，一個小型簡易爆炸裝置在奈洛比機場的一家知名餐廳裡爆炸，造成一個金屬垃圾桶以及天花板受損，但無人受傷。這起於週四晚間的土製炸彈爆炸案損傷非常小，而機場隨後立即恢復正常運作。

劫機 hijack

hijack 有「劫持（飛機或其他運輸工具）的意思，動詞和名詞同形，意思也相同。此外，動詞 hijack 也可做「操控；把持」解釋，例如 be hijacked by extremists（被極端分子所操控）。

新聞這樣說

An alleged attempt to hijack a London-bound Air India flight was made on Friday, according to an email sent to Jet Airways pilots. Several airlines have subsequently asked their crew to be on alert during flights.

一封寄給捷特航空機長們的電郵，聲稱週五企圖劫持印度航空飛往倫敦的班機。許多航空公司因此要求航空組員在飛行中特別提高警覺。

指紋 fingerprint

由於每個人的指紋都是獨一無二的（unique），因此警察可利用指紋來識別犯人。fingerprint someone 意指「採集（某人的）指紋」，fingerprint 在此當動詞用，另一種說法為 take someone's fingerprints，此處的 fingerprint 為名詞。

新聞這樣說

The team at the University of Surrey showed that chemicals produced when cocaine is broken down in the body could be detected in the fingerprint. They argue the test could be useful in prisons, drug abuse clinics and even for routine testing in the workplace.

一組薩里大學的小組發現，吸食古柯鹼在體內分解過程中所產生的化學物質，可由指紋檢測出來，他們主張這項檢驗可以實行於監獄、戒毒所，甚至是一般的職場中。

贖金 ransom

ransom 當名詞為「贖金」的意思，當動詞則是指「贖回」，片語 to hold somebody to ransom 有「綁架勒索」或是「脅迫」的意思。

新聞這樣說

Does paying ransom to a foreign kidnapper free one American but put more at risk? Not any easy question. But if you're someone like Nancy Curtis of Cambridge, Mass., you were never too interested in that debate. You wanted to save your son, Theo Padnos, who was taken hostage by al-Qaida in Syria in 2012.

付贖金給一位海外綁架犯可以換來一位美國人的自由、還是會讓更多人深陷危機呢？這不是個簡單的問題。但如果你是麻省劍橋的 Nancy Curis，妳絕對不會有其他想法，因為妳只想要找回妳那在 2012 年遭蓋達組織挾持的兒子 Theo Padnos。

恐怖主義的 terrorist

恐怖主義者（terrorist）即俗稱的恐怖分子，泛指使用暴力（use violence）以達到政治目的（political aims）的人。近年來由於許多回教國家和西方世界以及基督教之間的衝突，穆斯林（Muslim）常被人與恐怖主義（terrorism）連結。

新聞這樣說

Since 9/11, an average of six terrorist plots a year perpetrated by American Muslims resulted in 50 fatalities, according to the New York Times. But attacks by right-wing extremists averaged about 30 a year, a total of 337, between 2001 and 2012, resulting in 254 fatalities.

根據紐約時報指出，自 911 事件後，一年平均有 6 起的美國穆斯林恐怖攻擊，造成 50 人身亡；但右翼激進份子造成的攻擊一年約有 30 件，在 2001 至 2012 年期間一共有 337 起事件，造成 254 人身亡。

主謀 mastermind

一個犯罪案件，除了主謀之外，協助主謀實際執行犯罪的人稱做 accomplice（幫兇），僅參與策畫犯罪，卻沒有實際執行的人則稱為 accessory（共犯）。

新聞這樣說

The suspected mastermind of an attack on a Paris Jewish restaurant in 1982 that left six people dead and 22 injured has been arrested, officials in Amman and Paris confirmed on Wednesday. The man, Zuhair Mohammed Hassan Khalid al-Abbasi, 62, was taken into custody on June 1.

阿曼以及巴黎警方於週三時指出，1982 年一家巴黎猶太餐廳攻擊事件的嫌疑主謀，因當年造成 6 人身亡 22 人受傷，已被逮捕。62 歲的嫌犯 Zuhair Mohammed Hassan Khalid al-Abbasi 已在 6 月 1 日被拘留。

阻撓 foil

foil 當動詞時，表示「阻止；制止（違法之事）」，同義字為 thwart。此外，foil 也可做名詞，為「金屬薄片、鋁箔」的意思。

新聞這樣說

French authorities on Wednesday said they foiled an "imminent" terrorist attack on churchgoers after a man was arrested in Paris with an arsenal of weapons. The 24-year-old Algerian computer science student was only detained on Sunday because he shot himself in the leg, prosecutors said.

在一名配有大量軍火的男子於巴黎遭到逮捕之後，法國當局週三宣稱他們阻撓了一起針對上教堂禮拜之民眾可能的恐怖攻擊事件。據檢方說，這名阿爾及利亞的 24 歲電腦科技學生只在週日遭到拘禁，因為他開槍打傷自己的腿。

反恐行動的一大步

沒有一個人忘得了 2001 年 9 月 11 日所發生的悲劇，它震撼了全世界，動搖了所有宗教信仰以及善惡之分，這一天起，全世界有了一個共同目標：反恐任務。2011 年的 5 月 1 日美國時間晚間十一點三十五分，美國總統歐巴馬出現在全球新聞轉播，正式宣布基地組織 Al-Qaida 精神領袖賓拉登 Osama bin Laden 已被處死。這是史上最重要的反恐行動，而歐巴馬口中的「一小群勇敢的美國人」就是全世界最精密訓練、最具破壞力的超級軍隊 U.S. Navy SEALs，又稱海豹部隊。SEALs 代表的是 Sea, Air, Land Teams，他們受過最艱辛、最嚴峻的軍事訓練，在 911 事件後成為美國反恐行動最大主力，也影響了美國當代文化，不論電影、影集、小說，都將海豹部隊描繪成美國英雄。不論你怎麼看美國在反恐行動中的作為，不可否認的是，在美國自願兵役體制下，願意為國家、為正義、為和平犧牲的男女，都值得我們致上最大的敬意。

安檢層層把關

Lisa: Welcome to Taiwan, Mr. Smith! The company has sent me to be your guide [1]for the day. My name is Lisa.
史密斯先生，歡迎來到台灣！公司今天派我來接待你。我是莉莎。

Terry: Call me Terry, Lisa. Glad to meet you.
莉莎，叫我泰瑞就好。很高興見到妳。

Lisa: Was your flight OK? Was airport [2]security very strict?
這一趟飛行還好吧？機場安全檢查很嚴格嗎？

Terry: Of course. Since 9/11, security has been high everywhere. They even searched my shoes!
當然了。從九一一之後，到處都加強安全檢查。他們甚至還搜了我的鞋子！

Lisa: But they look like they were shined just five minutes ago.
但你的鞋看起來好像五分鐘前剛擦過似的。

Terry: You're very kind. Tell me, Lisa—has Taiwan had any problems with [3]terrorism?
妳誇獎了。告訴我，莉莎──台灣有恐怖主義的問題嗎？

Lisa: No, but some people are worried about it, especially since Taiwan is an U.S. ⁴⁾ally.
沒有，但有些人滿擔心的，尤其因為台灣是美國的盟邦。

Terry: I guess that would make Taiwan a target. But there haven't been any attacks, right?
我猜那或許會讓台灣成為攻擊目標。但到目前為止還沒發生任何攻擊吧？

Lisa: No, not yet at least. But some things have changed. Our airports are certainly a little more careful.
還沒有。但有些情況已經改變了。我們的機場的確格外小心了。

Terry: That's good. The whole world has changed a lot in the last few years.
那很好。過去幾年來全球都發生許多變化。

Lisa: ⁵⁾That's for sure. I almost went to Spain in March for a holiday, but then there were train ⁶⁾bombings!
的確。我三月差點就到西班牙度假，結果那邊就發生火車炸彈攻擊！

Terry: What a ⁷⁾tragedy that was. I sure hope there's an end ⁸⁾in sight to this horrible problem.
那真是一場悲劇。真希望不久之後這個駭人的問題能夠結束。

---

1. for the day 今天
2. security (n.) 安檢
3. terrorism (n.) 恐怖主義
4. ally (n.) 盟友，同盟國
5. That's for sure. 的確沒錯。
6. bombing (n.) 爆炸
7. tragedy (n.) 悲劇
8. in sight 視力所及之處
　　在此指「可見的將來」，也就是「不久之後」

好用短句　(MP3 39)

談反恐安檢
你還可以說

- Airport security is incredibly strict nowadays.

現在機場安檢都非常嚴格。

- Luggage is being checked very carefully, particularly for U.S.-bound passengers.

尤其是飛往美國的飛機，乘客的行李都被翻得很仔細。

- I switched planes in Japan the last time I went to the States. My bags got examined, and I almost didn't make my connecting flight.

我上次去美國在日本轉機，行李被抽檢，差點趕不上下一班飛機。

- I was asked to remove my shoes, but luckily I was wearing new socks.

我那次被要求脫鞋子，還好我穿的是新襪子。

- I've heard that in the future, we'll have to give fingerprints and photos if we want to fly.

聽說以後搭飛機還要按指紋並且拍照呢！

Nepal's Darkest Hours
尼泊爾的黑暗時刻

地震
earthquake

可簡稱為 quake，也就是「顫抖、搖晃」的意思。美國人也常用 temblor 來講地震，此字跟「顫抖」的另一個英文字 tremble 很相似。

新聞這樣說

One person has been killed in Taiwan's capital Taipei in a house fire following a 6.6 magnitude earthquake. The quake struck near Japan's Yonaguni on Monday morning. Buildings swayed in Taipei and people were seen rushing on to the street, but no significant damage was reported.

在台灣首都台北市中有一人葬身於規模 6.6 地震所引起的一場家中大火。地震於星期一早晨襲擊日本與那國島，台北也受影響，人們紛紛從搖動的大樓中逃出，但並無報出任何重大傷害。

震央 epicenter

epi 字首有「在……之上」的意思，center 則是「中心」。震央並非地震真正源頭，而是地底下震源（hypocenter / focus）垂直向上於地表的對應位置。

新聞這樣說

At 1:47 a.m. on September 21, 1999, the island of Taiwan, located off the southeastern coast of mainland China, was shaken by a 7.6-magnitude earthquake. Its epicenter was located in Nantou County in central Taiwan, but serious damage occurred across the island.

1999 年 9 月 21 日凌晨 1 點 47 分，位於中國東南岸的台灣被一場規模 7.6 的地震襲擊，其震央位於中台灣南投縣，但全島皆承受巨大損害。

傷亡人數 casualty

指的是軍事、災害、事故等的傷亡者，多以複數 casualties 表示。heavy casualties 則是「傷亡慘重」的意思。此字由形容詞 casual「意外的、偶發的」之意思衍生而來。

新聞這樣說

The number of people killed in multiple gas explosions in Kaohsiung overnight increased to 22 as of 7:30 a.m. Friday, the National Fire Agency said. Another 270 people were injured. Twenty-six firefighters were among the casualties, including 4 fatalities.

內政部消防署公布至週五早晨 7 點 30 分，高雄氣爆死亡人數已達到 22 人，另有 270 人受傷，26 名消防人員也在受傷名單中，包括 4 名殉職人員。

餘震 aftershock

規模最大的地震稱為主震，在主震之後跟隨的地震則稱餘震。反之，主要地震之前所發生的小地震則是「前震」foreshock。fore- 字首是「……之前」的意思。

新聞這樣說

The west coast of Taiwan was shaken by a magnitude 5 earthquake at 4:38 pm yesterday. A magnitude 4.2 aftershock was detected 15 minutes later, with an epicenter less than 2m away.

台灣西海岸昨天下午 4 點 38 分受到規模 5 的地震襲擊，15 分鐘後偵測到一場規模 4.2 的餘震，震央距離不到兩哩。

人道救援 humanitarian aid

humanitarian 是從名詞 humanity「人類、人道」變化而來。「人道主義」humanitarianism 就是在說一種對人群抱有仁愛精神，不忍他人遭受不平等待遇的情懷。aid 是「救援、輔助品」的意思，常見的急救箱就叫 first aid kit。

新聞這樣說

The Taipei-based International Cooperation and Development Fund (Taiwan-ICDF) said it has selected 15 people interested in its overseas volunteer programs, which are aimed at providing developement, humanitarian aid and helping Taiwan's diplomatic allies and other countries with good ties with the country, as well as promoting bilateral exchanges.

台灣財團法人國際合作發展基金會選了 15 名對於跨國志工有興趣的志工加入，提供發展、人道救援以及促進台灣同盟國和其它國家外交，並推廣互惠合作。

震級 magnitude

地殼快速釋放能量時的震動，會產生地震波，使用地震儀便可測量出震波的規模。大家熟知的芮氏地震規模的英文則是 Richter (magnitude) scale。

新聞這樣說

Japanese forecasters had warned the 6.6 magnitude earthquake could cause a tsunami as high as one metre (three feet) affecting several islands in the Okinawa chain. But they lifted the alert around an hour later, with no abnormal waves recorded.

日本預測中心警告規模 6.6 的地震可能會在沖繩群島引起 3 呎高的海嘯，但並無偵測到顯著異常現象，一小時後便解除警報。

巨大災難 catastrophe

catastrophe （大災難）和cataclysmic （大洪水的，大災變的），都是以 cata-為字首。字首 cata- 有「完全、下降」的意思，相同字首的常見字彙還有 catalog （目錄，同 catalogue）、category （種類）。

新聞這樣說

The catastrophic gas blasts last night rocked the southern city of Kaohsiung, ripping a massive trench through the road and launching vehicles into the air and killed 25 people.

一場氣爆大災難震撼南台灣高雄，不但將道路炸出一大條坑道並將車子震到空中，還造成 25 人身亡。

災後狀況，餘波

aftermath

此字是 after + math 的組合字，math 可不是數學，而是古英文「掃滅、全面清除」的意思。aftermath 也指某事件發生的結果及其所帶來的發展。常用表達為 (in) the aftermath of（在……之後）、cope with the aftermath of ～（應付……的後果）

新聞這樣說

Mainland Affairs Council (MAC) Minister Wang Yu-chi announced his resignation yesterday in leak case aftermath. The Taipei District Prosecutors Office (TDPO) concluded their investigation of former MAC Deputy Minister Chang Hsien-yao and two others without prosecution.

陸委會部長王郁琦昨天因洩密案餘波而請辭，台北地方法院檢察署總結調查，將不起訴前陸委會副委張顯耀以及其他兩人。

天佑尼泊爾

2015 年 4 月 25 日，老天在這日帶給尼泊爾——世上最美麗國家之一——自 1934 年的 Bihar 地震以來最嚴峻考驗。一場規模 7.8 的地震震驚全國，造成超過 8,800 人身亡，兩萬多人重傷，甚至引發喜馬拉雅山聖母峰雪崩，導致 19 名登山者死亡，寫下聖母峰最致命的一頁。多座極具歷史意義、被聯合國教科文組織列入世界遺產的神廟、建築毀於一旦。第一時間的全球社群網站用戶紛紛以 #PrayForNepal 作為信息串流，再次見證了現今 social media 在新聞傳遞或是思想理念傳播的強大力量。

示範對話　(MP3 41)

為尼泊爾祈福

Jason: Did you hear about the earthquake that hit Nepal yesterday?
你知道昨天尼泊爾發生大地震嗎？

Cynthia: No. I've been too busy to watch the news. Was it serious?
不知道耶。我最近太忙沒時間看新聞。嚴重嗎？

Jason: Yeah. It had a magnitude of 7.8.
很嚴重，震度規模 7.8。

Cynthia: Wow—that is serious. Where was the epicenter?
哇！那真的是很嚴重。震央在哪呢？

Jason: In a rural area northwest of Kathmandu.
在加德滿都西北方的郊區。

Cynthia: Is there a major [1)]fault around there?
那裡有什麼大斷層嗎？

Jason: Yes. Two tectonic [2)]plates meet in Nepal—that's how the Himalayas formed.
有啊，兩塊板塊在尼泊爾相遇，所以才形成喜馬拉雅山。

Cynthia: Ah, right. Is the ³⁾death toll high?
喔，對齁。傷亡嚴重嗎？

Jason: I think there are over 3,000 confirmed dead so far, but they say the number will probably double.
我想已經有 3 千人確定死亡，但他們說人數可能還會加倍。

Cynthia: That's terrible. Was most of the ⁴⁾destruction in the country-side?
真是太慘了！地震造成的破壞大部份都在郊區嗎？

Jason: Well, rescue teams haven't been able to reach a lot of areas yet, but they say that some villages were almost completely destroyed. The death toll may actually be lower in the countryside though, because most people were working outdoors when the earthquake hit.
很多地方搜救隊伍還沒有辦法到達，但他們說很多村莊幾乎全部被摧毀。但在在鄉間的罹難人數可能會比較低。因為地震發生時，大部份的人都在外工作。

Cynthia: So there were more ⁵⁾casualties in Kathmandu?
所以加德滿都的傷亡人數會更多囉？

Jason: Yeah. The population ⁶⁾density is much higher there, and lots of the older buildings are made of brick.
是啊，在那人口密度比較高，而且很多古建築都是用磚頭建造的。

Cynthia: Oh, no. Have there been any big aftershocks?
喔，天啊。有任何大型餘震嗎？

Jason: Well, lots of small ones. But a lot of people are sleeping outdoors because they're worried a big one may hit.
有很多小餘震。但許多人都已因擔心大餘震襲擊而睡在外面了。

---

1. fault (n.) 斷層
2. plate (n.) 板塊
3. death toll (n.) 罹難人數
4. destruction (n.) 摧毀
5. casualty (n.) 傷亡人數
6. density (n.) 密度

好用短句　(MP3 42)

談尼泊爾地震
你還你還可以說

· A powerful earthquake struck between the capital Kathmandu and the city of Pokhara.

一場強烈地震襲擊首都加德滿都及博克拉市之間。

· The landmark Dharahara tower is one of the many buildings reduced to rubble in Kathmandu.

知名地標達拉哈拉塔是加德滿都眾多被夷為平地的建築物中的一座。

· The massive 7.9 magnitude earthquake hit Nepal with devastating force less than 50 miles from the capital, Kathmandu causing tremors in northern India as well.

規模 7.9 的強大地震以距離加德滿都不到 50 英里的強大破壞力震擊尼泊爾，震波也觸及了北印度。

· Tremors have been felt as far away as Bangladesh and Delhi.

震波一路延伸到孟加拉以及德里。

· Thousands of people died in the catatrophe in Nepal as survivors face lack of water, food, shelter.

數千人死於尼泊爾大災，而生還者則須面對食物與水、避難所短缺等難題。

The Controversy of Prisoner Abuse
虐囚爭議

Hit! 話題單字 (MP3 43)

scandal 醜聞

scandal 有「醜聞；醜行」的意思，例如：a financial/political scandal（金融／政治的醜聞），a scandal breaks 是指醜聞被眾人所知，意即「爆發醜聞」。scandal 也做「（關於醜聞的）傳言」或「流言蜚語」解釋，為不可數名詞，to spread scandal（散播謠言）。

新聞這樣說

The Apache Scandal was exposed after Taiwanese TV presenter Janet Lee posted photos on Facebook that showed her posing in the cockpit of an Apache helicopter.

台灣節目主持人李蒨蓉在臉書張貼一張她在阿帕契戰機駕駛艙的照片後，阿帕契醜聞也因而展開。

戰俘 prisoner of war (POW)

prisoner of war 是指「戰俘」，意即在戰場上被敵方活抓的軍人，用以做為戰爭交換條件的人質（hostage）籌碼。

新聞這樣說

America's only prisoner of war has been freed in Afghanistan after the US agreed to release five Taliban fighters held at Guantánamo Bay. President Barack Obama announced that Sergeant Bowe Bergdahl had been released nearly five years after he was captured near the Pakistani border.

在美國同意釋放居留在關塔那摩灣的 5 名塔利班戰士後，阿富汗隨之釋放了美國唯一戰俘。總統歐巴馬宣布被拘禁於巴基斯坦邊境 5 年的 Bowe Bergdahl 軍官已被釋放。

humanitarian 人道（主義）的

形容詞 humanitarian（人道主義的）是從名詞 humanity（人類、人道）變化而來。人道主義是指「對人群抱有仁愛精神，不忍他人遭受不平等待遇的情懷」。常見的用語有 humanitarian aid（人道救援）、humanitarian mission（人道任務）等等。

新聞這樣說

The president of Kiribati, the prime minister of Tuvalu, the premier of Niue and the foreign ministers of Australia and New Zealand are all attending the regional meeting of the World Humanitarian Summit.

吉里巴斯總統、吐瓦魯總理、紐埃首相以及澳洲、紐西蘭外交部長都將參與世界人道主義高峰會的地區會議。

以軍法審判
court-martial

court-martial 為動詞，意指「以軍法審判」，常以被動式表示，因某事遭受軍法審判，要說「be court-martialed for 某事」。court martial 則為名詞，指「軍事法庭」或「軍事審判」。注意此字複數型為 courts martial。

新聞這樣說

A few dozen members of the military were court-martialed for misconduct like the well-documented humiliations inflicted at Abu Ghraib prison in Iraq.

數十名軍人因在伊拉克的阿布格布來監獄罪證確鑿之強加虐囚等不當行為，而遭到軍法審判。

日內瓦公約
Geneva Conventions

日內瓦公約（Geneva Conventions）是指西元 1846 年到 1949 年間，各國於日內瓦簽訂，關於減輕戰爭對軍人和平民造成損害的一系列國際條約（treaty）。

新聞這樣說

In 2006, the U.S. Supreme Court ruled U.S. President George W. Bush didn't have authority, under military law or the Geneva Conventions, to set up military tribunals for terror suspects at Guantanamo Bay in Cuba.

2006 年美國最高法院裁決於軍法及日內瓦公約條款之下，美國總統布希無權在古巴關塔納摩灣舉行軍事裁決。

國安
national security

national 源自名詞 nation（國家）這個字，有「全國性的；國家的；國有的」等意思，常見的用語有 national holiday（國定假日）、national interests（國家利益）、national museum（國立博物館）等等。

新聞這樣說

China has passed a wide-ranging national security law expanding its legal reach over the internet and even outer space as concerns grow about ever-tighter limits on rights.

中國通過了一項涵蓋範圍廣泛的國安法，將其法律控制延伸至網路以及外太空，同時也引起人權日漸縮減的關注。

起訴 prosecute

prosecute 做及物動詞時，有「起訴；控告」之意，受詞為「人或組織」，也就是被起訴或控告的對象，to prosecute…for + something/ doing something（起訴某人或組織犯了某罪）。

新聞這樣說

Chinese authorities have arrested a former University of Iowa student in southeastern China and say they will prosecute him in the killing of his girlfriend in Iowa, where her body was found stuffed into the trunk of her car, Iowa City police said.

中國檢方已在中國東南部逮捕並將起訴愛荷華大學學生，愛荷華市警方表示他在愛荷華殺害其女友並將他屍體塞入後車廂。

prisoner abuse

虐囚

abuse 有「虐待」的意思，prisoner 是「囚犯、犯人」，合在一起便指「虐囚」，為不可數名詞。類似的用語還有 child abuse（虐待兒童）、sexual abuse（性虐待）、self-abuse（自虐）等等。

新聞這樣說

At a time when American media is still exposing incidents of Iraqi prisoner abuse by American soldiers, a militant Muslim website has posted a video of the revenge beheading of an American businessman. The conflict was officially declared over following the capture of Saddam Hussein, but it seems that the media is currently exposing a new form of the continuing conflict.

美國媒體正陸續爆料顯示美軍虐待伊拉克囚犯之際，一個回教民兵網公布了斬首美國商人的報復影片。美伊戰爭隨著海珊被捕而宣告結束，但現在似乎有另一種形式的戰爭正藉由媒體爆發。

殘酷的戰爭

從越戰、二戰到伊拉克戰爭，虐囚事件層出不窮，常見的手段有：

- 肢體虐待 physical abuse
- 精神虐待 psychological abuse
- 性虐待 sexual abuse
- 嚴刑拷問 enhanced interrogation
- 拷打 torture

戰爭本身就已經是人性黑暗殘酷性質的體現，對於戰俘的處置更是一件需要以人道主義謹慎處理的事件。

示範對話 (MP3 44)

虐囚醜聞

Allan: Look at these pictures. These soldiers are [1]peeing on this prisoner.
看看這些照片。這些士兵在這個犯人身上尿尿。

Beth: That's [2]disgusting. How could they do such a thing?
那真噁心。他們怎麼可以做這種事？

Allan: This is even worse. They're beating him with the [3]butts of their guns.
這張更糟哩。他們在用槍柄打他。

Beth: I thought those soldiers were supposed to be [4]liberating Iraq, not destroying it.
我還以為這些軍人是要去解放伊拉克，而非摧毀它。

Allan: As an American, how does it make you feel to see your country's troops acting this way?
身為一個美國人，看到貴國軍隊這種行徑，妳作何感想？

Beth: Well, when you give people power over life and death, you're [5]bound to create a lot of problems.
這個嘛，當你賦予人生殺大權時，就一定會製造出很多問題。

Allan: No offense, but it sure makes the American and British armies look bad.
無意冒犯，但這件事實在讓美國和英國軍隊顏面掃地。

Beth: None taken. Things will get a lot [6]tougher for Bush and Blair now.
我不在意。這下情況對布希和布萊爾來說越來越棘手了。

Allan: The war in Iraq is probably going to get worse.
在伊拉克的戰爭大概會變得更糟。

Beth: And more people will want to be [7]terrorists.
而且更多人想要變成恐怖分子。

Allan: The U.S. and British armies should prosecute any soldiers and officers involved with these crimes.
美國和英國軍隊應該起訴任何涉案的官兵。

Beth: I think they should make some government officials [8]resign.
我認為他們應該要讓一些官員辭職。

Allan: Either that or [9]withdraw from Iraq altogether.
不然就是乾脆從伊拉克撤軍。

Beth: It's too late to do that now. They've already [10]invaded. Now they have to get their jobs done before they can leave.
現在撤軍太晚了。他們已經入侵啦。現在他們得完成任務才能離開。

Allan: They should have never invaded in the first place.
他們一開始就不該入侵的。

Beth: Try telling that to Bush, Cheney and Rumsfeld. They didn't even listen when millions of people protested.
試著去跟布希、錢尼和倫斯斐說吧。之前幾百萬人抗議，他們都不肯聽了。

---

1. pee (v./n.) 尿尿，小便
2. disgusting (a.) 令人噁心的
3. butt (n.) (武器等) 較粗的一端
4. liberate (v.) 解放，使獲自由
5. bound to… (phr.) 一定會…
6. tough (a.) 棘手的
7. terrorist (n.) 恐怖分子
8. resign (v.) 辭職
9. withdraw (v.) 撤退，退出
10. invade (v.) 入侵，侵略
11. protest (v.) 抗議，反對

好用短句　(MP3 45)

談虐囚
你還要知道

- The prisoner abuse scandal has tarnished the reputation of the American military.

  虐囚醜聞讓美軍的名譽掃地。

- President Bush's approval ratings have gone down dramatically as a result of the scandal.

  布希總統因此醜聞而滿意度大幅下滑。

- Even though Rumsfeld has publicly apologized for the scandal, a lot of people still suspect that he knew about it all along.

  雖然倫斯斐已經為虐囚案公開道歉，許多人還是懷疑他早就知道虐囚的情況。

- The English newspaper *Daily Mirror's* chief editor was fired for publishing fake pictures of British soldiers abusing prisoners.

  英國《每日鏡報》總編輯因刊出造假的英軍虐囚照片而被開除。

- An American businessman in Iraq was beheaded by terrorists as retaliation against the prisoner abuse.

  一位在伊拉克的美國商人被恐怖分子斬首，作為對虐囚的報復。

Invasion of the Mainland Mistresses
二奶的逆襲

性病 STD

完整名稱是 sexually transmitted disease，也稱 STI（sexually transmitted infection），指藉由性交或性器接觸而傳染的疾病。有些性病也會因為共用針頭等行為而傳染給他人，或是經由生產、哺乳而傳至下一代。

新聞這樣說

A group of teenage boys are in the process of inventing condoms that change color when they come into contact with STDs like chlamydia or herpes. Muaz Nawaz, 13, Daanyaal Ali, 14, and Chirag Shah, 14, of London's Isaac Newton Academy are the brains behind the "S. T. EYE" condom.

一群年輕男生正在發明一種可以改變顏色來探測性病（如：泡疹和披衣菌）的保險套，來自倫敦 Isaac Newton 學院 13 歲的 Muaz Nawaz、14 歲的 Daanyaal Ali 以及 14 歲的 Chirag Shah 是 "S . T. EYE" 保險套的幕後智囊團。

私生的 illegitimate

legitimate 是「合法的；婚生的」，若前面加上「否定」的字首 il-，意思便完全相反了。il-是很常見的字首，通常接在 L 開頭的形容詞前面。

新聞這樣說

A district court has ruled that late tycoon Wang Yung-ching's three illegitimate children have bloodties with him and are thus entitled to inherit his assets.

地方法院裁決過世的大亨王永慶的 3 位私生子，由於其血緣關係，是法定繼承人。

mistress 情婦

養小三是 keep a mistress，養很多小三則是 keep a string of mistresses。相對於 master（男主人），mistress 其實在舊式英文的用法中是「女主人」或「女管家」的意思。

新聞這樣說

A Chinese man has been arrested for having 15 mistresses and taking money from all of them. The man is married and has an 18-year-old daughter. He allegedly dated more than a dozen women—including two sharing the same dorm.

一位中國男子因為有 15 位情婦還向她們拿錢而遭到逮捕，他已婚並有一個 18 歲女兒。據稱他不但同時交往超過 12 位女性，其中還有兩個女生同住一間宿舍中。

婚外情 (extra-marital) affair

除了「婚外情」之外，affair 還可表示「事件；事情」，通常用單數表示，與 event 同義。但是，做「事務；業務」解釋時，則需用複數表示，例如：foreign affairs（外交事務）。

新聞這樣說

South Korea's constitutional court ruled on Feb 26 that having an extramarital affair was not a crime, striking out a 62-year-old law that put adulterers in jail for up to two years.

南韓的憲政法院在 2 月 26 日判定婚外情不再是違法行為，推翻了長達 62 年通姦者須服刑兩年的法條。

通姦 adultery

adultery 是指已婚者的婚外性行為（extramarital sex），為不可數名詞，與某人通姦的說法為 commit adultery with somebody。

新聞這樣說

South Korea was one of only three Asian countries to still criminalize adultery, alongside Taiwan and the Philippines. All European nations have decriminalized adultery and, while it is not considered a criminal offence in most Western parts, it may still have legal consequences, especially in divorce proceedings.

南韓、台灣以及菲律賓是目前僅存仍將通姦視為犯罪的三個亞洲國家。所有歐洲國家都將通姦除罪，然而在離婚過程中，通姦行為仍須承擔法律上的後果。

離婚率 divorce rate

get a divorce（with somebody）、getting divorced（with somebody）、divorce somebody 都是表示離婚的說法。divorce 也有「使分離；使脫離」之意，例如：He is unable to divorce fantasy from reality.（他不能將幻想與現實分開）。

新聞這樣說

Taiwan saw a lower divorce rate in 2014 of a total of 53,144 divorces in 2014, down 0.8 percent from the previous year, according to the latest statistics released by the Ministry of the Interior Saturday.

台灣內政部週六發佈一項數據，指出 2014 年共有五萬三千一百四十四件離婚案，台灣離婚率比起前一年下降 0.8 %。

外籍配偶 foreign spouse

foreign 是形容詞，有「外國的；在國外的；對外的」等意思，spouse 為正式說法或法律用詞，意思是「配偶」。foreign 後面加 er，意指外國人（foreigner），外語是 foreign language，外幣則是 foreign currency。

新聞這樣說

Employers of foreign spouses of Taiwanese nationals will soon be required to contribute funds toward their pensions as part of the amended Labor Pension Act that cleared the Legislature on Tuesday.

外籍配偶的雇主，基於週二頒布之部分勞工退休金修正條例，必須支付外籍配偶員工之勞保。

兩岸夾流
cross-straits interaction

cross 有橫越之意，straits 是海峽，cross-straits 則指海峽兩岸。interaction between，做「互動」解釋，若接 with，則為「互相影響」的意思。

新聞這樣說

In 2007, there were no direct flights between Taiwan and China. Now, there are more than 800 such crossings per week. The government sees only positive in such interaction, both in terms of expanding markets and in reducing isolationism between the two competing visions of China.

2007 年時，台灣和中國之間還沒有任何直飛班機，現在一週則有超過 800 班航機穿梭海峽兩岸。對政府來說，這是一個正向改變，不但能拓展市場還能降低台灣孤立。

總統的小三

美國政治史上最有名的婚外情對象非瑪莉蓮夢露和莫尼卡陸文斯基莫屬。瑪莉蓮夢露這位傳奇女星當年和甘迺迪總統的緋聞至今仍是美國人津津樂道的話題，一曲「生日快樂，總統先生」透露了總統和性感女神的曖昧之情，雖然這段風流韻事從未受到證實，但隨著瑪莉蓮的逝世，許多消息將其死因指向甘迺迪家族以及政治陰謀，使這段婚外情更添神秘。莫尼卡陸文斯基則是 2016 年美國總統候選人希拉蕊柯林頓這輩子最不想提到的人，當年 22 歲的莫尼卡陸文斯基和 49 歲的柯林頓總統聯手上演一段美國政治史最大性醜聞。在 1995、1996 年間，總統和實習生的婚外情演變成史上第二位美國總統彈劾案，莫尼卡陸文斯基沾有柯林頓精液的藍色洋裝已經成為美國近代文化的指標性物件，第一夫人希拉蕊柯林頓在 2003 年出版的回憶錄中曾提到：「我一生做過最困難的決定，就是選擇維持這段婚姻以及參選紐約議員。」在柯林頓必須出庭作證的前一晚，希拉蕊柯林頓才知道婚外情的真相，她說：「身為總統的妻子，我當下真想扭斷他脖子。」

示範對話 (MP3 47)

中國小老婆

Lynn: You going to Hong Kong for business?
你要去香港出差？

Nate: No. Just stopping there [1)]en route to Shanghai.
不。只是過境要去上海。

Lynn: Imagine if there were direct flights and we didn't have to pass through Hong Kong.
想想要是有直航班機，我們就不必過境香港了。

Nate: That would be great, but aren't there all sorts of political problems [3)]involved?
那就太讚了，但不是牽涉到林林總總的政治問題嗎？

Lynn: Yes, there are. There are lots of reasons to restrict cross-Straits interaction.
是，的確有。有許多原因限制了兩岸交流。

Nate: But wouldn't it be nice for people from both sides to learn more about each other?
但要是兩邊的人能夠彼此多了解，不是挺好的？

Lynn: Sure, but apart from the political problems, there will be personal problems, too.
的確，但撇開政治問題，還會有個人的問題。

Nate: What do you mean, exactly?
妳真正想說的是？

Lynn: Have you heard about a lot of Taiwanese businessmen keeping mistresses in China?
你聽說過很多台商在中國養小老婆嗎？

Nate: Oh, I see what you're talking about. Imagine if all of them came over to find their men!
喔，我懂妳在說什麼了。要是她們全都跑來找她們的男人就慘了！

Lynn: Exactly! Taiwan's divorce rate would go even higher.
沒錯！台灣的離婚率就會變得更高了。

Nate: This is an 6)angle I've never thought about. Are many business-men scared?
我從沒用這個角度思考過。許多台商感到害怕嗎？

Lynn: Who knows? It would make for a fun opinion poll though.
誰會知道？但這會是個有趣的意見調查題目。

Nate: Do you have any idea how many businessmen keep mistresses over there?
妳知道有多少台商在那邊養小老婆嗎？

Lynn: I would guess a 8)majority, but of course it's hard to say. Do you?
我猜大多數都有，但這當然很難說。你有嗎？

Nate: Ha-ha, very funny. You have a nice flight.
哈哈，愛說笑。祝妳一路順風。

---

1. en route 在途中（＝ on the way）　2. direct flight 直航班機
3. involve (v.) 牽涉到，涉及　4. restrict (v.) 限制
5. interaction (n.) 相互影響，交流　6. angle (n.) 觀點，看事情的角度
7. opinion poll 意見調查　8. majority (n.) 大多數

好用短句 (MP3 48)

談小三
你還可以說

- It's said that 8 or 9 out of 10 Taiwanese business-men who go to mainland China without their families will take a mistress.

據說單獨前往大陸的台商，十之八九都會包二奶。

- These businessmen say they take a mistress out of loneliness and because the women there actively pursue them.

這些台商說他們包二奶的理由是寂寞，而且當地的女生也會主動示好。

- This leaves the partners of these Taiwanese businessmen that remain in Taiwan very ill at ease.

這種情況讓留在台灣的台商配偶非常擔心。

- Hence, if they can find a way to do so, most of these partners will choose to accompany their husbands to mainland China.

所以，許多台商配偶只要能找出方法，都會選擇跟著先生一起到大陸。

Waves of Charity
海嘯後的人性光輝

tsunami 源自日語的「津波」，是一種極具破壞力的海浪（wave）。當地震發生於海底（undersea earthquak），震波（seismic wave）會帶動海水（sea water），造成海面劇烈起伏，形成強大的波浪向前推進，進而將沿海地區（coastal areas）淹沒。

tsunami

海嘯

新聞這樣說

A decade ago, one of the largest earthquakes ever recorded struck off the coast of Indonesia, triggering a tsunami that swept away entire communities around the Indian Ocean.

十多年前的一場史上最大地震襲擊印尼海岸，並引起一場橫掃印度洋上眾多地區的致命海嘯。

急救 first aid

aid 意思是「協助、幫忙」，first aid 便指緊急狀況下的優先救援行為；first aid kit 則是「急救箱」。aid 也常用指輔助工具，例如做簡報用的「視覺輔助」就叫 visual aids。

新聞這樣說

As there were still many injured waiting to be rushed to hospitals by ambulance, the Ministry of Heath and Social Welfare mobilized medical personnel from Taipei, New Taipei, Keelung and Taoyuan to open the on-site first aid stations to provide emergency treatment.

衛福部在許多傷者仍在原地等待救護車救援的同時，招集了來自台北市、新北市、基隆以及桃園的醫療團隊在災難現場開設急救站，提供急救治療。

捐贈 donation

donation 為名詞，意指「捐贈（金錢、物品）」，英文用法為 make a donation to somebody/something（捐贈給某人或某組織）。常見的捐贈還有 organ donation「器官捐贈」、 blood donation「捐血」等。

新聞這樣說

A former Chinese vice minister's offer to help set up a mechanism to facilitate organ donations from China to Taiwan should be viewed with caution, considering its legal and political implications, officials and the head of an organ registry center said.

器官捐贈中心表示，前中國衛生部副部長提議要建立中國至台灣器官捐贈程序的機制，應被謹慎監督，特別是其中法律與政治性的考量。

生還者 survivor

survivor 從動詞 survive「存活、倖存」衍生而來，指從意外及災難中，倖存的生還者。survive 也有「比……活得久」（outlive）的意思，所以 survivor 也常用來指喪失近親的生者。

新聞這樣說

The number of survivors from the cruise ship which capsized in the Yangtze River on June 1 was revised to 12 following verification, making the final death toll at 442, local authorities announced at a press briefing on Saturday.

當地相關當局於週六的記者會上表示，長江翻船意外的生還人數目前統計為 12 人，總罹難人數達到 442 人。

災難 disaster

fire 當名詞時，可解釋為「火」、「爐火」、「火災」、「砲火」等意思，還可指「熱情」。與 fire 相關的片語非常多，不勝枚舉，例如：on/catch fire（著火）、make/build a fire（生火）、put out the fire（滅火）、under fire（遭受攻擊）。

新聞這樣說

The Ministry of Health and Welfare has activated its emergency response mechanism following the nation's worst amusement park disaster, in which a fire broke out at New Taipei City's Formosa Fun Coast water park on Saturday night, leaving nearly 500 people injured.

衛服部啟動了緊急反應機制，為的就是因應台灣史上最嚴重遊樂園災難，新北市八仙水上樂園的塵爆事件讓近 500 位民眾受傷。

樂捐 pledge

pledge 有「承諾、誓約」的涵義，跟 donate「捐贈」意思相近，但 pledge 通常指持續一段時間或承諾救助的捐獻。近年比爾蓋茲、巴菲特等全球超級富豪紛紛加入樂捐身後財產的慈善活動就叫做 The Giving Pledge。

新聞這樣說

The United States has pledged an additional $133 million in humanitarian assistance for South Sudan, where U.S. officials say a surge in fighting in recent months has caused conditions to deteriorate sharply.

美國已捐款美金一億三千三百萬至南蘇丹人道援助款項中，官員並表示最近幾個月的爭鬥使那地區的情況更加慘烈。

救濟 relief

relief 為名詞，有「緩和、減輕痛苦或不快」的意思。新聞用語中常見的「賑災活動」或「救援行動」英文則是 relief effort。effort 同樣是名詞，表示「努力」或「嘗試」，在此指「（人們為達某目的）有組織的行動」。

新聞這樣說

The premier on Monday said there was no need for a special provision bill, financial assistance through a special budget allocation and a dedicated agency to administrate post-disaster relief and reconstruction for Kaohsiung.

行政院長週一表示，高雄災後重建並不需要一個特別補助條款或是相關處理單位執行。

供人們躲避惡劣天氣或危險的「遮蔽物」或「避難處」都可以叫 shelter，例如 bus shelter（候車亭）和 bomb shelter（防空洞）。此外，收容無家可歸者或流浪動物的場所也是 shelter，即俗稱的「收容所」或「避護所」。

避難（所）
shelter

新聞這樣說

When a major earthquake triggers a giant tsunami in the U.S. Pacific Northwest, as experts predict, one coastal town will be ready. Residents of the small Oregon town of Cannon Beach are preparing to build the first tsunami-resistant shelter in the U.S.

若一場由地震引發的大海嘯，真由專家預測的襲擊美國太平洋西北方，位於奧勒岡 Cannon Beach 鎮的民眾會做好萬全準備，因為他們正要建造美國第一座海嘯避難所。

南亞浩劫

2004 年 12 月 26 號一場發生在印尼外海規模 9.1 的超級地震（史上第三大地震）造成南亞 14 個以上國家天搖地動超過 10 分鐘，這是史上持續最久的地震，它讓整個地球震動了約 0.4 英寸幅度，造成全球多處地震，最遠直達美國阿拉斯加，並且引發了史上最致命的海嘯。首當其衝的印尼、斯里蘭卡、印度以及泰國傷亡慘重，全南亞超過 14 國都受到影響，超過 22 萬人罹難。隔年 1 月 5 日正午，歐盟 25 成員國，超過 4.5 億公民全體為海嘯罹難者默哀 3 分鐘。災後，聯合國立即展開史上最大規模救災行動，全球貢獻超過 140 億的捐款。這一天也是瑞典自 1709 年後，史上最多國民在單一意外事件罹難的記錄，超過 543 位遊客斷魂於海嘯。這次災難以最殘酷的方式，點出東南亞、南亞等國家因觀光旅遊業過度開發海岸線而產生的危機，也讓各國家當局特別注意海嘯過後沿海城市的重建。

示範對話　(MP3 50)

海嘯捐款潮

Lady: Pardon me, sir. Do you have a minute?
對不起，先生。您有空嗎？

Jon: Make it quick, because I'm [1]in a hurry to get to work.
快一點，因為我正趕著去上班。

Lady: I understand, but millions of people need your help.
我了解，可是有上百萬人需要您的幫助。

Jon: Oh, you're working for the tsunami relief effort, aren't you?
喔，妳在為海嘯賑災募款，對吧？

Lady: Exactly. You can read Chinese? Or you were looking at the pictures?
沒錯。你會看中文？還是你看的是這些照片？

Jon: The pictures. You know, I have some friends down there working on relief efforts.
照片。妳知道嗎，我有幾個朋友在那裡賑災。

Lady: Really? Well, I'm out here [2]collecting [3]contributions.
真的嗎？我則是在這邊募款。

115

Jon: Where exactly would my money be going?
我的錢到底會用在哪裡？

Lady: We're a ⁴⁾Buddhist charity organization, and we've sent doctors down to help.
我們是一個佛教慈善團體，我們已經派醫生前去幫忙。

Jon: I suppose I can ⁵⁾spare some cash. Let me see. [*hands over a ⁶⁾bill*]
我想我可以捐些現金。讓我看看。（遞出一張鈔票）

Lady: Thank you so much. ⁷⁾Every little bit helps.
非常感謝您。每分每毫都有幫助。

Jon: I know. This disaster is ⁸⁾unprecedented. I know a lot of people who want to help but don't know how.
我知道。這真是場前所未有的災難。我知道有很多人想幫忙，但是不知從何幫起。

Lady: People around the world have been donating, and many governments have ⁹⁾gotten on board.
世界各地的人都在捐獻，許多政府也已加入。

Jon: I know. I just hope the money is going to the right places. Do you think Taiwan could be 10)at risk for tsunamis too?
我知道。我只是希望錢會用對地方。妳想台灣也會有海嘯的危險嗎？

Lady: We've had huge earthquakes, as you probably know. But the Pacific has tsunami warning systems.
你或許已經知道，我們曾經發生大地震。不過，太平洋有海嘯預警系統。

Jon: It's too bad the Indian Ocean didn't have one too.
真可惜印度洋沒有。

---

1. in a hurry 急著，急忙地
2. collect (v.) 募捐
3. contribution (n.) 捐助，捐獻
4. Buddhist (a.) 佛教的
5. spare (v.) 讓出，割愛
6. bill (n.) 鈔票
7. Every little bit helps. (phr.)
   即使一點點也有幫助
8. unprecedented (a.) 史無前例的
9. get on board (phr.) 參與，加入
10. at risk 處於危險中，有風險

好用短句 (MP3 51)

談海嘯賑災
你還可以說

- Nearly 300,000 people died in the tsunami.

將近三十萬人在那場海嘯中喪生。

- Countries across the world donated five billion dollars.

世界各國的捐款有五十億美元。

- But disaster zones have only received half the aid.

但目前抵達災區的捐款僅有一半。

- Many survivors are suffering from illnesses and stress.

許多生還者仍飽受疾病和恐懼之苦。

- Thailand's tourism industry also suffered a heavy blow.

泰國的觀光業更是損失慘重。

Hail to the New Chief
中國當家換人做

socialism
社會主義

social 做名詞時，為「社會」之意，做形容詞時，則是指「社會的」。字尾-ism 有「信仰、主義」的意思。。信奉社會主義的人則稱為 socialist（社會主義者）。

新聞這樣說

Ironically, across the straits, Taiwan shows that it is possible to combine prosperity and democracy, and indeed practice socialism—or at least European style social democracy—in a Chinese culture.

說來諷刺，兩岸之中的台灣證明了，即便在中國文化之下，經濟繁榮與民主制度和社會主義的實踐——至少是歐洲方式的社會民主，得以共存。

領導統御，領導人 leadership

字尾-ship 接於名詞之後，有「狀態；能力」的意思，名詞 leader 則有「領導者」之意。leadership 為不可數名詞，而 the leadership 則為「領導階層（統稱）」。

新聞這樣說

Taiwan's ruling party is going to have new leadership. Eric Chu, mayor of New Taipei City, is set to become the next chairman of Taiwan's ruling party Kuomintang (KMT) on Jan. 19 as party members cast their ballots to elect their new leader Saturday.

台灣執政黨主席即將換人，新北市市長朱立倫在 1 月 19 日星期六，通過黨員投票，將接手主席一職。

民主 democracy

字根 demo 是指「一般人」（common people），加上有「治理」（government）之意的字尾 -cracy，便是「由人民來治理」，意即「民主」。democracy 還有「民主政體／制度」與「民主國家」的意思，反義詞為 authoritarianism（獨裁主義）。

新聞這樣說

Hong Kong's government put together an electoral reform package based on Beijing's ruling. But pro-democracy legislators vetoed the bill, which requires the support of two-thirds of the 70-seat legislature to pass.

香港政府依照北京指示擬訂一份選舉改革的法案，然而追求民主的立法委員否定了這項需要所有 70 位立法委員裡超過三分之二票數才能通過的法案。

共產 communism

communism 為不可數名詞，指「共產主義」或「共產主義制度」，communist 則是「共產主義者」或「共產黨黨員」，當形容詞用時，則做「共產主義的」或「共產黨的」解釋。

新聞這樣說

In the space of scarcely one generation, Shanghai has transformed itself from a city of narrow lanes and decrepit buildings. It's commerce one crippled by decades of communism, is now a futuristic megalopolis of 23m people, packed with skyscrapers and luxury malls, and the undisputed financial capital of China.

在僅僅一個世代內，上海已從狹窄巷弄、荒廢建築物、共產制度下的腐敗經濟，轉變成 2 千 3 百萬人口、充滿未來感、滿載摩天大樓及高級百貨的超級都會，也是無可取代的中國財經首都。

統馭 reins

rein 的本意為用於控制馬匹的「（皮）韁繩」，引申有「駕馭；控制；統治」等意思，多用複數 reins 表示。keep a tight rein on somebody/something（嚴格控制某人事物）、take over the reins（接掌控制權、統治權）、hand over the reins（交出控制權、統治權）為常見的慣用語。

新聞這樣說

Baghdad's first female mayor is set to take the reins. Zekra Alwach, a civil engineer and director general of the ministry of higher education, becomes the first female to be given such a post in the whole country, where international rights groups have condemned women's rights abuses.

巴格達的第一位女性市長即將掌權統馭。Zekra Alwach，一位土木工程師及高等教育部部長，即將成為這個備受國際人權組織譴責的國家首位得到此職位的女性。

premier 總理，行政院院長

premier 這個字用於新聞報導（news reports）上，意指 prime minister（首相；總理），類似台灣的行政院院長，在加拿大指「省長」，在澳洲則是指「州長」。此外，premier 做形容詞用時，有「最重要的；最好的；最大的」等意思。

新聞這樣說

The premier of Taiwan, Jiang Yi-huah, has resigned after his ruling pro-China party suffered heavy defeats in local elections. The Kuomintang party (KMT) appears to have lost control of districts across the country, including the mayor's office in the capital, Taipei.

台灣行政院長江宜樺在親中黨派地方選舉的慘敗後辭職下台。國民黨似乎漸漸失去地方民心，甚至失去台北市長的寶座。

軍閥 warlord

warlord 由名詞 war（戰爭）和 lord（主人）組成，意指軍事團體（military group）的領袖，但這個軍事團體通常不合法（illegal），且與政府或其他團體作戰對抗，中文常譯作「軍閥」。

新聞這樣說

Vladimir the Great or the Grand Prince was a warlord who became the first Russian ruler to convert to Christianity in the late 900s—before insisting that his people did the same. That was the beginning of the Russian Orthodox Church.

弗拉基米爾一世是位軍閥，也是第一位在西元 900 末期成為基督徒的俄國統治者，隨後堅持其人民轉信基督教，這也是俄國東正教的開端。

下台 step down

指自行卸除職務並離開工作崗位，也可說成 step aside，不過 step aside 較偏向「放棄職位，轉而讓給別人」，step down 則有被迫下台的意味。

新聞這樣說

Taiwan's president on Tuesday said he was stepping down as chairman of the ruling party in a widely expected move that comes after the Kuomintang was trounced in local elections on the weekend.

國民黨在此次選舉慘敗，總統週二宣布他將會如外界預料，辭去國民黨主席一職。

古巴新方向

中國是目前世界上仍奉行社會主義的四個國家之一，其餘分別為越南、古巴國以及寮國。除了中國已晉升世界超級強國，古巴共和國的發展也是世界注目焦點。古巴自革命成功以來，外交政策一直奉行國際主義，為的就是爭取更多國際生存空間，更以其優異的醫療技術，為許多受災國家提供無償人道救援。車諾比核災中，就有超過 1.8 萬的孩童在古巴得到免費治療；然而，古巴政府對於人權的壓迫，一直受到國際人權組織撻伐。在 2008 年，古巴囚禁記者人數僅次於中國，古巴國內幾乎沒有任何政治言論自由，全國上下高度戒備監獄高達 40 座，並有超過 200 座勞改營。和美國緊張的外交關係中，首度在 2009 年看見曙光，歐盟率先與古巴恢復全面合作關係，美國總統歐巴馬則取消古巴裔美國人至古巴旅遊及匯款的限制，開放了長達超過 50 年的旅遊禁令，讓古巴移民得以探親；許多美國旅行社也推出套裝行程，促進兩國觀光。2014 年，歐巴馬及古巴領導人勞爾卡斯楚共同宣布，古美將恢復中斷超過半世紀的外交關係。

示範對話 (MP3 53)

中國新氣象

萬歲

Steven: Can I ask you a question? Have you been to China before?
我可以問妳一個問題嗎？妳有去過中國嗎？

Kate: Yes, actually. Why do you ask?
有耶。為何這樣問？

Steven: If you look at the TV news, you'll see that they're changing their leadership.
如果妳有看一下電視新聞，就會知道他們正在換領導人。

Kate: Oh yes, Jiang Zemin is stepping down and giving the reins to Hu Jintao.
喔，對，江澤民要下台，交棒給胡錦濤。

Steven: Do you think China will become more 4)democratic now?
妳覺得中國此後會變得比較民主嗎？

Kate: I don't see how this would make it more democratic.
我看不出來為何這樣會讓中國變的比較民主。

Steven: Are you sad to see Jiang go?
妳不想看到江澤民走？

Kate: Is anyone? He's a ⁵⁾geriatric case who shares responsibility for the Tiananmen ⁶⁾massacre.
會有人不想嗎？他是要為天安門大屠殺負起責任的老人幫之一。

Steven: I see you have strong opinions. You've spent a lot of time in China?
看得出來妳很有主見。妳在中國待了很久？

Kate: I spent about a year there and had to watch President Jiang on TV a lot.
我在那裡待了一年左右，而且常常在電視上看到江主席。

Steven: It beat watching President Chen, right?
總比看到阿扁總統好，對吧？

Kate: No, actually President Chen is more ⁹⁾entertaining. And the ¹⁰⁾media here is more free.
不，其實阿扁總統有趣多了。而且這裡的媒體也比較自由。

Steven: Well, that goes without saying.
嗯，那還用說。

Kate: So do you think Hu will make any big changes in China?
那你覺得胡錦濤會在中國發動改革嗎？

Steven: He seems younger and more ¹¹⁾in touch with the people.
他似乎比較年輕，跟人民接觸比較多。

Kate: I'll believe it when I see it.
我要親眼看到才會相信。

Steven: He and Premier Wen seem a little less ¹²⁾conservative than Jiang, too.
他跟總理溫家寶似乎也沒有江澤民那麼保守。

Kate: True enough. I guess we all have to hope for the best, because there's little we can do from here.
的確是。我想我們只能聽天由命，因為我們在這裡能做的畢竟有限。

---

1. leadership (n.) 領導，領導權
2. step down 下台，辭職
3. reins (n.) 統馭
4. democratic (a.) 民主的
5. geriatric (a.) 老番癲的
6. massacre (n.) 大屠殺
7. opinion (n.) 意見，看法
8. president (n.) 總統，主席
9. entertaining (a.) 令人愉快的，有趣的
10. media (n.) 媒體
11. in touch with 和…有接觸
12. conservative (a.) 保守的，守舊的

好用短句　(MP3 54)

談中國領導人
還可以說

- Jiang Zemin gave up his power over the military, leaving him with no more leadership positions.

江澤民交出軍權後，就沒有任何領導職務了。

- Even though he's stepped down, he still wields a lot of influence.

即使他下台了，仍然有很大的影響力。

- Even though China's gained a young leader, relations with Taiwan remain just as tense.

雖然中國換上比較年輕的領導者，可是與台灣的關係依舊很緊張。

- No matter who leads the country, the PRC still refuses to give up the threat of invading Taiwan.

不論國家領導人是誰，中國始終不願放棄武力犯台。

- Like Jiang Zemin, Hu Jintao was selected by Deng Xiaoping.

就跟江澤民一樣，胡錦濤也是鄧小平欽點的。

Chapter Four

Society & Life
社　　會
時事開口說

相信許多鄉土劇的靈感來源就是台灣的社會新聞，從民生食品安全問題、天災人禍到台灣人特色活動：排隊。每天轉到新聞台，社會新聞絕對包羅萬象、匪夷所思、千奇百怪，各家新聞台更是致力於創造出讓人啼笑皆非、唯恐天下不亂的驚悚標題。從社會新聞可看見一個國家的民族性以及社會風氣，更是所有台灣人閒話家常的主題。所以，你一定不能不知道如何用英文說出以下這些很有可能出現在下星期《世Ｘ情》劇情裡的台灣社會新聞。

Is Anything Safe to Eat?
黑心風暴

有毒的
toxic

常與副詞 extremely / highly / quite（非常、極度、相當）連用，需加在 toxic 的前面，be toxic to 為「對～有毒的」，反義字是 nontoxic。

新聞這樣說

Vietnam's agriculture ministry has ordered an exhaustive investigation into allegations that some black tea shipments to Taiwan were contaminated with the highly toxic compound dioxin.

越南農業局下令進行一項全面的調查，檢驗出口台灣的紅茶是否被含有毒性極強的戴奧辛物質汙染。

塑化劑 plasticizer

塑化劑的分子結構類似動物體內的荷爾蒙（hormone），因此被稱為環境荷爾蒙，長期接觸恐會提高女性賀爾蒙相關癌症的風險，也會影響孩童的發育，導致男童行為易有女性化（feminization）傾向。

新聞這樣說

Plasticizers are chemical additives used to make plastic more pliable, but they were found in food additives such as clouding agents—a food additive used to emulsify drinks and make them look more appealing—sparking a food scare.

塑化劑為一種化學添加劑，可以讓塑膠更加柔軟，但近來在食物中發現它被用作於起雲劑，一種可以乳化飲料，讓它們看起來更好喝，結果引起食品危機。

致癌的 carcinogenic

名詞為 carcinogen，意思是「致癌物」，相關的用語有 known carcinogen（已知的致癌物）和 potential/ suspected carcinogen（可能的致癌物）。

新聞這樣說

Antioxidant preservatives like BHA and BHT that are used to keep potato chips, chewing gum, cereals from going rancid can be carcinogenic. They are known to impact negatively on appetite and sleep, can damage the kidneys and liver, and can even cause hair loss.

用來防止洋芋片、口香糖、麥片腐壞的抗氧化劑如 BHA、BHT 皆可能致癌，他們不但會造成食慾不振、引響睡眠品質、損害腎臟以及肝臟，甚至會造成落髮。

摻雜的 adulterated

動詞 adulterate 有「攙雜；攙假」的意思，用法為 adulterate something with，多用被動式表現。

新聞這樣說

Leechi is among hundreds of Taiwanese bakeries and eateries that were found last week to have sold desserts and dishes made with substandard cooking oil. Most of them say they didn't know their Kaohsiung-based supplier, Chang Guann Co., might have adulterated lard oil with restaurant and slaughterhouse waste.

犁記以及其他上百家麵包店及餐廳上週被檢驗出使用次等油製作點心。其中多數都表示，並不知情位於高雄的油供應商強冠會將豬油摻雜餐廳以及屠宰場的回收油。

農藥、殺蟲劑 pesticide

也可稱作 insecticide。pest 是「害蟲」，字尾 -cide 有「殺害」的意思，合在一起就是用來去除害蟲的農藥，也就是殺蟲劑，類似的作法還有 herbicide（除草劑）。

新聞這樣說

Mainland China's department in charge of import food safety announced yesterday that it will strengthen inspections on pineapples from Taiwan, after some tested positive for a toxic pesticide.

中國大陸負責進口食物安全的部門昨天表示，在台灣進口的鳳梨驗出有毒農藥後，將會加強檢驗。

受污染的 tainted

動詞 taint 有「腐壞；汙染」的意思，也可做「毀損；玷汙（地位或名譽）」解釋，但多用被動式表示。tainted 則為形容詞，有「腐壞的；受污染的；被玷污的」之意。

新聞這樣說

Frozen seafood at popular buffet restaurants was reported to be tainted with chemical compounds exceeding allowable amounts, the Taipei City Department of Health (DOH, 台北市衛生局) revealed yesterday.

台北市衛生局昨天公布，人氣自助餐廳的冷凍海鮮街檢驗出超標的化學物質汙染。

餿水油 gutter oil

gutter 是指道路旁的「排水溝」或是屋頂上承接雨水的「簷槽」。當動詞時，為文學用語，意指（燭火）搖曳不定，gutter oil 表示逐漸變慢變弱，最終熄滅、停止。

新聞這樣說

Chang Guann Co (強冠企業), a food oil manufacturer in Greater Kaohsiung, yesterday apologized to the public after one of its lard products was allegedly found to be tainted with "gutter oil" illegally recycled by an unlicensed factory in Pingtung County.

位於高雄地區的油品公司強冠企業被爆出所生產的豬油產品使用了無證照屏東工廠回收的餿水油，生產了大量產品後，昨天和社會大眾道歉。

珍珠奶茶
bubble tea

珍奶是許多外國人對台灣小吃的第一印象。bubble tea 其實最早是指泡沫紅茶，而珍奶只是泡沫紅茶文化中的一個分支，後來因為實在太夯了，兩者漸漸地就混淆了。此外，珍奶還有許多其他說法，常見的有 pearl (milk) tea。

新聞這樣說

In Taiwan last month a banned industrial chemical was found in powdered starch used to make a variety of snacks and desserts. The affected products include flat rice noodles, rice cakes, tofu puddings, dumplings, and tapioca balls used to make the island's popular "pearl" bubble tea.

台灣上個月在許多甜食點心中的澱粉發現了受管制的工業用化學成分，受汙染的食品包括板條、米糕、豆花、餃子以及製作美味享譽全球的珍珠奶茶中的粉圓。

美國黑心漢堡肉

台灣食安風暴使得人心惶惶，其實，美國雖為全球食品最安全國家之一，還是曾在 2011 年爆發過「Pink Slime 漢堡肉」事件。美國的麥當勞當年被踢爆使用泡過氨水的寵物食用級碎肉製作漢堡肉，雖然這些氨水肉渣早已行之多年，但原料是充滿大腸桿菌、各種細菌的寵物食材，再加上人工化學藥劑，怎麼樣都不是令人安心的食品。這位踢爆者到各單位遊走、勸說，並利用自己的美食節目 *Food Revolution* 向美國民眾宣導這種食品的危險。最終，麥當勞宣布再也不使用 Pink Slime 出產的漢堡肉原料，而這位打垮全球最大連鎖速食業者的食安英雄，就是大名鼎鼎的名廚 Jamie Oliver。

示範對話　(MP3 56)

珍奶不敢喝

Jessica: Hey, Thomas. Where have you been?
嘿，湯瑪士，你跑去哪了？

Thomas: I went to the night market for my midnight snack. I brought you some pearl milk tea.
我去夜市買消夜啊，我幫妳帶了珍珠奶茶回來。

Jessica: Ooh. Thanks, but I don't drink that stuff anymore.
哇，謝啦，不過我現在不喝那種東西了。

Thomas: Why not? It's delicious!
為何不喝？很好喝耶！

Jessica: I guess you haven't heard about all the food scandals.
我想你一定是還沒聽過最近的食安醜聞。

Thomas: No.
沒有耶。

Jessica: Well, a few years back, a lot of bubble tea shops were caught using an industrial plasticizer in their drinks.
嗯，幾年前，很多珍珠奶茶店鋪都被抓到使用一種工業塑化劑。

Thomas: Is that bad?
那樣不好嗎？

Jessica: Yeah. It's supposed to be carcinogenic.
對啊，這會致癌耶！

Thomas: Ouch!
喔天啊！

Jessica: Then there was another scandal—inspectors found toxic [1] starch in 2)tapioca pearls, and a bunch of other products too.
然後又發生了另一件食安醜聞，督察員又發現很多粉圓以及其他產品都含有毒澱粉。

Thomas: OK, no more pearl milk tea for me then.
決定了，我不要再喝珍奶了！

Jessica: Good choice. Even the tea leaves may not be safe. 3)Banned pesticides have been found in tea leaves imported from Vietnam.
很好的決定，現在連茶葉都不一定安全，從越南進口的茶葉裡還發現一些禁止使用的農藥。

Thomas: Well, at least the fried chicken I bought is safe…right?
那，至少我買的炸雞是安全的，是吧？

Jessica: Wrong! There was also a huge gutter oil scandal. Food companies were caught adding 4)recycled waste oil, animal 5)feed oil—and even leather cleaner—to their cooking oil.
錯！地溝油醜聞才嚴重勒！一堆食品公司被抓到將回收油、動物飼料油，甚至是皮革清潔油加入食用油中。

Thomas: Eww! So what is safe to eat then?
矮額！到底還有什麼是安全的啊？

Jessica: That's a good question. I wish I knew the answer.
真是個好問題，我也希望我知道答案。

---

1. starch (n.) 澱粉
2. tapioca (n.) 粉圓
3. banned (adj.) 被禁止的
4. recycled (adj.) 回收的
5. feed (v.) 餵食

好用短句　(MP3 57)

談黑心食品
你還可以說

- In 2011, two Taiwanese companies were found to be adding the toxic plasticizer DEHP to clouding agents used in food and drinks

兩家台灣食品公司在 2011 年被發現在用於食物及飲料的起雲劑中，加入有毒塑化劑 DEHP。

- The tainted clouding agent was found in hundreds of products, including sports drinks, tea, juice, jam, sauces and pastries.

在上百種商品中發現受汙染的起雲劑，包括運動飲料、茶品、果汁、果醬、醬料以及甜點。

- In 2013, a number of Taiwese companies were caught adulterating their cooking oil products with copper chlorophyllin, an illegal coloring agent.

在 2013 年數家台灣公司又被抓到在他們的食用油裡摻入銅葉綠素，一種非法染色劑。

- Some companies were also adulterating their oil products with cottonseed oil, which can be toxic if not properly processed.

一些公司還將他們的油製品摻入棉籽油，若不妥善處理將會有毒。

- In the 2014 "gutter oil" scandal, Chang Guann Co. and Ting Hsin International Group were caught blending cooking oil with waste oil and animal feed oil.

2014 年的地溝油醜聞，則是強冠集團以及頂新集團被抓到將食用油摻入廢油以及動物飼料油。

Doughnut Dementia
排成這樣有事嗎？！

形容一股風潮或是一窩蜂的現象還可以用 fever、fad 來表示民眾的狂熱。若特指「時尚潮流」可用 vogue, fashion, trend。這些現象其實最簡單的說法就是 popular 或 trendy。

craze
風潮

新聞這樣說

We start in Portland at Voodoo

Doughnuts, where the bacon craze hit early on. They put bacon on a maple glazed donut a decade ago. Tourists are still lining up to get their donuts.

我們先從波特蘭的巫毒甜甜圈起程，在這裡，培根風潮很早就開始，他們早在 10 年前就在楓糖甜甜圈上放上培根，至今遊客還是絡繹不絕的排隊搶購。

加盟店 franchise

franchise 表示加盟業者或是代理商，直營分公司或分店則會用 branch 稱呼。另外展上各公司所設攤位則是 booth。

新聞這樣說

U.S. fast-food giant McDonald's said it would sell all of its 413 stores in Taiwan to a franchise operator as part of a plan to turn around the retailer. The sale would end over three decades of company-owned stores on the island where it has 20,000 employees.

美國速食界龍頭麥當勞，將售出全台 413 家店的經營權給加盟業者，全台麥當勞直營店已有 30 年歷史且有超過 2 萬名員工。

旗艦店 flagship store

flagship 原指海軍的指揮總艦，flag 是「旗」，ship 為「艦」；後延伸指連鎖集團中店面最大的商店。若要說公司或政府總部的話，常用字是 headquarters，如 general headquarters（總司令部）、company headquarters（公司總部）。

新聞這樣說

The U.S.-based Krispy Kreme Doughnuts launched its flagship store in Taipei on Thursday, attracting a long line of 500 shoppers scrambling for the golden ticket which offers free donuts for a year.

週四美國甜甜圈品牌 Krispy Kreme 在台北的第一家旗艦店開幕了，超過 5 百位民眾排隊爭取那張能夠免費吃甜甜圈一年的黃金禮券。

佔位 hold one's place

hold 本身具有「維持」之意，place 就是一個位置，所以 hold one's place 就是佔位。另外，排隊或列隊英文是 line，動名詞同形，如 form a line（排成直線）、line up（排隊）。

新聞這樣說

Can't wait to get the new iPhone 5S or 5C, but can't stand the thought of camping out for days or waking up at dawn? Instead, you can pay someone to hold your place in line.

等不及拿到 iPhone 5S 或 5C，但又很受不了徹夜排隊或是一早起來排隊嗎？其實，你可以花錢請人代排。

週年慶 anniversary sales

anniversary 是名詞也是形容詞，名詞是週年慶祝的意思，如 wedding anniversary（結婚週年）。形容詞則指「週年的」。

新聞這樣說

Top department stores have been making daily sales of up to NT$300 million during their anniversary sales. In Taipei city alone, department stores have seen recent turnovers of as high as NT$4 billion.

百貨業在週年慶期間，一天的業績就高達三億台幣，光是台北各家百貨公司這一波的週年慶活動，就創下高達四十億的營業額。看來，台灣的經濟似乎沒有新聞報導的這麼差。

美食 gourmet

gourmet 當形容詞用是「美食的」，也可當名詞指美食家或饕客。若是要強調「烹飪」技巧則會用 culinary 這個字。

新聞這樣說

Taiwan is a noted destination for world-class gourmet food and such a good place to live that one German expatriate gave up a high paid position to return, according to a report published Sunday by the *China Times*.

中國時報報導，台灣這個世界美食之都之迷人，讓一位曾在此居住的德國人放棄了高薪工作，再度來台灣生活。

代購助理 personal shopper

personal 本意是「個人的」，也可以引申成「貼身的」，所以加上 shopper，就是指私人代購。個人助理或秘書的職位稱呼可以說 personal assistant/ secretary。

新聞這樣說

Betty Halbreich, 86, has been a personal shopper at Bergdorf Goodman for 37 years and has dressed a wealth of famous people from Lauren Bacall to Joan Rivers, who was a close friend.

86 歲的貝蒂哈柏麗絲在波道夫古德曼百貨擔任代購助理超過 37 年，曾幫數不清的名人穿搭裝扮，包括洛琳白考兒和貝蒂的好友瓊瑞佛斯。

cut in 有打擾或中斷的意思，line 這裡則指直排的隊伍。英式英文中有另一個表達插隊的說法 jump the queue，例如：Patient lies to jump surgery queue.（病人為了先開刀說謊）。

插隊
cut in line

The injured student, surnamed Chang, along with his two friends had been descending an escalator at Taipei Main Station to transfer to MRT Line 5 when the black-shirted suspect cut in line, brushed past Chang, and injured the student with a sharp object, according to Chang's mother.

受傷的張姓學生母親說，當他和兩個朋友在台北車站準備搭手扶梯下至月台轉搭藍線時，一位黑衣嫌犯插隊並和張姓學生擦身而過，用利器傷害張姓學生。

英倫瘋刈包

在倫敦蘇活區的 Lexington Street，一條長長的隊伍讓英國人見識到台灣小吃的驚人魅力。Bao 是一家以極簡風格、清爽建築外觀，包裹著台灣小吃魂的倫敦最新熱門餐廳，店內販售刈包、豆乳炸雞、豬血糕以及台灣啤酒，最新一期 *Bloomberg Business* 刊登美食評論家 Richard Vines 在 Bao 的美食奇遇。傳統刈包的軟嫩麵皮、允指豬頰肉，加上又甜又鹹的調味，讓他讚不絕口，來自台灣屏東的豆乳炸雞的醬料更是讓他無法忘懷。這是台灣排隊美食在歐洲發揚光大的最大驕傲，Richard Vines 口中『這家餐廳就像是「用心」和「創意」兩個好朋友在這見面，並且決定要好好 have fun！』，就是台灣小吃最佳寫照啊！

示範對話　(MP3 59)

排到天荒
地老

Sandy:　This line is really long, isn't it?
　　　　這隊排得還真長，對吧？

Jim:　　I know, but my 1)co-workers can't live without their doughnuts.
　　　　對啊，不過我同事沒有他們的甜甜圈就活不下去。

Sandy:　Why did they send you to buy them?
　　　　他們為何派你來買？

Jim:　　We 2)drew lots, and I lost.
　　　　我們抽籤，而我輸了。

Sandy:　I see. Well, there are worse ways to spend an afternoon.
　　　　了解。好吧，還有更糟的方式度過下午時光。

Jim:　　I guess so. It's amazing how 3)trendy this place still is.
　　　　我想是吧。真驚訝這地方仍然如此流行。

Sandy:　Did you know that you can now hire people to wait in line for you?
　　　　你知道現在可以請人幫你排隊嗎？

Jim: That's 4)hilarious. You mean there are personal shoppers?
那太好笑了。妳是說現在有多拿滋代購助理？

Sandy: Yes. You can find students online who charge 500 NT per trip.
對。你可以在網路上找學生，每趟收五百。

Jim: Maybe I should just do that next time and save the wait.
也許下次我該這麼做，省點排隊等待的時間。

Sandy: If you're getting your salary anyway, does it even make a difference?
如果反正你的薪水還是照領，那有什麼差別？

Jim: I guess not. And this way, I get to chat with nice people like you.
我想是沒有。而且這樣子，還可以跟妳這種好人聊天。

Sandy: Ha-ha. Actually, I just heard that a 5)professional line waiter met his 6)fiancée while waiting in line here.
哈哈。其實，我最近還聽說專業排隊的人還在這裡認識他的未婚妻。

Jim: That's not surprising. What else are you going to do for three hours?
那並不意外。不然三個小時你還能做什麼？

Sandy: And how else will you trust someone to hold your place when 7)nature calls?
還有上廁所時要找誰幫你占位？

Jim: Good question. Speaking of which, I'll be back in five minutes, OK?
好問題。說到這個，我五分鐘就回來，可以嗎？

---

1. co-worker (n.) 同事
2. draw lots (phr.) 抽籤
3. trendy (a.) 流行的，時髦的
4. hilarious (a.) 爆笑的
5. professional (a.) 專業的
6. fiancée (n.) 未婚妻，未婚夫即 fiancé
7. nature calls (phr.) 要上廁所

好用短句　(MP3 60)

談排隊
你還可以說

· This line is a bit too long.	這隊排得也未免太長了吧。
· What is this line for?	這是在排什麼隊？
· Is this where the line starts?	排隊從這裡開始嗎?
· Where are we supposed to line up?	我們到底要排哪裡啊？
· How long have you been in line?	請問你排多久了？
· Can you hold my place for a second? I'll be right back.	可以幫我留一下位子嗎？我馬上回來。
· No cutting in line.	請不要插隊。
· You didn't see there was a line?	你沒看到大家都在排隊嗎？

Typhoon Damage
可怕的颱風

landslide
土石流

slide 有「滑動」的意思，landslide 則是指土石滑落、坍方。在政治用語中，此字則表示某人或某方陣營在選舉中獲得大多數的民意支持。相似的字還有 mudslide（山崩，泥流）和 avalanche（雪崩）。

新聞這樣說

A driver had a lucky escape after a boulder narrowly missed a car in a sudden landslide caused by heavy rain in Taiwan. The incident was captured by a dashboard camera on another vehicle travelling along the coastal road in the north of the country.

台灣的一位駕駛幸運地逃過因為大雨造成土石流落下的大石頭，而這一切都被另一位行經濱海公路駕駛的行車紀錄器錄下來。

泡水車 flood-damaged car

flood-damaged 可視為複合形容詞，由名詞 flood（洪水）和動詞 damage（損害）組合而成，意即「洪水損壞的」，後面再加上名詞 car，便成為我們所說的泡水車了。

新聞這樣說

Honda destroying 1,000 flood-damaged cars in Thailand to reassure customers. Japanese automaker Honda yesterday began destroying more than 1,000 cars in Thailand to reassure customers that no vehicles damaged in the country's recent flood crisis will ever be sold.

Honda銷毀了在泰國一千輛的泡水車以保障顧客。日本車廠本田昨日開始銷毀一千輛在泰國的泡水車，以保證當地消費者不會購買到近日水災所造成的黑心泡水車。

水土流失 soil erosion

erosion 為不可數名詞，意指經由自然力量造成的「侵蝕」，意即地質學所說的「侵蝕作用」。此外，也用於表示權力、權威或信心的「逐漸喪失、削弱」，通常用 the erosion of ～ 表示。

新聞這樣說

The over-excavation of low-lying hills has defaced many parts of Taiwan's natural terrain, causing soil erosion and endangering indigenous species like the leopard cat, yellow pond turtle and mountain scops owl.

過度開挖造成許多淺層山丘地土壤流失，更讓許多原生種，例如：豹貓、黃喉擬水龜、黃嘴角鴞面臨絕種危機。

疏散 evacuation

不可數名詞，evacuate 為其動詞，有「疏散；撤離」的意思，常與介系詞 from 或 to 連用，兩者語意剛好相反，from 是從～撤離，to 則是撤離到～。

新聞這樣說

A series of events will be held Saturday to commemorate the evacuation of thousands of troops and civilians to Taiwan from the Dachen Islands off eastern China 60 years ago, the organizers said Thursday.

這周六將會舉辦一系列活動，以紀念 60 年前數千名從中國沿海的大陳島疏散到台灣的軍隊以及平民。

（洪水）氾濫 flooding

flooding 是表示淹水的名詞用法，意指雨水或河（湖）水淹沒了陸地。在醫學用語上，則是指產後大出血。flooding 源於 flood 這個字，flash flood 是指突如其來的水災。

新聞這樣說

Taiwan is bracing itself for Typhoon Matmo to strike on Tuesday night, giving damaging gusts of wind, torrential rain and a storm surge to the coast. In preparation for the storm, the Taiwanese military is collecting and distributing sandbags to guard against the expected flooding.

台灣正準備面臨颱風麥特母週二晚間的侵襲，將帶來強勁的暴雨、暴風以及大潮。為了準備面臨這場暴風可能帶來的洪水，軍方正積極收集、發散沙袋。

登陸 make landfall

登陸為氣象學（meteorology）用語，意思是指在海上形成的颱風眼（eye）越過海岸線（coastline）。相關的用語包括：發佈海/陸上颱風警報（issue a sea/land warning）、解除颱風警報（lift a typhoon warning）。

新聞這樣說

Typhoon Noul is brushing Taiwan's east coast and will not make landfall, officials say. However, school and work was suspended for residents in outlying islands, as a precaution.

官方指出，掃過台灣的紅霞颱風將不會登陸，只會掃過台灣東海岸。然而為了安全起見，偏遠地區的的離島學校及公司仍停班停課。

緊急應變 emergency response

emergency 當名詞時，可做「緊急情況；突發事件；非常時刻」等解釋。日常生活裡，有許多跟 emergency 相關的用法，例如：emergency exit（緊急出口，逃生門）、emergency room（急診室）、emergency brake（手剎車）。

新聞這樣說

In a statement issued shortly after 5 p.m. local time by TransAsia, it said three people died at the scene and a further 10 in hospital. A number of other passengers were taken to local hospitals and the airline set up an emergency response center.

復興航空下午 5 點發布一項聲明，表示 3 位乘客當場身亡，10 位則送醫不治，其他乘客也陸續送至當地醫院，航空公司也成立緊急應變中心。

天災
natural disaster

雖然部分的天災（natural disaster）可以預期並事先做好防範工作，但多數時候，人力依舊無法勝天，大自然的反撲往往都是 devastating / destructive（毀滅性的）和 catastrophic / disastrous（災難性的）。

新聞這樣說

The devastating 921 Earthquake 10 years ago, as well as environmental disasters that have hit the nation since, must be understood as a warning sign not only from the perspective of disaster management, but also for the unique threat it poses to Taiwan's unofficial, yet undeniable, world heritage status.

10 年前的 921 大地震，加上之後的各種天災，必須被視為台灣救災處理不足的警訊，更是一個對台灣不可否認的世界遺產地位一大威脅。

台美大洪災

2009 年的莫拉克颱風是台灣氣象記錄史上最致命的颱風，其破紀錄的雨量造成中南部嚴重土石流，被納入全球百大最致命洪災的八八水災就這樣完全掩埋高雄縣小林村，造成將近七百人罹難，重創台灣農業，而此次防災救災不力也導致馬政府聲勢大幅下滑。美國史上最嚴重的水災則要回溯到 1927 年的密西西比大洪災，當年，隨著前一年夏季的超級暴雨，密西西比河支流達到最大負荷，不斷湧出的河水沖破 Mounds Landing 的河堤，在 145 處支流以及超過 7 萬平方公里的土地造成嚴重淹水，全美超過 10 州受到影響，其中阿肯色州有超過 14%的土地遭河水淹蓋，超過 240 人罹難。

示範對話　(MP3 62)

缺德泡水車

Paula and Jerry meet at [1]*auto shop 保羅和傑瑞在修車廠碰面*

Paula: Hey, Jerry. You're getting some work done on your car too?
　　　嗨！傑瑞。你的車也需要修理嗎？

Jerry: Yeah. I'm getting a new [2]muffler and having the tires rotated.
　　　是啊。需要一個新的消音器，還要把輪胎對調。

Paula: How long have you had your car?
　　　你的車買多久了？

Jerry: I just bought it, actually. It was so cheap I had to wonder if it was
　　　stolen or something.
　　　其實才剛買。便宜到我都要懷疑是不是贓車之類的。

Paula: Who knows? Maybe it was.
　　　天知道？說不定是。

Jerry: Is car theft very common in Taiwan?
　　　汽車竊盜在台灣很普遍嗎？

Paula: Quite common, especially since Typhoon Morakot.
蠻普遍的，尤其是在莫克拉颱風之後。

Jerry: Why would a typhoon make car theft more common?
颱風為何會使汽車竊盜更加普遍？

Paula: Thousands of cars were damaged by flooding, and 3)shady 4)car dealers bought and resold a lot of them.
颱風之後的洪水讓許多車受損，黑心車商會蒐購並轉賣許多受損的車輛。

Jerry: Wow. That's bad news for car buyers.
哇，買車的人真是悽慘啊。

Paula: That's right. And some 5)gangsters also switched the 6)plates onto other stolen cars for resale.
對啊。有些歹徒還會把車牌換到其他偷來的車上轉賣。

Jerry: Could my car have been 7)tampered with? Any way I could find out?
我的車會不會被亂搞過？我有什麼辦法查明？

Paula: I don't know. But you don't want to be driving a car that's in bad shape, 8)let alone one reported as stolen.
不知道。但最好不要開一輛狀況不好的車，更別說是備案的失竊車。

Jerry: What a mess. Maybe I should go back to the shop and see what the deal is.
實在很糟。或許我該回店裡把這件事問個清楚。

Paula: Be careful. They may be 9)in cahoots with gangsters.
小心點。他們說不定跟黑道有勾結。

Jerry: Wow. I hope this typhoon doesn't 10)end up 11)soaking me, too.
哇，希望這個颱風不要最後也把我淋成落湯雞。

---

1. auto shop 汽車用品店
2. muffler (n.) 消音器
3. shady (a.) 不光明正大的
4. car dealer 汽車商人，賣車的人
5. gangster (n.) 幫派分子
6. plate (n.) 車牌
7. tamper (with) 動手腳，竄改
8. let alone 更不用說…了
9. in cahoots with 與…合夥，與…共謀
10. end up 結果變成…
11. soak (v.)（口）向…敲竹槓

好用短句　(MP3 63)

談颱風
你還可以說

- After the floods, quite a few flood-damaged cars showed up on the market.

  水災過後，市場上出現許多泡水車。

- There are a lot of shows on TV telling people how to spot water-damaged cars.

  許多電視節目都在教人如何分辨泡水車。

- Shady used car dealers clean the cars up to make them look like new.

  黑心的中古車商會把車整理得跟全新的一樣。

- To fix up flood-damaged cars, some shady dealers buy parts from car thieves.

  為了翻修泡水車，有些黑心車商還會跟偷車賊買零件。

- And because of this, the number of carjacking cases has increased significantly.

  汽車失竊案件因此大增。

- There are also a lot of shows on TV telling people how to avoid getting their cars stolen.

  還有許多電視節目教人如何避免汽車被偷。

Where's the Beef?

不是你想的牛肉

Hit! 話題單字 (MP3 64)

台灣的疾病管制署（Centers for Disease Control）為國家級的防疫（epidemic prevention）機構，隸屬於衛生福利部（Ministry of Health and Welfare），簡稱疾管署。

CDC 疾病管制局

新聞這樣說

Before SARS, who knew that the CDC even existed? These days, the CDC, whether Taiwan's or America's, is a household name.

以前誰注意疾病管制局的存在？但如今因為 SARS，不管是台灣或美國的疾管局，瞬間都成了人人知曉的熱門單位。

禽流感 bird flu

禽流感（avian flu 或 bird flu）病毒存在於受感染禽鳥的呼吸道飛沫及排泄物（excrement）中，人類會感染主要是因為吸入（inhale）或是接觸到禽流感的病毒顆粒，潛伏期（incubation period）可長達十四天之久。

新聞這樣說

Last month, because of mad cow disease, everyone was afraid of imported American beef. This time it's bird flu that has everybody scared of East Asian poultry. Few people have actually gotten sick, but it looks like the economy's caught a serious case of the flu.

上個月因為狂牛病，大家怕美國進口的牛肉；這次則是因為禽流感，大家怕東亞國家的家禽肉品。真正染病的人少之又少，但病毒引起的經濟損失卻很大。

鈉 sodium

鈉是一種化學元素（chemical element），是人體必需的礦物質營養素，主要透過飲食攝取，尤其是俗稱食鹽的氯化鈉。現代人飲食口味普遍偏重，容易造成腎臟與心血管疾病（cardiovascular disease）。

新聞這樣說

While it is healthy to maintain a diet low in sodium, fat and oil, a recent article published by the Taiwan Society of Cardiology and the Taiwan Hypertension Society suggests that sodium-free diets can increase the risk of hypertension and cardiovascular disease.

雖然低鈉、低脂、低油飲食習慣是健康的，但根據台灣心臟及高血壓協會日前發表的一篇文章指出，無鈉飲食可能會增進新血管疾病及高血壓的發生。

致污物
contamination

做「汙染」或「致污物」解釋，常與 environmental（環境的）、bacterial（細菌的）、radioactive（放射性的）、chemical（化學的）、food（食物）等字連用，動詞為 contaminate。

新聞這樣說

Due to concerns over food safety, netizens implored I-mei, who came out on top during the nation's food contamination scandal last year, to purchase the management rights to McDonald's for its business integrity.

最近台灣麥當勞易主，網友們擔心接下來食安又要有問題，紛紛請求在上一波食安風暴全身而退的義美接手。

消毒
disinfection

disinfection 為不可數名詞，disinfect 為其動詞形式，同義字為 sanitize，消毒水則是 disinfectant。電腦中毒時，disinfect 則是指「移除病毒」。

新聞這樣說

Freaked out by SARS, everyone's buying alcohol and bleach and disinfecting everything. Is all this actually effective, or are people just trying anything to calm themselves down?

SARS 猖獗，人人聞「煞」色變，家家戶戶買酒精、漂白水猛消毒，但這究竟是真的有效，還是只求圖個心安？

大豆蛋白
soy protein

protein 為「蛋白質」，是構成人體細胞（cell）的主要成分之一，也是飲食中不可缺少的重要營養成分，依照攝取來源可分為動物性蛋白質（animal protein）和植物性蛋白質（vegetable protein）。

新聞這樣說

Soy protein is often hailed as a "green" replacement for meat. However, it is the use of soy within the meat industry that is largely responsible for the emissions and carbon footprint of livestock production.

大豆蛋白常被稱做肉品的「綠色」替代品，然而在肉類產業裡大豆的運用卻是畜牧業碳排放及碳足跡的最大禍源。

肌腱 tendon

中文稱做「腱」或「肌腱」，是一種連接肌肉到骨頭的軟組織（soft tissue），具有很好的支撐力及柔軟度。Achilles tendon 則是指位於小腿後側的肌腱，又稱「阿基里斯腱，是人體中最強壯的肌腱。

新聞這樣說

You can get anything from dumplings to beef tendon, but the won tons are a must. Add roast pork, and some duck, too, if you're really hungry. Your bill will still be less than $10.

你可以點任何東西，從餃子到牛腱，而雲吞更是必點美食，如果真的很餓，再加點烤豬、烤鴨，最後帳單還是少於美金 10 元。

重組肉
restruc-tured meat

重組肉意指用蛋白黏合的碎肉（chopped/ minced meat），較不具經濟價值，常見於香腸（sausage）、熱狗（hot dog）等加工肉品（processed meat）或是加工過的魚肉製品。

新聞這樣說

A new system for restructured meat labeling started on Dec. 17. The menus or food packaging for any restructured beef, pork, fish and chicken items sold in restaurants, snack outlets and supermarkets need to state that they must be cooked well if they are to be eaten.

一個新的重組肉標示系統將在 12 月 17 日上路，所有餐廳、便商或超市販賣的牛肉、豬肉、魚肉以及雞肉都必須標示為重組肉，並提醒消費者需煮熟食用。

牛排這樣點

新鮮現煎的牛排是上帝給人類的禮物，一塊煎的粉嫩多汁、外酥內軟的牛排真的可以療癒心靈。以下附上一張各個部位牛肉及熟度的英文名稱，讓你在英語系國家輕鬆點一份完美牛排。

一分熟 rare
三分熟 medium-rare
五分熟 medium
七分熟 medium-well
全熟 well-done

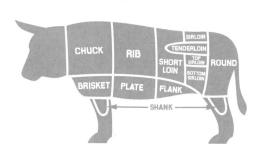

牛肉在哪裡

A man sits down with a [1]vegetarian dish at a night market table
一個男士端著一盤素菜在夜市的餐桌坐下

Glen: You didn't order the beef here, did you?
妳沒有點這裡的牛肉，對吧？

Sandra: Well, actually I did. And it tastes lovely. I really like night market food.
呃，其實我有。而且味道很棒。我真喜歡夜市的食物。

Glen: You obviously haven't been watching the news lately. You know—the stories on restructured beef?
妳最近顯然沒有看新聞。妳知道——那些關於重組牛肉的報導嗎？

Sandra: Uh, no. Could you [2]fill me in?
呃，沒有，你能跟我從頭說起嗎？

Glen: Well, it seems that lots of places are selling beef that's been restructured.
嗯，似乎有許多地方在賣重組過的牛肉。

Sandra: Does that just mean they take a lot of little bits of meat and mix them together?
這只表示他們把許多小塊肉拿來湊在一起嗎？

Glen: It'd be nice if that were all it was. People are adding things like soy protein to the meat after they remove the tendons from it.
如果只是這樣就好。那些人把肉裡的筋去掉之後，在裡面加入大豆蛋白之類的東西。

Sandra: Well, whatever they've done, it's really tasty.
呃，不管他們做了什麼，還真是蠻好吃的。

Glen: But ³⁾potentially bad for you. The added soy ⁴⁾ups the meat's ⁵⁾sodium ⁶⁾content and makes it more likely to have problems with bacterial contamination.
但對身體有潛在的危害。加入黃豆會提高肉的鈉含量，並讓肉更容易遭到細菌感染。

Sandra: Hmm, maybe I should just buy my beef at steakhouses then.
嗯，或許我該只在牛排店消費牛肉了。

Glen: They're even worse right now. Several ⁷⁾chains were selling this cheap meat at more expensive ⁸⁾chuck steak prices.
現在牛排店更糟糕。幾家連鎖店之前在用嫩肩肉的價格販賣這種便宜肉。

Sandra: You know, I think all this ⁹⁾disturbing news has made me lose my appetite.
你知道嗎，我覺得這些煩人的新聞已經讓我失去胃口了。

---

1. vegetarian (a.) 素菜的，吃素的
2. fill sb. in 告知某人錯過的消息
3. potentially (adv.) 潛在地，有可能地
4. up (v.) 升高
5. sodium (n.) 鈉
6. content (n.) 含量，內容
7. chain (n.) 連鎖店
8. chuck steak 牛頸部至肩胛之間的肉，有些牛排店稱做「嫩肩肉」
9. disturbing (a.) 使憂慮的，使不安的

好用短句 (MP3 66)

談重組牛
你還可以說

- With the intense news coverage on restructured beef, steakhouses that normally have lines of people waiting outside their doors are finding their restaurants surprisingly empty.

重組牛肉的新聞高度曝光，讓原本需要排隊的牛排店都門可羅雀。

- It is not necessarily true that restructured beef is harmful to one's health.

重組牛肉對健康不必然有害。

- Because restructured meat is processed, it is more susceptible to bacteria.

由於重組肉是經過加工的，也因此更容易遭細菌汙染。

- So when eating restructured meat, it's best to make sure that it's well-cooked.

所以當食用重組肉時，最好確定它是全熟的。

- Chains that sell restructured steaks all claim to use quality meat.

提供重組牛排的連鎖店都以品質為號召。

- When waiters ask customers how they want their steaks cooked, this makes them mistakenly think that they're being served high-quality meat.

但侍者問客人牛排要幾分熟時，會誤導客人以為那是高級牛排。

Inaccurate Weather Forecasts

不太準的氣象局

在氣象預報中，有很多用到 storm 的詞彙，像是 thunderstorm「雷暴或雷雨」、snowstorm「暴風雪」tropical storm「輕度颱風」、hailstorm「雹暴」等等。

沙塵暴
sand-storm

新聞這樣說

After a long dry summer, the coldest winter on record, and then seemingly endless rains, hopes were high for a nice and easy transition into spring. But no such luck—a sandstorm had to come first.

好不容易度過苦旱的夏天、破紀錄低溫的寒冬、下個沒完的陰雨，原本以為終於要春暖花開，沒想到沙塵暴就先來了。

限水
water rationing

缺水（water shortage）時，為了保障大家在乾旱（drought）時期都有水用，限水是必要手段。rationing 為不可數名詞，意指「定量配給」，除了可與 water 搭配使用外，也能加在 power 的後面，做限電（power rationing）解釋。

新聞這樣說

Water rationing is back! Last year's water shortage ended only six months ago, and Taiwan's reservoir water levels are already dangerously low. This is beginning to seem like a never-ending nightmare. Will it ever end?

又要限水了！去年全台水荒才結束半年，今年水庫又開始拉警報了。這個似乎永無止境的惡夢，究竟何時會結束？

熱浪 heat wave

heat wave 意指在某段期間內不尋常的酷熱天氣，反義詞是 cold wave「寒流」。熱浪來襲時，需注意適時補充水分，避免外出，以免中暑（heatstroke）。

新聞這樣說

This hasn't just been Taiwan's hottest summer ever—it might just be the world's hottest summer in history. Weather scientists across the northern hemisphere are worried that the current heat wave may be caused by man made pollution.

不只在台灣連連創下高溫記錄，這個夏天或許是人類有史以來最熱的夏天。最令北半球的天氣科學家憂心的是，這次的熱浪可能是人類自己製造污染得來的結果。

中央氣象局 Central Weather Bureau

weather 這個字的本意是「天氣」，並由此衍生許多有趣的用法，身體不舒服的時候，除了說 I feel sick 之外，也可以說 I feel under the weather。

新聞這樣說

Taiwan's Central Weather Bureau (CWB) has issued its first typhoon warning of the season. Forecasters issued a sea warning for Typhoon Noul at 8:30 am on Sunday. Forecasters say that Noul was centered some 600 kilometers south-southeast of Taiwan's southernmost point of Eluanbi.

中央氣象局發了今年第一個颱風警報，周日上午 8:30 發布紅霞海上颱風警報。氣象局表示，紅霞目前中心點位於峨鑾鼻南南東 600 公里處。

乾旱 drought

drought 與 dry 這個字息息相關，因為長期欠缺雨水（rainfall），導致土壤太乾燥（dry），無法提供農作物生長所需的水分，嚴重時可能造成饑荒（famine）。

新聞這樣說

Taiwan has begun rationing water supplies to more than one million households as it tackles the island's worst drought in years. Water supplies will be cut off entirely for two days each week, on a rotating basis, in several northern cities.

台灣為了因應幾年來最嚴重的一場旱災，開始了對於超過一百萬住戶的限水，在限水期間，北部幾個城市一週內將被斷水兩天。

午後雷陣雨 afternoon thundershower

另一種說法是 afternoon shower with thunder。「雷陣雨」thundershower 指的是伴隨雷聲（thunder）和閃電（lightning）的短暫暴雨（brief rainstorm）。

新聞這樣說

The drought in southern Taiwan is likely to persist through May despite some afternoon thunder showers over the past few days, an official with the Water Resources Agency said Monday. Taiwan's dry season usually ends when the plum rains begin in May.

經濟部水利署一位官員表示，即使這幾天有午後雷陣雨，全台缺水情況將會持續到 5 月。台灣的乾季通常結束於 5 月梅雨季節的開始。

空氣污染
air pollution

pollution 為「汙染」之意，可分為 air pollution「空氣污染」、water pollution「水污染」、soil pollution「土壤污染」、noise pollution「噪音污染」等，其動詞型式為 pollute。

新聞這樣說

EPA warns of high air pollution levels in nation's south. Southern Taiwan will continue to experience poor air quality as a result of pollutants being carried on a cold air mass from China, the Environmental Protection Administration (EPA) said.

行政院環境保護署警告民眾：台灣南部將會持續遭到嚴重空氣汙染，主因是冷鋒將大量中國內陸汙染源帶來台灣。

暴雨
torrential rain

torrential 有「急流的；洶湧的；猛烈的」之意。關於下雨天的用詞，常見的還有 drizzle「毛毛雨」、shower「陣雨」、thundershower/thunderstorm「雷陣雨」、downpour「傾盆大雨」等等。

新聞這樣說

A moist air current dumped torrential rain on southern Taiwan yesterday, prompting the closure of schools and offices in Greater Tainan and Greater Kaohsiung, where sporadic flooding has been reported.

一股潮濕氣流造成南台灣暴雨不斷，也讓大台南及大高雄地區許多學校及公司因為淹水停課。

問天氣八大句型

- What's the weather like out there?
  外面天氣如何？
- How is the weather out there?
  外面天氣如何？
- Is it supposed to rain on Monday?
  星期一會下雨嗎？
- Is it supposed to be sunny this weekend?
  這個週末是不是晴天？

- Is it raining where you are?
  你那邊有下雨嗎？
- Is it hot / cold outside today?
  今天外面熱 / 冷嗎？
- What does the weather forecast say?
  天氣預報怎麼說？
- What's the temperature today?
  今天的氣溫幾度？

示範對話　(MP3 68)

氣象預報
愛騙人

Alice and Chad are standing on an MRT platform 艾莉絲和查德站在捷運月台

Alice: Oh no! Look at those dark clouds over there!
喔不！你看那些烏雲！

Chad: Yeah. It looks like it's gonna rain later. But you never know.
喔，看起來晚點要下雨了，但也很難說啦。

Alice: I should never have believed the weather [1]forecast. It said there was only a 15% probability of rain, so I didn't bother to bring my umbrella.
我真不該相信氣象預報的，他們說今天只有百分之十五的機率會下雨，所以我連傘都沒帶。

Chad: Well, it said on the CWB's website that there's a 15% chance of afternoon thundershowers. Won't you be at work in the afternoon?
嗯，中央氣象局網站是有說下午會有百分之十五的午後雷陣雨機會，但妳不是下午會在工作嗎？

Alice: Yeah. But what if I want to go out for lunch?
是啦，但萬一我想出去吃午餐呢？

Chad: I'm sure your office has a ²⁾courtesy umbrella you can borrow.
妳公司一定會有愛心傘可以借用啦。

Alice: That's true.
這倒是。

Chad: But you should do what the locals do. Since the weather reports are so unreliable, I always have a ³⁾fold-up umbrella in my back-pack. And I keep a rain ⁴⁾poncho under the seat of my scooter.
但我覺得妳應該學學當地人的作法。既然氣象預報不太可靠，我背包裡一定會有一把折疊傘，機車座墊下一定會有雨衣。

Alice: That's what I'll do on my lunch break—go shopping for a fold-up umbrella. Then I can just ignore the weather forecasts!
我午餐休息時就來這麼做！我要去買摺疊傘，然後完全不用理氣象預報!

Chad: Well, with typhoon season coming, you probably don't want to ignore them completely.
這個嘛，颱風季節要來了，應該也不要完全不管氣象預報啦。

1. forecast (n.) 氣象預報
2. courtesy (q.) 愛心的
3. fold-up (a.) 摺疊的
4. poncho (n.) 雨衣

好用短句　(MP3 69)

談天氣
你還可以說

- The government's weather reports haven't been very accurate recently.

  最近中央氣象局的天氣預報好像都不太準。

- They've gotten their typhoon warnings wrong several times.

  好幾次關於颱風的預測都不正確。

- They put out a heavy rainfall warning for what turned out to be a sunny day.

  發布大雨特報，結果卻是大晴天。

- When they say the weather will be good, it often rains heavily.

  說天氣好，卻常常下大雨。

- Maybe it's best to just assume the opposite of what they predict will be true.

  也許最好的方法就是相信與氣象局相反的說法就行了

Medical Disputes
醫療疏失

dispute 指事件的爭議，特別用來表示強烈反對意見時使用。表達「反對、不同意見」的其他相近字還有 controversy（爭議）、quarrel（爭吵）及 disagreement（意見不一）。

dispute
糾紛

新聞這樣說

The most common reaction in a medical dispute is to blame the individual medical workers involved rather than the system.

當面對醫療糾紛時，最常見的反應就是直接責怪醫療人員，而非整個醫療體制。

弱勢族群 disadvan-taged groups

disadvantaged 是形容詞也是名詞，通常指「社經條件不利、政經地位低落」，也能當「身心有礙的」，比 handi-capped（殘障）較為委婉。也可直接用 the disadvantaged 表「弱勢族群」。

新聞這樣說

Disadvantaged groups get ignored during election season and then insulted afterwards. Our dear politicians must be disadvantaged when it comes to under-standing disadvantaged groups.

弱勢族群的權益，在選舉時得不到政治人物的關注也就算了，選後還得忍受他們嘴裡吐出的歧視評論。也許我們的政治人物對弱勢族群的觀察力，許多只有弱視的程度。

虐待兒童 child abuse

abuse 有「虐待」的意思，動詞和名詞同型，「自虐」則是 self-abuse。abuse 也可做「濫用」解釋，例如：drug abuse（藥物濫用）、alcohol abuse（酗酒）。

新聞這樣說

The delayed treatment of a battered four year-old girl opened a huge can of worm's for Taiwan's health care system and the ethics of individual doctors. From the abusive father to the lying doctor, the dark side of humanity was exposed for all to see.

受虐女童變成醫療人球一案，不僅顯示醫療體系有重大缺失，也讓部分醫生的醫德受到質疑。整件事從施暴的父親到說謊的醫生，在在顯示人性的黑暗面。

酒駕 drunk driving

drunk 是動詞 drink 的過去式和過去分詞，drink 除了有「喝」的意思，也可做「喝酒」解釋，喝醉的英文叫做 be/get drunk，喝醉了開車是很危險的事，更是違法（illegal）的事，千萬別輕易嘗試。

新聞這樣說

Taiwan will enter a "zero tolerance" era on drunken driving Thursday when the world's toughest standards for alcohol levels in motorists go into effect.

隨著史上最嚴格的駕駛酒測開始執行，台灣將進入「酒駕零容忍」時代。

賠償金 compensation

因事故所得到的補償、理賠英文是 compensation；動詞用法是「compensate for + 某事」。公司給員工的薪資福利，包括獎金、保險、退休金、有薪假等等也是用這個字，完整說法是 compensation package。

新聞這樣說

In recent years, the number of medical disputes has risen rapidly and the industry's regulatory body now reportedly handles an average of 430 cases every year. One prominent medical dispute in 1996 concluded with record compensation of NT$43 million (US$1.42 million) this year.

近年來，醫療糾紛案件發生率攀升，據說主管機關一年平均要處理 430 件案例。發生在 1996 年的重大糾紛並創下了四千三百萬台幣賠償金的紀錄。

監護權 custody

custody 是指「父母離婚後對小孩監護和照顧的權利」，而離婚夫妻在法庭上爭取孩子的監護權，英文是 custody suit，也可以說是 custody battle。此外，custody 還能表示「拘留，監禁」的意思。

新聞這樣說

A custody fight between two families became an incident between two countries. Poor Iruan became stuck between two sets of relatives, two nations, and the yapping jaws of the media. We hope Iruan is now enjoying his time out of spotlight.

從兩個家庭爭監護權，演變成兩個國家的外交事件，小憶樺被雙方親屬、兩國政府、以及大批媒體一再傷害的鬧劇，終於落幕了。

醫療疏失 malpractice

字首 mal- 表示「壞」的意思，practice 則是指醫師或律師等依其專業所完成的工作，由此可知，medical malpractice 意思是指醫生在專業工作上有疏失，也就是醫療疏失。

新聞這樣說

Academia Sinica and members of the medical community on Tuesday called for the revision of a law that treats medical malpractice as a criminal act, amid an increasing shortage of doctors.

由於日漸短缺的醫生人力，中央研究院以及一群醫療界成員週四呼籲應該修改一項將醫療疏失視為刑事犯罪的法案。

壯陽藥 drugs for erectile dysfunction

erectile 為「可直立的」，與動詞 erect（使直立；豎立）相關。dysfunction 則是指「功能障礙；機能失調」。erectile dysfunction 為醫學術語的「勃起功能障礙」，即俗稱的「陽痿」（impotence）。

新聞這樣說

Move over Viagra. Now that Levitra and Cialis are hitting the market, men won't just be invigorated, but so will the global market for erectile dysfunction medicine. Such a little pill can make such a big difference.

威而剛請讓位，隨著樂威壯和犀利士的相繼問世，不只壯了男性的雄風，更壯了全球的壯陽藥市場。果然小小藥丹，大大威力！

美國健保小知識

說到醫療健保，這項對台灣人而言再理所當然不過的保障，對於美國人來說可是金字塔頂端高收入人口才能享有的奢侈福利。美國醫療設施以及醫療保險大多由私人機構經營，每個人需要依照自己的經濟能力購買相對應的健保，也因此常發生個人保險無法受益於家人，或是根本負擔不起剩下的高額自付額，高就醫門檻導致許多低收入戶家庭生不起病，預估每年起碼有超過四萬人死於缺乏醫療保險。

示範對話 (MP3 71)

醫師不好當

Sheila: Ready to lose? This shot is going to be beautiful. Darn, I missed.
準備好輸球了嗎？這一球一定漂亮的啦。可惡，我打歪了。

Allan: Ha-ha. I'm going to beat you so badly, you might just ¹⁾end up in the hospital.
哈哈，我才要痛宰妳，搞到妳最後可能要上醫院。

Sheila: Speaking of hospitals, did you hear about the president's son-in-law?
說到醫院，你有聽說總統女婿的事嗎？

Allan: Well, I saw that he's getting ²⁾sued for malpractice.
嗯，我看到他因為醫療過失被控告。

Sheila: Yeah, that's it. I don't think the family ³⁾has a strong case though.
是啊，就是那件事。但我覺得那家人的說法接下去實在很難站得住腳。

Allan: What's the deal anyway? He performed ⁴⁾surgery on the woman's back, and she died?
到底是怎麼回事？他幫那位婦人動背部手術，她就死了？

Sheila: Over a month later from heart 5)fibrillations. The doc that saw her said it had nothing to do with the previous surgery.
一個月過後死於心臟纖維性顫動。為他看診的醫生說那跟之前的外科手術無關。

Allan: So, why is the family suing him then?
所以呢，這家人為何要控告他？

Sheila: Maybe because he's famous?
會不會是因為他有名？

Allan: It just goes to show that 6)fame's not always a good thing.
這表示有名氣不永遠是一件好事。

Sheila: Welcome to the world of fame and politics. 7)Talk about a soap opera!
歡迎進入名氣與政治的世界。實在是跟肥皂劇沒兩樣。

Allan: Actually, it reminds me of lawsuits in the States.
其實，這讓我聯想到美國的訟訴案件。

Sheila: And the Japanese soap opera — White Pagoda. An 8)oncologist is too proud to take advice from other doctors and a patient of his dies.
以及那齣日本偶像劇——《白色巨塔》。一位癌症專科醫生太傲慢聽不進其他醫生的建議，以致於他的一位病患死亡。

Allan: Does he go into politics after that?
他在那之後從政了嗎？

Sheila: No, the family sues and wins, and in true soap opera style, the doctor then finds out he has cancer.
不，病患家屬上訴並且勝訴，接著非常符合肥皂劇風格，這位醫生發現他得了癌症。

Allan: So are you saying Chao Chien-ming will go 9)under the knife soon?
所以妳是說趙建銘很快就需要被開刀囉？

---

1. end up (phr.) 結果變成
3. have a strong case （爭論時）有強力的論點支持
6. fame (n.) 名氣，聲望
8. oncologist (n.) 腫瘤科醫師

2. sue (v.) 控告，lawsuit (n.) 訴訟案件
4. surgery (n.) 外科手術
5. fibrillation (n.) （醫）纖維性顫動
7. talk about… (phr.) 真是…
9. (go) under the knife (phr.) （口）接受外科手術

好用短句 (MP3 72)

談醫療疏失
你還可以說

· When there are disputes over medical treatment, the patient's family is always in a helpless position.	發生醫療糾紛時，病患家屬都會非常無助。
· And hospitals may only be willing to protect their own hospital staff.	醫院也可能會袒護醫療人員。
· If the case goes to court, it often drags on for years.	告上法院又經常纏訟多年。
· Some families of patients that die scatter ghost money at the hospital entrance.	有些死者家屬還會在醫院門口撒冥紙。
· When there are reports of medical treatment in the news, everyone tends to feel bad for the families.	看到醫療糾紛的新聞，大家都會覺得家屬很可憐。
· But at the same time, people can't help but wonder if it's not just money that the families are after.	但同時又忍不住懷疑他們是否在為錢抗議。
· Things would be better if there were a fair arbitration body to handle medical treatment disputes.	要是能有一個公正的醫療糾紛仲裁單位就好了。

Chapter Five

Education &
Culture
教　育
文化簡單聊

說到台灣教育，每一次教育部領佈最新教綱或是考試制度，就像讓台灣家長看一部恐怖片一樣。而且還不是看完會覺得很刺激、很興奮的恐怖片，是一部拍得又臭又長到很恐怖的恐怖片。在這樣的情形下，望子成龍、望女成鳳的父母只能把小孩放學立刻送到補習班，英文、數學、物理、化學、國文全部再上一次，回到家學校功課、補習班功課寫完立刻上床睡覺，這些變成了我們培養未來社會棟樑的方式。教育是發揮人類潛能最重要的一環，是孩子成長中最舉足輕重的階段，教育也最終決定了一個國家的文化。用英文跟老外聊聊台灣教育文化，或許是刺激你我思維及視野的最好方式！難道你不好奇外國人怎麼看待我們的文化嗎？

The Army Wants You
兵役改改改

Hit! 話題單字 (MP3 73)

---

volunteer military 自願役

volunteer 為名詞，指自願參加者、志願者、義工。自願役是指符合條件之人民自願投入軍隊，以軍人作為職業。

新聞這樣說

The implementation date for an all-volunteer military has been pushed back two years from 2015 to 2017 because of recruitment difficulties, the Ministry of National Defense announced yesterday at a press conference.

國防部昨天在記者會宣布，全自願制兵役實行將由 2015 延後兩年至 2017 年實施。

軍事院校 military academy

academy 為名詞，有學院、專科學校、協會的意思，比如大家熟悉的奧斯卡金像獎 Academy Awards，別稱奧斯卡（Oscars）。

新聞這樣說

"While historical mistakes may be forgiven, historical truths must not be forgotten," Ma said, adding that Taiwan must make sure that a similar war will never happen again. Ma made the comments during a graduation ceremony held at the R.O.C. Military Academy in Kaohsiung yesterday.

馬總統在高雄中華民國陸軍軍官學校的畢業典禮上表示：「歷史錯誤可以被原諒，但絕不可被遺忘」，並表示台灣絕對要盡全力不讓戰爭再次發生。

退伍 discharge

dis 有相反或否定的意思，charge 在這裡當名詞有責任的意思；discharge 當名詞為出院、解僱、退伍排放，相關字詞應用: discharge from the military 退伍/the hospital 出院、榮譽退伍 honorable discharge，不榮譽退伍 dishonorable discharge。

新聞這樣說

The MND has launched a series of downsizing programs over the past decade. The continuing downsize has forced many middle-aged military personnel to discharge from the military prematurely.

中華民國國防部在過去 10 年間發動了一連串人事縮減專案。這樣持續縮減下讓許多中年軍人被迫提早退役。

徵兵（制）draft

同意字為 conscription，而透過此機制徵得的士兵叫做 conscript。

新聞這樣說

"The draft was a win-win for the state and for youth. The state had people to serve the country and young people learned basic life skills and the necessary qualifications to get a job," says retired Gen. Allard.

退休的 Allard 將軍指出，徵兵制是對國家以及年輕人雙贏的局面，國家有人民保護，而人民得以在軍中學習到基本生存技能以及找工作能力。

義務役 compulsory military service

compulsory 是形容詞，指強制性的、義務的、必修的。目前世界上如台灣、以色列、南韓等有義務役制度。其他「義務」相關的用語有：義務教育 compulsory education、投票義務 compulsory voting。

新聞這樣說

Gen. Bai Chieh-lung, a human resources official, said that as the Taiwan military will be transformed into a fully voluntary one before January 2017, the military will enlist a last batch of conscripts to serve their compulsory military service before the end of this year.

白捷隆將軍表示，台灣軍方將在 2017 年一月前完成自願役轉型，軍方將在年底前徵招最後一批義務役役男。

緩役 deferment

defer 為動詞，有延期、推遲的意思；加上 ment 即為名詞。

新聞這樣說

Glenn King graduated from high school in 1942 and began studying engineering at the University of Wyoming. That qualified him for a full deferment from the military draft—until the president changed the rules. "While I was at the university, Roosevelt signed the order to draft 18-year-olds—me," King remembers.

Glenn King 於 1942 年高中畢業並進入懷俄明大學就讀工程學系，這讓他符合緩兵制度，直到總統改變法規。「當我還在讀大學的時候，羅斯福總統簽訂了徵招 18 歲青年入伍的法案」，King 憶道。

新兵訓練營 boot camp

boot 用在軍隊中就是招募與基本訓練的意思，因此新兵訓練也可以稱為 recruit training 或 basic training，參予的新兵稱作 recruits。在軍隊或球隊中稱菜鳥為 rookie。

新聞這樣說

Brian Kash, 32, signed up for the Marine Corps at 17, had his first day of boot camp Sept.11, 2001, and was deployed to Iraq. When he returned from Iraq he decided to make a career of the military, with a goal of becoming a Navy Seal.

32 歲的 Brian Kash 在 17 歲時加入海軍陸戰隊，並在 2001 年 9 月 11 號加入新兵訓練營，隨後便被派駐至伊拉克，當他從伊拉克返國時，他決定要投入職業軍旅生涯，並成為一位海豹精英成員。

alter 即有變化的意思；alternative 在這裡是形容詞，指兩者（或若干）中擇一的、非此即彼的、供選擇的；也可做可數名詞，指選擇、二擇一。

替代役
alternative service

新聞這樣說

Under a new program called the "industry reserves alternative service," conscripts serve a three-year stint that is salaried according to market rate during the last two years. In the first year, wages are distributed based on the conscript's level of education and range from NT$19,500 to NT$28,000.

在新制產業替代役制度下，役男服役三年內的薪資是以該產業近兩年平均薪資值為基準，第一年的薪資則以該役男教育程度高低作為準則，薪水範圍約為台幣一萬九千五百元到二萬八千元。

台美兵役比一比

大學快畢業的男生最擔心的就是台灣瞬息萬變的兵役制度，以及一直以來存在軍中的多種不合理官僚潛規則。跟台灣比起來，美國兵役制度可是完全不同。美國兵種分為陸軍 Army、海軍 Navy、海軍陸戰隊 Marine Corps、空軍 Air Force 以及沿海防衛隊 Coast Guard。 通常軍隊會在高中校園以及大學內進行招募，只要年滿 17 歲，並取得父母之一或是監護人同意，就可以申請進入軍隊。

示範對話 (MP3 74)

當兵到底要當多久

Elise and Zhang are watching the Changing of the Guard at Chiang Kai-shek [1]Memorial Hall. 伊莉絲和小張在中正紀念堂看衛兵交接

Elise: I swear, every time I see something like this, I am just amazed at how much [2]discipline these guys have to have.
我敢說，每次看到這樣的情景都讓我對這些如此訓練有素的傢伙感到驚訝。

Zhang: I'm sorry. Were you talking to me?
對不起，妳剛剛在跟我說話嗎？

Elise: Oh, sorry. Not really. I was just talking to myself. But, aren't they [3]incredible?
喔，對不起。也不是啦。我只是自言自語而已。不過，他們真是不可思議吧？

Zhang: The guy there, on the right, is my brother. He's going to be finishing his military service in a few weeks.
在右邊那傢伙是我弟弟。他再幾個星期就服完他的兵役了。

Elise: Oh, really? How long do you have to serve in Taiwan?
喔，真的嗎？你們在台灣要服役多久？

Zhang: Good question. That's something that is being 6)debated right now. It was three years, then two and a half, and now it's two, but they want to make it one year by 2008.
好問題。那是現在一直在討論的事。原本是三年，然後是兩年半，現在是兩年，不過他們想要在二○○八年時減成一年。

Elise: Is that 7)mandatory service?
那是義務役嗎？

Zhang: For now, it is. Guys normally go in just out of college, and serve for two years. By the time you get out, and go to look for a job, you've already forgotten everything you learned in school.
目前是。男生通常大學一畢業就要去服役兩年。當你退伍去找工作時，你已經忘光在學校所學的東西了。

Elise: I can believe it. It seems like such a waste of time.
我相信。似乎很浪費時間。

Zhang: Well, it has its good points, too. You get to learn a lot about how to 8)deal with a lot of different kinds of people.
嗯，當然也有好處。你可以學習如何跟不同的人相處。

Elise: But not everyone wants to learn how to be a soldier.
不過不是每個人都想學如何成為軍人。

Zhang: True. That's why the government is going to try out a volunteer military, like they have in the U.S.
沒錯。所以政府即將要試辦自願役，就跟美國的一樣。

Elise: Wow, that's 9)awfully 10)daring of the Taiwanese government, with China 11)breathing down your neck and all.
哇，台灣政府還真是大膽，中國對你們這樣虎視眈眈都不怕。

Zhang: Who knows? Maybe it will work. My only hope is that, by the time my son grows up, he won't be required to serve if he doesn't want to.
天知道？也許會行得通。我唯一的希望是，當我兒子長大的時候，如果他不想當兵，他就可以不用當。

---

1. memorial (a.) 紀念的
2. discipline (n.) 訓練，紀律
3. incredible (a.) 不可思議的，驚人的
4. military service 兵役。
5. serve (v.) 服兵役
6. debate (v.) 爭議
7. mandatory (a.) 義務的，強制的
8. deal with… 應付…
9. awfully (adv.) 非常地
10. daring (a.) 勇敢的，大膽的
11. breathe down sb's neck 嚴密監視某人

好用短句 (MP3 75)

談兵役
你還要知道

· Every Taiwanese male has to serve in the military.

在台灣每個男生都必須當兵。

· In the past, people said you weren't a man till you did your service.

以前大家都覺得當過兵的才是男人。

· Nowadays, everyone wants to get out of serving.

現在大家卻想逃避兵役。

· This is because people think military service is a waste of time.

這是因為大家人為當兵很浪費時間。

· Another reason is that older soldiers often bully the younger ones.

還有老兵常常欺負新兵也是一個原因。

· Some new recruits commit suicide because they can't get used to military life.

有些新兵因為不適應軍隊生活而自殺。

· Actually, military service is pretty easy these days, and the time of service keeps getting shorter.

其實現在當兵很輕鬆了，役期也越來越短。

· But for people who are compelled to serve against their wishes, the shorter the time the better.

但是對於非志願當兵的人而言，役期還是越短越好。

The Ethics of Suicide Reporting
新聞媒體職業道德

畏罪自殺
murder-suicide

murder 是「謀殺」，其他各種殺人罪行相關說法還有：「畏罪潛逃」escape punishment、「過失殺人」negligent homicide、「蓄意謀殺」intentional homicide。

新聞這樣說

Authorities said depression and failing health were the likely causes of a recent suspected murder-suicide in Taichung, with the bodies of a man and his son found on a hillside road.

相關當局表示，憂鬱症以及健康問題可能是最近台中畏罪自殺嫌犯的原因，他與兒子雙雙被發現陳屍在山路邊。

憂鬱症 depression

press 原意為「壓」，de 字首有「向下」或「表負面」之意，故 depress 當動詞有使人沮喪的意思，跟 discourage 相似。名詞 depression 跟 melancholy「鬱悶」意思相近，憂鬱症的醫學術語即是 melancholia。

新聞這樣說

Afflicted by depression, more and more people are choosing to take their lives. Their friends and family are then left to suffer unspeakable pain. Some of them are even posting their plans on the Internet. The government should think of some bold and practical ways to remedy the situation.

受憂鬱症之苦，越來越多人走上自殺一途，因而留給親人朋友無法言喻的悲傷。有人甚至在網路上公布他們的自殺計畫。政府機關應該想出更有力及可落實的政策來修補現況。

諮詢 counseling

counsel 當動詞用時是提供諮詢，如 The teacher counsels troubled students（老師向問題學生提供輔導）。易混淆字 consult 則是尋求諮詢，如 The company consults a big consulting group on its future business development（公司向顧問公司諮詢事業發展的意見）。

新聞這樣說

Earlier this week, DPP city councilors Tuan Yi-kang said that less than 20 percent of the calls they placed in a recent survey of three of Taipei's hotlines got through. The city has six hotlines for individuals seeking suicide counseling.

本週稍早，民進黨市議員段宜康表示，在最近一項針對生命熱線調查中，不到 20% 的電話被接通。而台北有六個生命熱線專門幫助想要自殺的人。

熱線 hotline

hotline 為電話專線，許多聯絡資料上常出現：information hotline「咨詢專線」、 customer service hotline「客服專線」等。若要在專線後附上號碼則用「hotline at 電話號碼」表示。

新聞這樣說

A suicide hotline prevented 143 people from killing themselves last year, the Department of Health (DOH) said at a press conference yesterday. The suicide counseling service hotline, jointly run by the DOH and the Lifeline Association, Taipei, received 61,284 calls in 2009, the department said.

在昨天記者會中，衛生福利部表示，由衛生福利部以及生命線協會共同主辦的自殺防治專線去年使一百四十三人免於自殺，並在 2009 年接了六萬一千二百八十四通自殺防治電話。

自殺 commit suicide

犯罪的動詞常用 commit，如 commit atrocity（犯下暴行）、 commit adultery（通姦）、commit a murder（犯殺人罪）。commit to 則是允諾或誓言，如 She is not ready to commit to anyone. (她還沒準備要訂下終身)

新聞這樣說

Four siblings, aged between five and 14 and left unattended by their parents for months, apparently committed suicide by drinking pesticide in southwest China, the government and state media said Friday.

中國媒體指出，西南部的四個兄弟姊妹，5 歲至 14 歲，在遭到父母遺棄數月後喝下農藥自殺。

模仿，抄襲 copycat

模仿行為或動作的其他字詞有：mimic, imitate，如：He tries to mimic a British accent. （他嘗試模仿英國腔）。另一個相近字 simulate 則是「模擬」的意思，譬如飛行模擬機就是 flight simulator.

新聞這樣說

In another study published in 2003, researchers found that extensive newspaper reporting on charcoal burning suicides in Taiwan contributed to a rapid rise in so-called "copycat" suicides by this method.

2003 年的一份研究中在指出，媒體對於燒炭自殺的密集報導，造成仿效自殺效應的疾速提升。

喪失親屬的 bereaved

bereavement 是喪親，喪親之痛則可用 agony of bereavement。be bereaved of + 某人，是指失去了親人。而「寡婦」是 widow，鰥夫則是 widower；失去父母也可以 parentless 形容。

新聞這樣說

Tokyo Electric Power Co. has been ordered to pay 27 million yen ($219,500) in compensation to the bereaved family of a male evacuee who committed suicide after being displaced due to the 2011 Fukushima nuclear disaster.

東京電力公司必須支付二千七百萬日圓的賠償金給一位因福島核爆案件被調職而自殺的員工家屬。

自殺傾向的
suicidal

自殺傾向亦可說 suicidal tendency，而有殺人傾向則是 homicidal tendency。cida 字根是殺人的意思，sui 字首在拉丁文中指自己（self），homo 則是人，所以 suicide 是「自殺」而 homicide 是「殺人」。

新聞這樣說

Experts say spring can make people feel short-tempered and empty or even suicidal . They even have a term for it—"Springtime Depression". So it should come as no surprise that over ten people "including the editor of a well-known men's magazine" killed themselves in just a few days time. Hopefully springtime depression will soon give way to summer elation.

專家說春天容易使人煩躁空虛甚至有自殺欲望，造成「春季憂鬱症」，果真短短幾天內就發生十幾起自殺案件，就連知名男性雜誌總編輯也在最近輕生。不論是上吊、服毒或是燒炭，這些人求死的毅力比求生的勇氣還強。

給自己一個機會

人生是很艱難的一段旅程，路上佈滿了痛苦、煎熬、挑戰和失意，但只要有一口氣在，生命的道路上還會有歡樂、笑顏、愛情和親情。所以，當你覺得自己無法承擔這些痛苦時，請你轉向身邊的親人、專業人士或是一位聊得來的陌生人，尋求幫助。記得：求助並不可恥，求助是成熟、負責且勇敢的行為。美國自殺防治協會等一連串自殺關懷協會特別製作了一份 Recommendations For Reporting On Suicide 的準則，提供給各大媒體及社會機構，教導他們確實且負責的自殺新聞報導，內容包含：

1. 請以理性且最低限度地渲染成分編寫頭條。
2. 請不要刊登死亡方式、自殺凶器等血腥照片；以學校照片、家庭合照等配合自殺防治專線取而代之。
3. 請不要用「飆高」、「感染性」等字眼描述自殺率。
4. 請不要說出「毫無預警自殺」等字眼，謹慎報導可能導致自殺的行為及情緒轉折，並教導民眾如何避免此情緒或如何尋求協助。
5. 請將自殺新聞歸類為全民健康相關新聞。
6. 請勿節錄或是立刻訪問當眾目睹自殺案件之毫不相關的民眾。
7. 請不要出現「自殺不成」、「成功取得煤炭而自殺」等字眼，請不要把自殺當作一件可區分為成功與否的事件。

示範對話 (MP3 77)

自殺報導的限度

Kim: You look kind of confused by the TV news.
你似乎被電視新聞弄糊塗了。

Jason: You bet I am! Are they holding a [1]séance right now?
妳說的完全沒錯！他們在辦通靈法會嗎？

Kim: Yes, for a famous actor who killed himself. The media has [2]gone completely nuts.
是啊，是為一個自殺的明星辦的。媒體已經完全瘋了。

Jason: What else is new? News here has always been [3]weird.
還會有什麼新鮮事？這裡總是報怪新聞。

Kim: It's not just weird now. It's [4]downright dangerous.
現在不只是奇怪——根本已經十分危險了。

Jason: Are you talking about the risk of people committing copycat suicides?
妳是指造成群眾跟風自殺的危險？

Kim: Exactly. After Leslie Cheung jumped to his death, Hong Kong's suicide rate [5]shot way up.
一點也沒錯。張國榮跳樓身亡之後，香港的自殺率突然攀升了。

Jason: Doesn't that happen every time a public figure kills himself?
每當公眾人物自殺，不是都會發生這種情況？

Kim: There are ways to report on it without causing more problems.
其實有辦法在不造成更多問題的情況下做報導。

Jason: How? Doesn't the public want to know what happened?
要怎麼做？大眾不都想知道發生什麼事嗎？

Kim: Of course, but the public doesn't need to see so many [6]gory photos, or learn easier ways to do it themselves.
當然，但大眾不需要看到這麼多恐怖的照片，或得知更簡便的方法去自我了斷。

Jason: Is there any hope of the media learning to be more responsible?
有可能指望媒體學著更負責任嗎？

Kim: There are [7]WHO [8]guidelines about suicide reporting. Europe and even Korea have done a really good job of suicide reporting.
世界衛生組織有針對自殺新聞的報導準則。歐洲、甚至韓國在報導自殺新聞方面就做得很好。

Jason: Well, maybe Taiwan can do it then, too.
呃，那麼或許台灣媒體也可以做到。

Kim: I hope so. And the government should improve mental health services [9]while they're at it.
希望如此。而且政府也應該順便加強心理健康的服務。

---

1. séance (n.) 通靈法會
2. go nuts (phr.) 發狂
3. weird (a.) 奇怪的
4. downright (adv.) 完全地，徹底地
5. shoot up (phr.) 突然高升
6. gory (a.) 令人毛髮悚然的，血腥的
7. WHO = World Health Organization 世界衛生組織
8. guideline (n.) 準則
9. while sb.'s at it (phr.) 順便

好用短句 (MP3 78)

談新聞媒體道德
你可以說

- It seems like there's stories in the news about someone committing suicide every day of the week.

台灣的電視新聞幾乎天天都有自殺消息。

- And news reporters seem not only describe the suicide methods in detail, but even speculate about the reasons behind the suicide.

新聞記者不但會仔細描述自殺方法，還會猜測自殺原因。

- Reporters even go so far as to ask the victim's family members how they feel or try to get images of the bereaved breaking down and crying.

新聞記者甚至誇張到去追問死者家屬的「感想」，或拍攝失去親人的家屬傷心痛哭的景象。

- Reporters claim they're just protecting people's "right to know," but does anyone really want to know these details?

記者都宣稱自己是為了維護大眾「知的權利」，但真的有人想知道這些嗎？

Cyberbullying
網路霸凌

Hit! 話題單字 (MP3 79)

bullying 作名詞指恃強欺弱的行為、霸道；bully 可作形容詞、名詞及動詞，同樣為惡霸、欺侮及橫行霸道的意思。

霸凌
bullying

新聞這樣說

TV personality and model Peng Hsin-yi, more commonly known by her stage name Cindy Yang, on Tuesday committed suicide in her Taichung residence by reportedly inhaling helium, leaving behind a suicide note blaming her decision on coworkers and bullying on the Internet.

藝人及模特兒彭馨逸，以其藝名楊又穎聞名，於週二在台中自家吸入過多氫氣自殺身亡。因遺書中將自殺原因歸咎於同事及網路霸凌。

恐同症
homophobia

homo 為名詞，是對同性戀者較貶低的稱呼；phobia 也是名詞，指恐懼症、懼怕。

新聞這樣說

Holding white signs reading: "How many more have to die?" dozens of supporters attended a demonstration rally held by the Lobby Alliance for LGBT Human Rights on International Day against Homophobia and Transphobia, on Ketagalan Boulevard yesterday.

一群支持者在昨日聯合國國際日參與 LGBT 人權遊說團體在凱達格蘭大道上的遊行集會，手舉寫有「還要死多少人？」的白色看板，抗議恐同症與恐變性人者。

羞辱 humiliate

humiliate 為動詞，同義字有 embarrass、disgrace、shame。

新聞這樣說

The commencement of the 23rd Tokyo International Film Festival last weekend was tainted with cross-strait drama, when mainland Chinese film representatives publicly humiliated the Taiwan film industry attendees by demanding that they present themselves as "Chinese Taipei" instead of "Taiwan."

第 23 屆東京國際電影節開幕式蒙上兩岸政治陰影，中國電影代表團公開羞辱台灣電影產業與會者，要求台灣代表團將「台灣」改為「中華台北」。

恐嚇 threaten

threaten 為動詞，作威脅、恐嚇：threaten + to v 或 + with；同義字有 warn、caution。

新聞這樣說

China has developed a large new drone—known as the Shen Diao or Divine Eagle—which could threaten Taiwan. Unveiled over the past few days, it is made by Shenyang Aircraft Corp and is a high-altitude long-endurance uncrewed aircraft that makes potential targets in Taiwan more vulnerable.

由中國瀋陽工業集團發展出的高海拔、長程飛行神鵰無人戰機，讓台灣成為可能目標並帶來威脅恐嚇。

性騷擾 sexual harassment

sexual 為形容詞，指性別的、兩性的、性的。harassment 為名詞，即騷擾、煩擾的意思。相關詞有 electronic harassment，指在網路上聊天使用攻擊性或騷擾的言詞、或用 email 寄送色情的、無用的電子郵件。

新聞這樣說

Heavy media coverage in Taiwan of a former Sunflower Movement leader's confession of sexual harassment and the seeming acceptance of his actions has led several women to break their silence and open up online about their past sufferings.

隨著媒體大幅報導太陽花學運領導人陳為廷性騷擾事件，他僅於表面上承認性騷擾的作為，讓很多女人決定挺身而出說出自己相關遭遇。

操控 manipulation

manipulate 為其動詞，有操作熟練、權勢操縱、做手腳的意思；字尾 -ation 表示「行動、行為」。說人「愛掌控、控制欲高」則可用 manipulative 來形容。

新聞這樣說

What is Media Manipulation? If you don't know, you should. Because media manipulation currently shapes everything you read, hear and watch online.Today, with our blog and web driven media cycle, nothing can escape exaggeration, distortion, fabrication and simplification.

什麼是媒體操控？如果你還不知道，你必須知道這個掌控了我們閱讀、聆聽以及收看一切的手段，現今社會這個由部落格以及網路串起的媒體生態，任何資訊會被誇大、曲解、捏造以及簡化。

蓄意的 deliberate

deliberate 可作形容詞或動詞，作形容詞有慎重、深思熟慮及蓄意的意思；作動詞時為仔細考慮、商議的意思，deliberate + about／on／upon。

新聞這樣說

In a press conference held yesterday, Premier Jiang Yi-huah said that evidence shows that the storming of the Executive Yuan by students on Sunday night was a deliberate act led by the "Black Island Nation Youth Front."

昨日記者會上，行政院長江宜樺表示，週日晚間學生佔領立法院之行為是一場由「黑色島國青年陣線」所蓄意發起的活動。

社群媒體 social media

social 為形容詞，指社會上的、交際的；media 指大眾媒體。social network 「社群網絡」為其相關字，指人與人建立起來的社交圈。而我們現在常聽到的 social networking site「社交網站」即是一種讓人們得以聯繫、交流的網路互動平台。

新聞這樣說

With a population of 23 million and growing use of social media tools, Taiwan has garnered the interest of online social media companies. Facebook recently announced that Taiwanese were now the biggest users of Facebook in Asia, while Twitter said it was looking for people to help boost its presence in Taiwan and Hong Kong.

擁有二千三百萬人口（並還在快速成長中）使用社交軟體的台灣，吸引了許多社群網站公司的注意。facebook 最近宣布，台灣成為全亞洲使用戶最多的國家，推特則提及要尋求人才來推廣在台灣及香港的能見度。

Tyler Clementi 事件

網路霸凌已是一個全球執法及教育單位須立刻正視的社會問題。2010 年的「Clementi 自殺事件」引起全美、甚至全球對於網路霸凌議題的關注。當時 18 歲的大一新鮮人 Tyler Clementi 在進入紐澤西 Rutgers 大學讀書的前一刻和家人出櫃，雖獲得父親接受，卻和信仰虔誠的母親產生歧異。在進入大學宿舍後，又因為室友在電腦上偷偷開啟錄影功能，錄下他和約會對象接吻的畫面，甚至在社群網站上散佈影像，並邀請所有網友一起觀賞下一次偷拍直播。事發 3 天後，Tyler 選擇跳下華盛頓大橋結束生命。這件悲劇在全美引發一連串反霸凌運動，包括總統歐巴馬、國務卿希拉蕊都因此事件發表全國性演說。許多美國高中、大學也因為 Tyler 事件建立了「零霸凌」教育主旨。Clementi 的死雖成了美國反霸凌運動歷史上最黑暗的一頁，但也激起了全國人民向校園、網路霸凌說「不」的勇氣。

示範對話 (MP3 80)

正視網路霸凌

Sheldon: Who's that pretty girl on the TV?
電視上那個漂亮的女孩是誰啊?

Angela: Cindy Yang. She was an actress and model.
楊又穎。她曾是位演員及模特兒。

Sheldon: Was?
曾是?

Angela: She committed suicide last week.
她上週自殺了。

Sheldon: Really? She looks so young.
真的嗎?她看起來好年輕。

Angela: Yeah. She was only 24.
是啊,她才 24 歲。

Sheldon: Do they know why she did it?
有人知道她為什麼要這麼做嗎?

Angela: Yes. She left a suicide note. She was really [1]depressed because of negative comments about her on Facebook. Lots of [2] anonymous posters said mean things about her, calling her [3] phony and [4]hypocritical.

179

嗯，她留了遺書，她因為臉書上的一些負面言論感到很沮喪，很多匿名的網友貼文，講她壞話，說她做作、虛假。

Sheldon: That's the problem with social media—people say things about other people online that they would never say to their faces.
這就是社群網站的問題，人們總是對其他人說些現實生活中不敢當著他們面說的話。

Angela: Exactly. It's especially bad for teenagers—lots of teens are getting 5)harassed and even threatened all the time. In her note, Cindy said she hoped her death would help raise awareness about cyberbullying.
沒錯，這對青少年來說更是嚴重，很多年輕人會在網路上遭到騷擾，甚至是恐嚇。在楊又穎的遺書中，她提到她希望藉由她的死，人們能正視網路霸凌問題。

Sheldon: Well, it looks like it's working.
嗯，看來確實起了作用。

Angela: Yeah. Lots of entertainers and politicians are speaking out against cyberbullying, and there's even talk about passing new laws.
對啊，很多藝人和政治人物都出面反網路霸凌，甚至還有人說要建立法規。

Sheldon: There was a similar case in the U.S. a few years ago. A college student watched his roommate kissing another guy on a webcam and then talked about it online. Then, a few days later, his roommate committed suicide. It started a national 6)debate about cyberbullying, but the laws haven't changed much since then.
幾年前美國也發生過類似的事件。一個大學生用網路攝影機偷窺他的室友和另一個男生親嘴，還在網路上討論這件事。幾天後，他的室友就自殺了，這件事引起了全國對於反網路霸凌的聲浪，只是後來法律沒有多大的改變。

Angela: Well, I guess there's a fine line between bullying and free speech.
嗯，我想霸凌和言論自由真是一線之隔啊。

---

1. depressed (adj.) 憂鬱的
2. anonymous (adj.) 匿名的
3. phony (adj.) 做作的
4. hypocritical (adj.) 虛假的
5. harass (v.) 騷擾
6. debate (v.) (n.) 辯論

好用短句 (MP3 81)

談網路霸凌
你還可以說

- The issue of cyberbullying received widespread attention after the suicide of Cindy Yang.

經過楊又穎自殺事件後，網路霸凌議題受到廣泛注目。

- Many people have urged the government to pass a law against cyberbullying to restrict online abuse.

許多人督促政府通過法案來約束網路霸凌。

- The minister of Education said that he would back legislation against cyberbullying if it was introduced.

教育部長聲明若一旦要立法反網路霸凌，他會支持法案的通過。

- But the vice premier said that the government had no plans to promote anti-cyberbullying legislation.

但行政院副院長說政府並無宣導反網路霸凌的法案計畫。

- Some civil rights advocates worry that a law against cyberbullying would restrict freedom of speech.

一些公民權益組織擔心這種反霸凌法會限制人民言論自由。

The Ugly Truth
日本不願面對的過去

贖罪
atone-ment

atone 為 atonement 的動詞，atone for an error 指為了一個錯誤贖罪或補救。另一常見於報導中的字是 penance，動名詞同形，a work of penance 是指宗教的贖罪、苦行。

新聞這樣說

About 30 percent of for-mer South Korean wartime sex slaves have received atonement money from a private Japanese fund, the fund's former executive director said Thursday, revealing for the first time the exact number of beneficiaries.

大約 30% 的戰時南韓慰安婦，從一個日本私人基金會得到贖罪賠償款項，該基金會前執行總裁也於週四首度公布正確的受益者數量。

暴行 atrocity

brutality 為 atrocity 最常見的同義詞，形容詞為 atrocious，同義字也有許多如：monstrous, brutal, barbarous, heinous 都是指殘暴的、暴力的；另外 autocracy 則是獨裁。

新聞這樣說

Japanese Prime Minister Shinzo Abe said Monday that Japan would reflect on its atrocities during World War II in his statement to be announced in August to commemorate the 70th anniversary of its end.

日本首相安培晉三週一時表示，為紀念二戰結束七十週年，他將在八月發表聲明，內容將提到日本會反省其於二戰時期所做出的暴行。

南京大屠殺 Nanjing Massacre

massacre 是屠殺的總稱，其他較接近的說法有 slaughtering（濫殺），random killing spree（隨機殺人），二戰時德國納粹對猶太人的集體屠殺則是 genocide（種族清洗）。

新聞這樣說

"History cannot be forgotten, and countries should learn from history and make efforts to promote peace in the region", a Taiwanese official said Saturday, the 77th anniversary of the start of the Nanjing Massacre committed by Japanese troops in China during the Second Sino-Japanese War (1937-1945).

在第 77 屆南京大屠殺紀念日這天，日本軍隊於中國抗日戰爭時在中國境內進行屠殺。一位台灣官員週六時表示：「歷史無法被遺忘，各國應該向其歷史學習，並努力宣傳和平理念。」

掩飾（罪刑、過錯）

whitewash

whitewash 拆解成兩個單字後，white 及 wash，就能看出由「洗白」所衍伸的「掩飾錯誤」之意；其他動詞如 cover, conceal, overlook 也是指掩蓋或是忽略某項事實。

新聞這樣說

The Obama administration has successfully signaled to the Chinese that the U.S. supports Japan's administrative control of the Senkaku Islands. But his administration also has reportedly called for restraint from Japan as well, and even criticized Tokyo publicly for actions that seem to whitewash Imperial Japan's actions in World War II.

歐巴馬執政團隊成功的讓中國政府知道美國支持日本之於釣魚台列嶼行政權力的掌控，但也要求日本自制以及譴責日本試圖掩飾二戰時期帝國主義的種種行為。

國家主義者

nationalist

nationalist 與 nationalism 所代表的是單一民族主義傾向的國家主義。而英雄電影所宣導的「愛國情操」，可以用 patriotism（愛國情操），patriot（愛國者）與 patriotic（愛國的）來形容。

新聞這樣說

Japanese nationalists have labeled Angelina Jolie a racist and there have been calls for her to be banned from the country for directing the movie *Unbroken*. However, activists attempting to encourage Japan to face up to its brutal imperial past say criticizing *Unbroken* is taking "denier history to a new level."

日本國家主義者宣稱執導《永不屈服》的安潔莉納裘莉為一種種族歧視者，並要求禁止讓裘莉入境日本。然而要求日本正視其殘酷帝國主義過往的人權分子則說，批評《永不屈服》一片無疑是將歷史否認帶到另一境界了。

歷史竄改

historical revisionism

revision 是修訂本或修改的意思，延伸去的 revisionism 是指重複修正或重新詮釋，字尾 ism 長表示一個信仰或行為準則的意思，如：terrorism「恐怖主義」、plagiarism「剽竊」。

新聞這樣說

Prime Minister Abe has made numerous controversial remarks on whether there was actual coercion involved to recruit women into sexual slavery by the Japanese military, and even questioning the definition of "invasion" and "aggression" in Japan's past. Korea and Japan have faced diplomatic tensions because of Abe's right-wing tendency toward historical revisionism.

對於二戰時日本軍方是否有強迫微召慰安婦的指控，日本首相安培晉三一再發表爭議性的評論，甚至對其過去所謂的「侵佔」及「侵略行動」存疑。日韓兩國也因為安培晉三右翼政治立場，傾向歷史竄改，而陷入緊張關係。

杯葛 boycott

boycott 音譯為杯葛亦較常作為政治術語，日常生活中則是抵制的意思，比較生活的同義字詞為 refuse, resist（拒絕）；而國際航空上武器或物品禁運則是用 embargo 這個字。

新聞這樣說

A campaign to boycott Ting Hsin food products picked up momentum yesterday as food conglomerate tycoon Wei Ying-chung made his first public appearance since the latest tainted oil scandal erupted to apologize to the nation.

杯葛頂新集團食品的運動在昨天達到高點，加工食品大亨魏應充在黑心油風暴後首度露面向大眾道歉。

慰安婦 comfort woman

慰安婦的軍營因存在於戰時，故也可以用 comfort battalion 或 military brothel（軍妓院）來稱呼；目前，性工作者則泛稱 sex worker。

新聞這樣說

The issue of "comfort women," a euphemism by which the victims are known in Japan, has long haunted Tokyo's ties with South Korea. Relations remain chilly even as the Asian neighbors near the 50th anniversary of diplomatic ties on Monday.

慰安婦，一個戰時受害者的委婉名稱，長久以來為日韓關係蒙上一層陰影，兩國關係在周邊亞洲國家邁入 50 年的外交關係之際仍然冷淡。

德國的轉型正義

二戰後簽署的波茨坦協定開始了一連串「去納粹運動」（denazification）。德國開始整肅全國上下各機構的納粹份子，努力洗刷歷史罪名。這種民主國家對於過去歷史大屠殺、發動戰爭等違法行為的彌補，稱作「轉型正義」（transitional justice）。在一份 2015 年四月所進行的民調中，十位德國人中，有四位覺得德國已贖罪完畢，不需再肩負起更大的道德責任。

示範對話 (MP3 83)

帝國主義的過去

Sam: Hi, are you German?
嗨，妳是德國人嗎？

Eva: Yes. You could tell from the book cover?
對。你是從書的封面看出來的嗎？

Sam: Of course. I've been reading a lot about German history recently—World War II stuff.
當然。我最近讀很多關於德國的歷史，二次世界大戰的東西。

Eva: That was a long time ago. Germany has changed a lot.
那是好久以前的事了。德國已經改變了很多。

Sam: I know. I think you've done a much better job of [1]addressing your history than Japan has.
我知道。我覺得你們在處理歷史方面做的比日本好太多了。

Eva: I don't know much about it, but I heard that their textbooks don't talk much about what happened.
我知道得不多，不過我聽說他們的課本沒有提太多過去發生的事？

Sam: No, they sure don't. It's made a lot of people here and in China very angry.
對，他們的確沒有。這讓這裡和大陸的很多人非常生氣。

Eva: This could never happen in Germany. Sometimes, I feel like we're still 2)atoning for our past.
這絕對不會在德國發生。有時候，我覺得我們仍然在為過去贖罪。

Sam: I don't understand why Japan still plays this game.
我不懂日本怎麼還在玩這一套。

Eva: Maybe they don't want to admit what they did.
也許他們不想承認他們做過的事。

Sam: I guess so, but this is causing major 3)diplomatic problems.
我想是吧，可是這引起了很大的外交問題。

Eva: And educational ones, too, I suppose.
我想，還有教育的問題。

Sam: Yeah. If their students don't understand history, what kind of citizens will they make?
對。如果他們的學生不了解歷史，那將來會成為什麼樣的公民？

Eva: Is there anything anyone can do about this?
有人有方法可以解決嗎？

Sam: People have talked about boycotts. And there have been violent 4)protests in China.
有人一直在談論抵制。而中國則有過暴力抗議。

Eva: It sounds like they're 5)going a little far.
聽起來他們似乎有點過火了。

Sam: Maybe, but those who don't learn the mistakes of history are 6)doomed to repeat them.
或許是，不過沒從歷史上學到教訓的人注定會重蹈覆轍。

---

1. address (v.) 處理，討論
2. atone (v.) 彌補，贖罪
3. diplomatic (a.) 外交的
4. protest (n.) 抗議
5. go too far (phr.) 太過分
6. doom (v.) 決定命運，注定

好用短句 (MP3 84)

談篡改歷史
你還可以說

· Japan has long tried to deny its history.

日本對於過去的歷史一直採取否認態度。

· Their textbooks only touch lightly on their past sins.

他們的教科書只輕描淡寫帶出過去的罪行。

· International reaction to this historical revisionism has been extremely negative.

國際間對於這種篡改歷史的行為極度不齒。

· The countries most upset are those that suffered under Japanese colonial rule.

尤其曾被日本殖民欺壓的國家更無法忍受。

· Japan's post-World War II behavior has been quite different from that of Germany.

日本在第二次世界大戰後的態度與德國大相逕庭。

· Germany has apologized for its mistakes and earned the world's forgiveness.

德國勇於承認錯誤的行為獲得國際間的諒解。

· Maybe Japan should learn from Germany's willingness to frankly confront its past.

或許日本應該學學德國的勇於誠實地承認錯誤。

· Then, Japan's future generations could learn the truth about what happened.

那麼一來，日本的下一代就能得知過去真正發生的事。

Medicine East and West
中醫—奇蹟製造者

經絡
meridian

也稱為 channel network。meridian 除了經絡以外，也是地理上的經線，prime meridian 就是指「本初子午線」；而緯度則是 latitude，赤道叫做 equator。

新聞這樣說

Whereas acupuncture uses hair-thin needles to direct and channel body energy to improve the flow of ch'i, acupressure uses gentle, firm pressure of the fingers and hands to stimulate points along the meridians to release the blocked energy.

針灸利用細如髮的針刺入穴道，疏通身體內的經氣，而指壓按摩則是用手指和手溫柔有力地按壓，以刺激經絡上的穴道，釋放受阻的能量。

瀕臨絕種的
endangered

danger 是危險，en 當字首表動詞化，ed 當字尾則表被動。所以 endangered 就是「被放入危險中」衍生為瀕臨絕種之意。若指真正「滅絕」則可用 extinct。

新聞這樣說

Traditional Chinese Medicine (TCM) claims all manner of ailments including back ache, poor memory and even cancer can be cured by the natural world. It is often believed that the more endangered the animal is, the greater the healing affect it will have.

傳統中醫協會會指稱所有病痛，從背痛、記憶衰退到癌症都能夠被大自然的力量療癒，越是瀕臨絕種的動物，其療效往往越是被誇大。

療法，藥物
remedy

後面常接介係詞 for 指某病痛的療法，如：I know a remedy for your headache（我有治療你頭痛的藥）。而病痛「治癒」可用 cure 或 heal 表示。

新聞這樣說

Last year three million Britons took herbal remedies to treat everything from fever to joint pain. But renewed debate about the safety of these remedies was sparked last week following the news of an EU crackdown on herbalists and Chinese medicine practitioners who operate unregulated at present.

去年有約三百萬的英國人以草藥治療一切病痛，從高燒到關節，但由於上週有關歐盟取締草藥醫生與中醫師不按規定行醫的消息傳出後，關於草藥的爭議便再度被掀起。

針灸 acupuncture

針灸所針的穴道稱為 acupuncture point 或 acupoint，針灸師則是 acupuncturist。另外，利用按壓穴道的指壓按摩則稱為 acupressure。

新聞這樣說

Acupuncture has spread around the world since originating in China, but conventional Western medicine has remained steadfastly skeptical. Although there is now good evidence that acupuncture can relieve pain, many of the other health benefits acupuncturists claim are on shakier ground.

針灸自發源於中國以來已席捲全球，然而傳統西醫對於其療法仍是抱持懷疑態度，雖然已有證明針灸對於疼痛治療的功效，但其他中醫師宣稱的功效仍是不被西醫廣泛接受。

偽科學 pseudoscience

pseudo 是「偽」的意思，如 pseudonym（筆名或假名），pseudo- 常用於科學、工程專有名詞如動植物的「偽足」pseudopod、程式語言的「虛擬碼」pseudo-code 等。

新聞這樣說

"I will stop calling traditional Chinese medicine (TCM) a pseudoscience if any TCM practitioner can accurately detect pregnancy simply by taking their pulse, as their ancient system claims they can," promised an outspoken critic of TCM.

一位公開批評傳統中醫療法的的人士保證，「若是傳統中醫業者真能誠如他們所聲稱，靠把脈精準診斷出一位女性懷孕與否，我就不再說中醫是偽科學。」

另類醫學 alternative medicine

alternative 通常指「替代方案」，形容詞則是「替代的」或是「另外的」。所以 alternative rock（另類搖滾）、alternative medicine（另類醫學）便因而得此譯名。

新聞這樣說

Alternative medicine has grown into a $3.5 billion industry supported by four out of five Australians, who admit to taking anything from vitamin supplements and echinacea to using acupuncture and homeopathy. The problem is very few of these products are tested in the same way prescription drugs are reviewed.

每五個澳洲人中就有 4 位支持另類醫學療法，使其成為一種高達三十五億美金的產業，這些支持者服用維他命補充劑以及紫錐花，甚至是針灸以及同類療法。但最主要的問題在於只有極少數醫療食品有經過處方藥物般的規格審核。

風水
feng shui

其他常見中國命理民俗文化還有 palm-reading（看手相）、八字（eight characters of horoscope）。而「算命」通稱 fortune-telling，所以算命師就叫 fortune-teller。

新聞這樣說

Feng shui—literally meaning "wind-water"—is influential in many parts of Asia, where people adjust their lives, homes and offices based on its rules to maximize their luck and wealth.

英文 feng shui，按中文字面解釋為「風」及「水」，在亞洲地區極具影響力，人們依照風水來調整自己的生活、家裡裝潢以及辦公室擺設，以招來更多好運以財富的。

草藥
herbal medicine

herb 泛指香草植物，所以 herbal 就是形容詞；medicine 除了當藥物以外也是指醫學，所以醫學院的英文是 medical school 或是 school of medicine。

新聞這樣說

There's growing acceptance that herbal medicines could be effective for medical conditions, but the scientific evidence to vault such a treatment into an approved drug is often lacking.

雖然大家對於草藥療效有漸漸接受的趨勢，但要讓草藥成為核准藥品的科學根據卻仍相當缺乏。

劉海若火車意外

劉海若為台籍前鳳凰衛視主播，以她專業形象及甜美笑容在兩岸三地具有相當知名度，然而，2002 年 5 月 10 日的一場英國火車車禍，改變了一切。當年劉海若和林家欣、巫佳靜三人在英國乘坐火車旅遊時，車廂出軌翻覆，另外兩人當場身亡，劉海若重傷昏迷，一度被英國醫師判定腦死，放棄治療。當下劉海若家人決定將她轉回北京宣武醫院治療，北京腦科專家凌鋒招集一組中西合併的醫療團隊為她治療，期間，北京知名中藥行同仁堂也提供安公牛黃丸給劉海若服用，兩個多月後她神奇地甦醒，這件醫療事件被全球醫界視為醫學奇蹟，也讓這種傳自清朝宮廷神秘中藥聲名大噪。

(MP3 86)

中醫好神奇

Jeff: Mr. Green should be getting here any minute.
格林先生應該隨時會到。

Sylvia: Oh, he's always late. Let's see what's on the news. *[turns on TV; it's a report on Liu Hai-roh]*
喔，他老是遲到，我們來看看有什麼新聞。（打開電視，在報導劉海若）

Jeff: I heard about this woman! She was [1]brain-dead, right?
我聽說過這個女生！她原本腦死了，對吧？

Sylvia: She was in a [2]coma for two months.
她一度昏迷兩個月。

Jeff: But she looks pretty good! Talking and everything!
但她看起來挺好的！能說會動的！

Sylvia: Her [3]recovery has been pretty [4]miraculous.
她的復原非常神奇。

Jeff: She was sent to a hospital in Beijing, right?
她之前被送到北京的醫院是吧？

Sylvia: Yes, and they used a 5)combination of Eastern and Western medicine to treat her.
對，他們中西醫並用來治療她。

Jeff: That kind of mix is really popular in the States right now.
這種綜合療法目前在美國很受歡迎。

Sylvia: Really? Americans know about stuff like acupuncture and Chinese herbs?
真的？美國人知道針灸和中藥這些玩意兒？

Jeff: Of course. People just 6)eat stuff like that up. And feng shui is very popular, too.
當然啦。大家都卯起來吃。而且風水也很流行。

Sylvia: 7)No kidding. Maybe I should tell my doctor friends to go work in the States.
真的是。或許我該叫我那些當中醫的朋友到美國工作。

Jeff: They'd have a lot of competition, especially in California!
他們會有很多競爭對手，尤其在加州！

Sylvia: You know, back when she was 8)comatose, the doctors almost donated Liu's organs.
你知道嗎，當初她昏迷時，醫生差點把劉海若的器官捐出去了。

Jeff: Wow! Good thing they didn't. She'd wake up without a heart. *[the door opens]*
哇咧，還好他們沒那麼做！否則她醒過來時心臟就不見了。（門打開）

Sylvia: It's Mr. Green. Quick! If he catches us watching TV, he'll donate our organs, too!
是格林先生。快！要是被他抓到我們看電視，他也會把我們的器官捐出去！

---

1. brain-dead (a.) 腦死的
2. coma (n.) 昏迷，in a coma 表示「昏迷中」
3. recovery (n.) 復原
4. miraculous (a.) 神奇的
5. combination (n.) 組合，混合
6. eat up 大吃，吃光
7. No Kidding. (phr.) 真的是
8. comatose (a.) 昏迷的

好用短句　(MP3 87)

談中醫
你還可以說

- Tongrentang has been a famous Chinese herbal pharmacy for over three hundred years.

同仁堂是一間很有名的中藥店，有三百多年歷史。

- Tongrentang provided medicine to the Qing imperial family for nearly two hundred years and continues to employ secret imperial remedies.

同仁堂為清朝皇室提供藥品將近兩百年，至今仍擁有許多宮廷祕方。

- Liu Hai-roh was given Tongrentang medicine while she was comatose.

劉海若昏迷期間吃了同仁堂的藥。

- The medicine is useful for preventing stroke-related paralysis.

那種藥對預防中風病人癱瘓很有效。

- The medicine came even more famous after Liu recovered.

劉海若醒過來之後，那種藥就變得更出名了。

- Liu Hai-roh was a news anchor in Hong Kong.

劉海若原本是香港的新聞主播。

- She suffered a severe train wreck when traveling with friends in England.

她和朋友一起去英國玩時，發生嚴重火車車禍。

- Two of her friends died, and Liu was pronounced brain-dead.

另外兩位朋友都傷重死亡，劉海若則被宣布腦死。

- But her friends and family refused to give up. They sent for a doctor from Beijing to bring her back and save her.

但劉海若的親友不肯放棄，請了一位北京醫生去把她帶回來，並救了她。

Making Priority Seats a Priority
讓座的美德

Hit! 話題單字 (MP3 88)

priority seat
博愛座

priority 是優先的意思，博愛座的功用是給有需要的人士「優先使用」，所以英文才會是 priority seat。若餐廳看到寫有 reserved seat 則是預訂席、courtesy seat 是禮遇席。搭飛機或輪船時的優先登機則稱為 priority boarding。

新聞這樣說

Disappointed with students occupying priority seats on the MRT, the Taipei City Department of Education is launching a campaign this week to urge students to respect the disadvantaged and yield their seats to people in need.

因為對學生族群的霸占博愛座行為感到失望，台北市教育局正準備規劃一場宣導尊重弱勢團體以及宣導讓座行為的活動。

公德心 common courtesy

common 有公共的、共通的意思，courtesy 則是禮儀，故兩者表示公共場域公德心。另外 public-mindedness 是指「心在公眾」所以也是公德心的意思。

新聞這樣說

I have witnessed many instances where cyclists do not stop at stop signs, wear earbuds, ride side by side on narrow roads, do not use hand signals and generally do not use either common sense or common courtesy.

我曾多次目睹自行車騎士看到停車標誌卻不停車，戴著耳機，肩並肩騎在狹小的道路上，也不會使用手勢示意，完全沒有公德心也沒常識。

同情心 compassion

同情心 compassion 字面上與 sympathy 相同，但文意 compassion 除了同情還有實際行動，但 sympathetic look 僅用來形容同情的眼神。另外 empathy 則是同理心。

新聞這樣說

The Argentine pope, visiting his home continent for the second time since becoming pontiff in 2013, landed in Ecuador Sunday on a mission to reach out to the region's poorest and most marginalized with a message of compassion for the weak and respect for the environment, reports say.

報導指出，阿根廷籍的教宗將會在 2013 年踏上自當選教宗以來第二場返鄉旅程，周日會先由厄瓜多開始，拜訪南美洲最貧窮、最邊緣化的地區，以同情貧困以及尊敬其環境為此旅程傳達之訊息。

禮節 etiquette

etiquette 是較為正式的禮節、禮儀的通稱,似 formality(正式的規矩)。此字若用於基本禮貌則與 courtesy、decency 相近。

新聞這樣說

The etiquette of cell phone use is certainly an evolving one. When is it OK to talk on your phone and when is it not? When do you leave a message? When you're sitting with a group of friends is it OK to take a call, make a call, text?

行動電話禮節是一種越發重要的趨勢,何時應該打電話?何時應該留言?和朋友碰面時,何時應該接打電話或發送簡訊,何時不應該?

懷孕的 pregnant

pregnant 是常用的字詞,另外還可以用 She is expecting a baby 來表示女子有身孕。其他相關字如:人工受孕 artificial impregnation、男子不孕是 infertile man 或是 man of infertility。

新聞這樣說

The poll of 1,000 Americans found commuters are annoyed by people who don't offer their seat to people with disabilities, the elderly or pregnant women, and the messy eater who leaves crumbs behind, and the passenger who gets too comfortable and uses the spare seat for their luggage.

在一份一千位美國通勤者的問卷調查中,發現人們最無法忍受看到身障人士、老人或孕婦還不讓位的人、吃東西掉滿地的乘客,以及把行李放在身旁空位的旅客。

公開信 open letter

open letter 常見於報紙上,而報上的讀者專欄則是 opinion column,特別專欄是 special column,報紙社論則為 editorial。

新聞這樣說

The students later wrote down their opinions on the guideline changes on the back of an open letter to Minister of Education Wu Se-hwa, which they threw across the ministry's gates. The act was a plea to the minister to stop treating their appeals with indifference, they said.

學生接著在寫給教育部長吳思華的公開信的背後寫上他們的訴求,並丟向教育部大門,此舉主要是位了抗議教育部對於他們訴求的忽視。

大眾運輸工具 public transportation

大眾運輸交通亦可稱為 public transit 或 public transport,形式包括 city bus(市區巴士)、trams(輕軌列車)、rapid transit(捷運系統)等等。

新聞這樣說

Taiwan has listed a budget of over NT$5 billion (US$160 million) to improve public transportation networks and facilities this year after noticing that the percentage of public transportation use has grown only slowly in the past several years.

台灣今年編列了台幣五十億的預算來加強公共交通運輸設施,主因為過去幾年大眾交通工具使用率成長緩慢。

個人主義
individualism

individual 型名同型都是個人（的），individualism 與 individualistic 則是表示個人主義（的）。個人主義的反義是集體主義 collectivism 與 collectivistic，collective 表示集合的意思，如 collective farm（集合式農場）。

The Japanese education minister has denounced Western-influenced individualism in schools, saying allowing too much freedom was like eating too much butter, newspapers said yesterday.

日本報紙昨日報導，日本教育部長譴責學校裡實行受西方影響的個人主義，並表示給予學生太多自由，就像是吃太多奶油一樣不健康。

I'll Ride With You

2014 年雪梨咖啡廳人質事件造成南半球的恐慌，槍手 Man Haron Monis 在 Lindt Café 挾持 18 名人質，並強迫人質揮舞伊斯蘭黑旗，隨後更向警方要求 ISIL 旗幟，包括槍手在內其有 3 人罹難。這件挾持事件是否該被列入恐怖攻擊的意見分歧，然而，在雪梨社會卻因為此悲劇引發了一波伊斯蘭教徒擔憂報復行為的恐懼，因而不敢搭乘大眾運輸工具。一位電視主播在 tweeter 上發佈了一則發文，他說他在 facebook 上看到一個小故事：一位搭乘火車的雪梨人看見坐在身旁的伊斯蘭教女乘客，看見車廂人越來越多，便默默地低下頭，拿下她的頭巾，下車後，這位雪梨人立刻跑上前和伊斯蘭女乘客說：「請妳把頭巾戴上，我會陪著妳搭車」。這位教徒立刻哭了出來，並緊緊的抱著她長達一分鐘，隨後又默默地離開。這件事經由各種社群媒體傳播在雪梨發酵，在 12 小時內，tweeter 上便出現了超過 15 萬次的 #illridewithyou 串流字，成為最新雪梨社會運動，不同種族的居民紛紛放上自拍照，告訴擔憂的伊斯蘭乘客、路人，「若你需要人陪你坐車，我會陪著你」。I'll Ride With You 運動成為社群媒體正面力量的最好證明，也讓全球看見雪梨這城市是如何運用人性的光明，面對恐怖攻擊以及反伊斯蘭情節。

示範對話　(MP3 89)

全民讓座運動

Al: Hey, Jessica. You know, those are priority seats—they're 1)reserved for the elderly and 2)infirm.
嗨，潔西卡。妳知道嗎，那些位子是博愛座，要留給年老體弱的人坐的。

Jessica: I'm sick, too. Look at me. See how white my face is?
我身體也不好。你看到我的臉有多白嗎？

Al: That's your natural color, isn't it? Don't be silly.
那是妳天生的膚色，不是嗎？別傻了。

Jessica: Oh, all right. I guess I'll stand up.
喔，好吧。我想我還是站起來好了。

Al: That's very kind of you. I know it's common to not give up your seat in New York.
妳人真好。我知道在紐約不讓位是很正常的。

Jessica: I guess it's more of a 3)dog-eat-dog world where I come from.
我想我的故鄉是個比較冷酷的地方吧。

Al: But these days, Taiwanese kids are doing the same thing.
不過最近，台灣小孩也正在做同樣的事。

Jessica: Why is that, do you think?
你認為為何會這樣？

Al: I think people are just getting more individualistic.
我想大家都越來越個人主義了吧。

Jessica: Has there been a 4)backlash yet?
有引起反彈嗎？

Al: Yes. The 5)Ministry of Education sent a open letter to universities, asking students to be more polite.
有。教育部發給各大學一封公開信，請學生要更有禮貌。

Jessica: Is that kind of thing effective?
那種方法有效嗎？

Al: Of course not. Everyone laughed at the letter, and the minister even denied responsibility for it.
當然沒有。大家都在笑那封信，而且部長甚至拒絕為它背書。

Jessica: That's pretty funny. Well, what'll work then?
那真是蠻好笑的。那到底怎樣才行得通？

Al: I just got you out of the reserved seat, didn't i?
我不就讓妳從博愛座起來了嗎，是不是？

Jessica: True enough! I guess 6)guilt works, ha-ha.
的確是！看來讓人內疚還是很有用，哈哈。

Al: Of course. All right, this is my stop. See you later!
當然。好了，我要在這站下車。再見喔！

---

1. reserved (a.) 預訂的，指定的
2. infirm (a.) 體弱的
3. dog-eat-dog (a.) 自相殘殺的
4. backlash (n.) 反動，反彈
5. ministry (n.)（政府）部
6. guilt (n.) 內疚，罪惡感

好用短句　(MP3 90)

談讓座
你還可以說

· People wrote letters of complaint to the Ministry of Education.	有民眾寫信去教育部投訴。
· They complained that students on buses don't show any compassion for the elderly or pregnant women.	抱怨學生在公車上看到老人、孕婦都缺乏同情心。
· The nicer students pretend to be asleep and don't give their seats up.	有良心一點的學生，不讓位還會裝睡。
· The ruder ones don't even bother pretending, but still don't give up their seats.	臉皮厚一點的，連裝都不裝，根本不讓位。
· After receiving the complaints, the Ministry responded in a robotic manner.	教育部收到投訴後的反應非常公式化。
· Instead of addressing the problem in terms of education, they just published an open letter.	他們不去檢討從根本教育著手，只發了一封公開信了事。
· And everyone who read the letter just laughed.	看了那封信的人無不大笑。

Chapter Six

Entertainment & Sports

影視
運動談八卦

TV

大家都愛看娛樂新聞，不論是緋聞、醜聞、慾照、走光、暴走，只要加上明星的名字，銷售量立刻飆升，有的明星深知狗仔隊的存在就是魚幫水、水幫魚，時不時會被「不小心」拍到一些不該被拍到的東西，通告就可以多上好幾個；有些「則」認為自身才華是藝術的表現，因而不屑虛浮不實的名聲，狗仔就是他們最大敵人。不論如何，娛樂新聞的存在已經成為當代文化現象的一部份，學好娛樂關鍵字，才能說出最口語、最具時代感的超有梗英文。

Linsanity is back

林來瘋席捲全台

代言 endorse-ment

endorsement 為動詞 endorse 的名詞型式，endorse 有「（公開）贊同、支持、認可」的意思，也可指「（在支票背面）簽名、背書」的動作。名人透過廣告表達認同與喜愛特定產品或服務的代言行為，也可以用 endorse。

新聞這樣說

Taiwanese smartphone maker HTC Corp. (宏達電) said Tuesday that it has signed an endorsement agreement with local rock band Mayday (五月天) for the third consecutive year.

台灣智慧手機製造商宏達電於週二表示，已和本土樂團五月天簽下連續第三年的代言合約。

轉播權 broadcast rights

right 在此處做「權利」解釋，若以複數 rights 表示時，特指書籍、電影、電視節目、音樂之類的版權。the rights to 後面接物品，例如：the rights to the new book. （這本新書的版權）。

新聞這樣說

Copyright and related rights, particularly those relating to broadcasting organizations like broadcast rights, underpin the relationship between sport and television and other media.

著作權以及相關權益，特別是和轉播有關的轉播權，支撐著運動賽事與電視及其它媒體之間的關係。

血統 ancestry

ancestry 多以單數表示，意指「祖先」或「血統」。of…ancestry 表示「擁有……的血統」，例如：Her mother is of French ancestry. （她母親有法國血統）。

新聞這樣說

Whether in language, architecture or way of life, links among indigenous peoples of the Philippines and Taiwan are undeniable, with both sides tracing their ancestry to the Austronesian migrations across the Pacific Islands thousands of years ago.

無論是在語言、建築或生活方式方面，菲律賓原住民和台灣原住民之間的連結是無庸置疑的，兩者血統皆源自數千年前太平洋島嶼上的南島語系移民。

選秀 drafted /
非選秀 undrafted

draft 當名詞時指「（職業運動的）選拔制度」，當動詞時則是「選派」的意思。

新聞這樣說

Players are able to sign with teams as undrafted free agents, which can be a good thing because it allows them to pick their spot instead of being assigned somewhere without any input.

球員可以非選秀自由球員身分和球隊簽約，如此對他們是好事，能給予他們選球隊位置的空間而不會在毫無準備下被分發。

雙重國籍 dual nationality

另一個說法是 dual citizenship，若想清楚表明有哪些國籍時，可以在 dual 和 nationality 的中間加上國籍形容詞，例如：He has dual British and South African nationality.（他有英國和南非的雙重國籍）。

新聞這樣說

Both of Jeremy Lin's parents were born in Taiwan and hold dual nationality of the ROC and the U.S. Jeremy Lin was born in California and has U.S. citizenship, but he has been offered dual citizenship in the ROC as well by the Ministry of Foreign Affairs.

林書豪雙親皆為擁有台美雙重國籍的台灣人，林書豪則是出生於美國加州並擁有美國國籍，而台灣外交部也提供了台灣國籍給他。

表帥 representative

representative 意指「代表性的」或「典型的」，但也可做名詞用，意指「代表；代理人」，後接 of 與所代表的人事物或組織。例如：a representative of the U.N.（聯合國的代表）。

新聞這樣說

The UK has changed the name of its representative office in Taiwan from the British Trade and Cultural Office to the British Office to better reflect its services. "This is purely a change of title. It is not a change of functions," UK Representative to Taiwan Chris Wood said yesterday.

為了更能體現服務性質，英國在台辦事處將其名稱由「英國在台經貿文化辦事處」改為「英國在台辦事處」，英國在台代表表示這只是一個名稱的更動，並不影響其職責。

公眾形象 public image

public image 只能用單數表示，前面可搭配如創造（create）、加強（enhance）或改善（improve）等動詞使用。

新聞這樣說

The Ministry of National Defense has produced three short films to give the public a closer look at everyday life in the military and enhance the military's public image, which has been tarnished by recent scandals.

國防部日前因醜聞而形象敗壞的國軍，製作了三段短片來向大眾解釋國軍的軍旅生活，以提升公眾形象。

sport 後面接名詞時，需用複數表示，例如：a sports team。sensation 為可數名詞，但做「狂熱」或「轟動」解釋時，常搭配動詞為 cause 或 create（cause/create a sensation），意即「造成／引起狂熱或轟動」。

運動狂熱
sports sensation

新聞這樣說

It's hoped that having a sports sensation like Lin will give Taiwan some of the international attention it so often craves. "At Jeremy's games, Taiwanese fans hold up Taiwan's national flag," says Mr Lee. "It's very rare for Taiwan to be able to display its international flag at such high-profile events."

希望林書豪帶起的運動狂熱，能為台灣帶來期盼已久的國際關注，得已在如此備受矚目國際賽事上，看見台灣國旗飄揚是件不容易的事。

林書豪語錄

林書豪激勵了許多年輕人，特別是他所代表的意涵，一位台灣籍的美國球員在 NBA 大放異彩，實屬難得。他堅定的家庭觀念以及宗教信仰也讓他言談間的一字一句，都俱有值得學習參考的意義，以下節錄幾句林書豪名言，讓大家學習英文也能學習 Jeremy 激勵人心的態度：

· Suffering produces character and character produces hope and hope does not disappoint us.

· I'm not playing to prove anything to anybody.

· It's not that much about who starts; I think it's more about who finishes and how you play with the time you're given

· My best career decision was probably not giving up when I wanted to. God as well as my family and friends were there for me during my toughest times.

示範對話　(MP3 92)

豪小子回來了

Victor: Whoa! It looks like Linsanity is back!
哇！看來林來瘋又要再度燃起了！

Sally: Linsanity?
林來瘋？

Victor: You know—Jeremy Lin, the basketball player.
你知道啊，就是那位籃球員林書豪啊。

Sally: I seem to remember something about that a few years back.
What's so special about him?
噢，我好像記得幾年前有這麼一回事。他有什麼特別的嗎？

Victor: Well, he was the first Taiwanese player in the NBA.
他是第一位 NBA 台籍球員。

Sally: Wasn't he born and raised in the U.S.?
他不是在美國出生長大的嗎？

Victor: Yeah, but he has dual nationality. Both of his parents immigrated from Taiwan.
是啊，但他有雙重國籍。他的父母都是從台灣移民過去的。

Sally: Interesting. Didn't he play for the Knicks?
真有趣。他是尼克隊的吧？

Victor: Yeah. He was undrafted out of Harvard, and ending up signing with the Golden State Warriors. But he didn't play much in his rookie season, and joined the Knicks a year later.
是啊，他在哈佛選秀時沒被選中，後來跟金州勇士隊簽約。但他菜鳥階段並沒有什麼上場機會，一年後就轉到尼克隊了。

Sally: That's when Linsanity started?
結果就變林來瘋了嗎？

Victor: Yep. He led the Knicks on a seven-game winning streak in 2012 and became an instant sensation.
對啊，他在 2012 年帶領尼克隊連贏 7 場，掀起一陣旋風。

Sally: I don't remember hearing about him since then though.
但之後好像就沒聽過他的消息了。

Victor: Well, he played for the Houston Rockets for two seasons, and got traded to the Lakers last year—but he's mostly been a back-up player.
這個嘛，他為休士頓火箭隊打了兩個賽季，結果去年又被交易到湖人隊，但他大部分是擔任遞補球員角色。

Sally: So why do you think Linsanity is back?
那你怎麼會覺得又要再度掀起林來瘋？

Victor: I just read that he's on Forbes list of top 100 highest paid athletes this year. And he's coming to Taiwan again this summer. It's always Linsanity when he visits Taiwan!
我讀到他是今年富比士百大年收最高運動員之一，而且他今年夏天又會來台灣。每次他來絕對是一陣林來瘋啊！

好用短句 (MP3 93)

談林書豪
你還可以說

- Born in California to Taiwanese immigrants, Jeremy learned basketball from his father at the YMCA as a kid.

林書豪生於加州，雙親為台灣人，他從小就和爸爸在基督教青年會學籃球。

- Jeremy played on his high school basketball team, and as captain in his senior year led the team to win the state title.

林書豪高中最後一年時擔任籃球校隊隊長，並帶領球隊贏得州冠軍。

- While playing basketball at Harvard, Jeremy became the first player in the history of the Ivy League to record at least 1,450 points, 450 rebounds, 400 assists and 200 steals.

當他在哈佛大學校隊打球時，他成為長春藤名校第一位擁有1450分、450籃板球、400次助攻以及200抄截的紀錄保持人。

- Linsanity began when Jeremy led the Knicks on a seven-game winning streak in February 2012.

林書豪旋風開始於 2012 年，林書豪帶領尼克隊取得七連勝紀錄。

- After playing two seasons for the Houston Rockets and one season for the L.A. Lakers, Jeremy signed a two-year contract with the Charlotte Hornets in July 2015.

在和休士頓火箭隊合作兩季以及湖人隊一賽季後，2015 年 7 月，林書豪和夏洛特黃蜂隊簽下兩年合約。

Political Talk Shows
電視名嘴亂說話

political slant
政治傾向

slant 本意是「傾斜」，美式口語上則特指「偏頗的報導」或「偏見」。「偏見」其他常見字有 bias 和 prejudice。

新聞這樣說

Underscoring cable news' more overtly political slant, 26% of respondents also said they didn't trust Fox News "at all" as a news source, the highest among the national TV news outlets mentioned in the survey. MSNBC came in second at 24%.

在一項新聞媒體的民調中，26% 的受訪者強調，有線電視新聞的政治傾向更是明顯。表示「一點都不」相信福斯新聞網報導的比例是全國電視新聞媒體中最高的，其次是MSNBC。

政治打壓 political pressure

政治打壓是國家的 politics「政治」和 policy「政策」不公所致，political 即是這兩個字的形容詞。pressure 是「壓力、壓迫」；而「抗壓」就可以說「某人 works well under high pressure」。

新聞這樣說

Under Chinese control since 1997, Hong Kong faces direct political pressure from Beijing aimed at limiting democratic rights, press freedom and freedom of expression through a gradual process of "mainlandization."

從 1997 年香港回歸中國開始，香港得直接面對北京當局施予的政治打壓；打壓民主權利、媒體自由、言論自由，一切都是一場逐漸「內地化」政策的過程。

隱私權 privacy

它的形容詞是 private「私密的」，所以「私事、個人隱私」是 private matters，也可說 personal matters。

The health of Taiwan's KMT presidential candidate Hung Hsiu-chu raised public concern Tuesday in the wake of reports that she has been treated for stage 1 breast cancer. Yu Tzu-hsiang, spokesman for Hung's campaign office, declined to comment on the reports, saying that personal health is a matter of privacy.

國民黨總統參選人洪秀柱的健康問題引起廣泛注意，特別是她曾接受第一期乳癌治療的新聞曝光後，洪秀柱競選辦發言人游梓翔則表示不會做出任何評論，個人醫療紀錄是其隱私權。

客觀的 objective

形容詞是「如實的、客觀的」的意思，也可當名詞指所訂定的「目標」，亦是詞性中「受詞」的意思。「客觀性」英文則是 objectivity。

新聞這樣說

Former Taipei deputy mayor King Pu-tsung will take up the position of chief executive officer of Next Media's new TV station from Monday and promised objective reporting on the government despite being a close aide to President Ma Ying-jeou.

週一前台北副市長金溥聰表示將接下壹傳媒電視台執行行長一職，並保證，即使身為馬總統的心腹，仍會以公正客觀角度報導政府相關新聞。

吐槽 rant

英文並沒有完全相對應的概念，意思最接近的字是 rant，指「嚷嚷，針對某議題大做文章」。

新聞這樣說

Last month Singapore teenager Amos Yee was found guilty scene imagery and "wounding religious feelings," after posting a YouTube rant in which he criticized the recently deceased Lee Kuan Yew, the nation's widely revered first prime minister. Today Yee was scheduled to receive his sentence.

上個月一名新加坡青年 Amos Yee 在 YouTube上發布了一支影片而被定罪，影片內容是吐槽並批評剛逝世不久且廣受愛戴的前新加坡總理李光耀。Amos Yee 將於今天收到判決書。

收視率 rating

rating 除了收視率、收聽率還有很多意思，例如軍隊的階級、信用度、測驗等級分數等等。

新聞這樣說

Talk show host Lee Tao (李濤) has taken temporary leave as host of the 2100 Talk Show (2100 全民開講), TVBS said on Monday. Lee's decision has sparked speculation that he has left because of the show's dismal ratings.

TVBS 週一表示，李濤將短暫離開 2100 全民開講的主持崗位，而他的離開也讓很多人揣測是因為日漸下滑的收視率。

黃金時段 prime-time

prime 是形容詞，這裡意思是「最好的」，與 best 同義。prime-time 特指晚間 7 點到 10 點電視節目（TV programs）收視率最高的黃金時段。

新聞這樣說

CNN says the prime-time talk show Piers Morgan Live is coming to an end. Morgan succeeded Larry King in the 9 p.m. time slot three years ago, but his show has had lackluster ratings. CNN said Sunday that the show's final airdate has yet to be determined.

CNN 表示，黃金時段的脫口秀 Piers Morgan Live 即將結束，他在三年前取代賴瑞金成為九點時段主持人，然而收視率並不高。CNN 週日表示節目最後一集的播出時段仍未確定。

政論節目
political talk show

talk show 是請名人、名嘴一起討論某議題的「談話性節目」，前面加上 political「政治的，政黨的」，便是政論節目了。另外 tabloid talk show（八卦節目）或 late-night talk show（夜間綜藝節目）也是常見的談話性節目種類。

新聞這樣說

Some say the major source of chaos in Taiwan isn't blue or green in nature, but comes instead from the political talk shows that rise up to bite us on the nose every time we turn on the TV. The views are extreme; the discussion heated. And as such, it is really a bit difficult to assert that Taiwan's current political chaos has nothing to do with those talk shows.

有人說台灣最大的亂源不是藍色，也不是綠色，而是每天打開電視就看得到的政論節目。這些節目立場偏激，言論辛辣，要說台灣現在政治亂象不干他們的事，還真是有點說不過去。

美國政治名嘴

美國電視節目最受歡迎的類型除了影集、實境節目，還有脫口秀。脫口秀對於美式文化影響非常重要。政論節目在美國也是以脫口秀方式呈現，Jon Stewart 的 The Daily Show 絕對是其中最具影響力節目之一。以新聞時事、政治人物、政府政策及媒體現象為嘲諷內容，搭配藝人、樂手或是政治人物訪談，Stewart 的機智幽默，以及節目中為政治時事和人物下的註解，已成為當代美國人談論到相關話題常常會引述的來源。Stewart 接手 The Daily Show 的 16 年期間，連續 10 年靠著此節目獲得日間艾美獎最佳喜劇劇集，更在 2005 年獲得葛萊美最佳喜劇專輯，2015 年將會是 Stewart 主持 The Daily Show 的最後一年，也讓人更期待光榮卸下主持棒的他，會再以什麼方式為美國人民帶來歡笑。

示範對話　(MP3 95)

政論節目每天吵

Cary shows up at Teri's house for a date; her roommate answers the door
凱瑞來泰莉家找她約會；她的室友來應門

Bette: I'm sorry, Teri had to go buy something at the store. She'll be right back.
抱歉，泰莉得去店裡買點東西。她馬上回來。

Cary: Shall I wait outside?
我該在外面等嗎？

Bette: You can come in and watch TV if you like.
如果你想要，可以進來看電視。

Cary: Do you have cable? I don't really ¹⁾care for Taiwanese ²⁾soap operas.
你們有裝有線電視嗎？我不是很想看台語連續劇。

Bette: Come in and let's see what's on. *[turns on the TV]*
進來，我們來看看電視在播什麼。（打開電視）

Cary: How can there be a political talk show on at 8 p.m.?
晚上八點怎麼會有政論節目？

Bette: You don't have political shows during prime time in the States?

你們美國在黃金時段不會有政論節目嗎？

Cary: Of course not. ³⁾Networks want shows like Friends or Seinfeld. It's all about the ratings.
當然沒有。電視聯播網想播的是像《六人行》或《歡樂單身派對》的節目。全都是因為收視率。

Bette: But you do have political shows, don't you?
但你們有政論節目，不是嗎？

Cary: Yeah. Nightline is on every night at 11:00, and there are some popular weekly news magazine shows like 60 Minutes and 20/20.
有啊。每晚十一點有《夜線新聞》，也有一些受歡迎的新聞週刊節目，像是《六十分鐘》和《二十/二十》。

Bette: Do they ⁴⁾feature grandstanding hosts like Wang Ben-hu or Sisy Chen?
那些電視聯播網會主打像汪笨湖或陳文茜這種煽動人心的主持人嗎？

Cary: No, we don't really have any ⁵⁾equivalents. There are no talk show hosts who are also ⁶⁾congressmen.
不會，我們其實沒有類似那樣的主持人。沒有脫口秀主持人身兼國會議員的。

Bette: But doesn't Jerry Springer ⁷⁾dabble in politics?
但是傑瑞史賓格不也涉足政治？

Cary: Ha-ha. I guess so, but he's no Sisy Chen.
哈哈，或許吧，但他跟陳文茜比差得遠。

Bette: I think politics sometimes ⁸⁾trump commercial considerations in Taiwan.
我覺得在台灣，政治有時會凌駕商業考量。

Cary: It's not surprising, is it? Politics seems like a national religion here.
這沒什麼好驚訝的，不是嗎？政治在這邊有點像全國性的宗教。

Bette: I guess that means TV is your national religion.
我猜這表示電視是你們的全國性宗教了。

---

1. care for (phr.) 喜歡或想要某事物   2. soap opera 肥皂劇
3. network (n.)（電視）聯播網   4. feature (v.) 以…作為宣傳號召
5. equivalent (n.) 等同物   6. congressman (n.) 國會議員
7. dabble (v.) 涉獵，涉足   8. trump (v.) 勝過

好用短句　(MP3 96)

談政論節目
你還可以說

- Political talk shows on TV started out as call-in shows.

  政論節目最早是以 call-in 的方式在電視上出現。

- Later, they started with a host inviting reporters, political figures and academics onto the show.

  後來,漸漸演變成由主持人邀請記者、政客或學者上節目。

- But regardless whether shows have a call-in or interview format, the political slant of each talk show is usually pretty obvious.

  但不論是 call-in 還是對談,政論節目的政治傾向都非常明顯。

- Political talk show hosts always say how fair and objective they are.

  政論節目的主持人整天都把公平、客觀掛在嘴邊。

- Yet what the shows actually spend their time on are the political rants that audiences love to hear.

  但其實節目中講的都只是政治狂熱觀眾想聽的話。

- Although the call-in format is no longer a main one used on political talk shows, it has now become something used on television news.

  call-in 雖然不再是政論節目的主流,卻變成電視新聞會使用的節目形式。

When News Isn't News
狗仔趕不走

Hit! 話題單字 (MP3 97)

anchor
主播

anchor 原意是固定船身的錨，也指賴以支撐的人、靠山。男主播是 anchorman，女主播則是 anchorwoman。

新聞這樣說

Controversy raged following a recent spat between the *Liberty Times* and former TVBS news anchor Lee Yen-chiou , with Lee accusing the newspaper of using sexually offensive content to launch personal attacks against her.

前 TVBS 主播李艷秋控訴自由時報使用充滿性別歧視的字眼對她進行人身攻擊，雙方近期所引發之口角引起相當的爭議。

狗仔隊
paparazzi

單數「狗仔」叫做 paparazzo，常簡寫為 pap。此字源自於義大利語，是指專門偷拍名人私生活的攝影記者。另一個相似字為 shutterbug，原本是指以拍照為嗜好的攝影愛好者，但在小報新聞中，遂成為 paparazzi 的另一種說法。

新聞這樣說

Luc Besson's production company has denied reports that the film-maker and star Scarlett Johansson are to end a film shoot in Taiwan early after becoming the target of aggressive local paparazzi, according to Variety.

根據綜藝報報導，盧貝松的製片公司否認盧貝松和女影星史嘉雷喬韓森是因為台灣狗仔的窮追猛打而被迫提早結束在台灣的拍攝。

緋聞，花邊
gossip

此字不一定得用在名人身上，只要是談論他人私事的行為都稱為 gossip。形容八卦相當「有料」，則可說 juicy gossip。

新聞這樣說

Hearing juicy gossip about famous people apparently fires up the brain's pleasure center in the same way as eating the finest food or even winning the lottery. And it's not good news that gives us the biggest buzz. Tales about stars' troubles are what we crave.

據說聽到名人八卦可以開啟腦內愉悅分子，好比吃到美食或是贏得樂透的感覺，而且讓我們欲罷不能的不是名人的正面新聞，而是他們面臨的困境。

名人 celebrity

此字多指娛樂圈（show biz）及政商名流，帶有名利共享的意味。另一個類似的字是 public figure「公眾人物」，為比較中性的說法。

新聞這樣說

The social media sensation of dumping ice water on celebrities and posting a video online to raise awareness of a paralyzing disease has spread to Taiwan, with political figures and celebrities taking on the task and challenging more to participate.

日前國外名人將自己淋冰水的影片上傳到社群網站以喚起大眾對漸凍人的重視，這股熱潮也傳到了台灣，一堆政治人物以及藝人紛紛接受挑戰和挑戰別人。

小報 tabloid

小報最愛談八卦（gossip/dirty laundry），將名人私生活公諸於世。沒人喜歡被別人在背後議論自己的私事，更何況是一群不認識的民眾，希望新聞工作者也要有同理心，設身處地（put oneself in someone's shoes）為受訪者著想一下。

新聞這樣說

Hung, who filed three separate lawsuits against political pundit Clara Chou, author Windson and the tabloid Next Magazine, also stated that while it was fine to vet an election candidate, it was unjust to smear another's reputation.

洪秀柱對於名嘴周玉蔻提出三項告訴，讓小報壹週刊也表示，要公開審視總統候選人是可以的，但像周玉蔻這種毀謗以及刻意抹黑他人名譽是不被接受的。

誹謗 slander

指製造謠言（spread rumor）的行為、詆毀他人名譽的言論（defamatory statement）。

新聞這樣說

This unlikely couple made headlines in 2013, when news of their relationship broke. When The New Paper spoke to Taiwanese lyricist Li Kuncheng back then, he was adamant about protecting his girlfriend from slander. His girlfriend, Lin Jing-en, then a high school student, is 40 years his junior.

五十七歲的李坤成以及十七歲的林靖恩在 2013 年登上新聞頭條。相差四十歲的戀情讓林坤城堅定要保護還在讀高中的女友不被公開誹謗。

超級名模 supermodel

時尚伸展台（runway）上的超級名模經常都以超瘦（super-skinny）的紙片人模樣出現，但在國外一般認為，這樣看起來病懨懨，不是健康良好的形象。

新聞這樣說

On the evening of July 20 at the Formosa Regent, a 21-year-old office worker from the southern city of Pingtung won the championship in the first Ford Supermodel of the World—Taiwan, putting her in the media spotlight.

7 月 20 號晚上在晶華酒店舉行的第一屆福特世界超模選拔賽上，來自屏東的 21 歲上班族女生贏得冠軍，成了媒體鎂光燈的焦點。

名詞 sensation 指造成轟動的人、事、物。sensational 則有故意製造轟動效果的意味在，這種行為就可稱為 sensationalism「譁眾取寵」。

煽情的
sensa-
tional

新聞這樣說

With the introduction of tabloid-type publications in recent years, major Chinese-language papers here have reorganized to follow a tabloid business model, Professor Su said. Such reorganizations included establishing paparazzi teams to uncover and follow scandals, and increasingly sensational coverage of crime and entertainment news.

蘇教授說，隨著小報形式刊物大舉進攻台灣，台灣主要報章雜誌也跟進這種增設狗仔部門、追查醜聞以及煽情報導犯罪或娛樂新聞的產業模式。

黛妃的殞落

1997 年 8 月 31 號，全世界的目光都鎖定在史上最受愛戴王妃——戴安娜王妃逝世的新聞，一場在巴黎隧道躲避狗仔追逐的飛車戲碼，造成了震驚世人的意外。9 月 6 號，全球電視轉播戴妃的葬禮吸引了超過二十億人口收視，超過一百萬人湧入倫敦街道目送戴妃最後一程，創下歷史紀錄。戴妃的一生充滿爭議，不論是和英國皇室衝突、和查爾斯王子痛苦的婚姻或是精彩婚外情，戴妃的一舉一動都是狗仔追族的對象，她是世上被拍過最多照片的女人，她的美麗、智慧、愛心、憐憫以及魅力征服了全世界，成為全球最受歡迎的皇室成員。然而，媒體的嗜血追逐導致了無法逆轉的悲劇，也讓全球名人齊聲撻伐狗仔。然而，公眾人物的隱私權以及狗仔的新聞媒體自由之間的平衡直到今日，還是一條模糊界限。

示範對話　(MP3 98)

新聞都在報這些?!

Jack: Can you tell me who that woman on TV is?
你可以告訴我電視上那個女人是誰嗎?

Hanna: That's Lin Chi-ling, Taiwan's top supermodel.
那是林志玲,她是台灣的首席超級名模。

Jack: If she's just a model, why is she on TV all the time?
如果她只是個模特兒,為什麼她會一直上電視呢?

Hanna: I think you've just answered your own question.
我想你已經回答了自己的問題。

Jack: But does she have any 1)news value at all? Is she as 2)entertaining as Hsu Chun-mei?
但是她有什麼新聞價值嗎?她跟許純美一樣有娛樂性嗎?

Hanna: No and no. But the media have decided to 3)manufacture a 4)rivalry between her and Stephanie Hsiao.
是都沒有。但媒體已經決議在她跟蕭薔間製造競爭。

Jack: Oh, yet another supermodel, I'm sure?
喔,又是另一個超級名模,對不對?

Hanna: Not exactly, but definitely another pretty face. The media loves them, and they love the media [5]back.
不盡然，但絕對是另一個美女。媒體喜歡她們，而且她們也喜歡媒體。

Jack: [6]I rub your back and you rub mine, right?
魚幫水，水幫魚，是吧？

Hanna: Exactly. Everyone wins, except for those of us who want to watch real news.
沒錯。大家都是贏家，除了那些想看真正新聞的我們。

Jack: Real news in Taiwan? Is it possible?
在台灣有真正的新聞？可能嗎？

Hanna: Nah. Even the TV anchors are [7]fodder for the tabloids.
不可能。甚至連電視主播也成了八卦報刊的素材。

Jack: You talking about Patty Ho?
妳是在說侯佩岑嗎？

Hanna: Of course. But even she [8]transcended the tabloids.
當然了。但是她甚至凌駕了八卦報刊之上。

Jack: Yeah! I heard that her kiss with Sean Lien was on the *China Times* front page!
是呀！我聽說她跟連勝文接吻上了《中國時報》頭版！

Hanna: Wow, you know a lot about Taiwan.
哇，你對台灣知道真多。

Jack: [9]Apparently not enough, if I had to ask you Lin Chi-ling's name.
似乎還不夠，若我還得問妳林志玲的名字。

Hanna: Don't worry. There'll be another supermodel to replace her in a few years.
別擔心。過幾年又會有另一個超級名模取代她。

---

1. news value 新聞價值
2. entertaining (a.) 使人得到娛樂的，有趣的
3. manufacture (v.) 製造
4. rivalry (n.) 競爭，對抗
5. back (adv.) 往回，回報以
6. I rub your back and you rub mine. 魚幫水，水幫魚
7. fodder (n.) （創作的）素材
8. transcend (v.) 優於，凌駕
9. apparently (adv.) 似乎

好用短句　(MP3 99)

談狗仔
你還可以說

· Taiwan's media have been reporting on Patty Ho and Lin Chi-ling almost daily.

台灣媒體最近幾乎天天都在報導侯佩岑和林志玲的新聞。

· In discussions of Taiwan's top beauty, Lin Chi-ling is often compared with Stephanie Hsiao.

林志玲也常被拿來跟蕭薔比，看誰是台灣第一大美女。

· Many people think Patty Ho is Taiwan's most beautiful news anchor.

許多人認為侯佩岑是台灣最美麗的女主播。

· Patty Ho was photographed dating Sean Lien, Lien Chan's son.

侯佩岑被拍到跟連戰的兒子連勝文交往。

Queen Oprah
權力女王歐普拉

巨擘
mogul

（在某產業中）有權有勢又有錢的「大人物、大亨」稱做 mogul，特別是指新聞媒體或影視產業。此外，mogul 還可以指雪地中一整片相鄰的小丘。

新聞這樣說

Hong Kong media mogul Jimmy Lai, a pioneer of animated news, plans to sell his Taiwanese business after allegedly suffering huge losses on the operation's TV branch, a report said yesterday.

根據報導指出，香港媒體巨擘以及動畫新聞先鋒黎智英因為其電視台部門大虧損，而決定賣出台灣經營權。

心靈
spirituality

spirituality 可做「精神（性）、靈性、心靈」等解釋，為不可數名詞。其形容詞為 spiritual，意指「精神上的、心靈的」或是「宗教的」。

新聞這樣說

In a 2013 segment of her program Super Soul Sunday, the high priestess of pop spirituality, Oprah Winfrey, told swimmer and nonbeliever Diana Nyad that if she was awed by the power of nature she was "not an atheist."

在她 2013 年節目《週日超靈》中，大眾心靈女權威歐普拉告訴身為游泳選手且及不信上帝的 Diana Nyad，只要她對大自然的力量感到驚奇，那她就不是一位無神論者。

非裔美國人
African-American

African-American 為可數名詞，做「非裔美國人」解釋。當形容詞時，則有「非裔美國人的」之意。值得注意的是，Native American 是指「美洲原住民」。

新聞這樣說

Dylann Roof, who police say opened fire and killed nine people during a prayer meeting at a historic African American church here, was arrested Thursday, more than 13 hours after the chilling attack.

狄倫魯夫在一所極具歷史意義的非裔美國人教堂中，槍殺了九名正在做禱告的民眾，他在週四，也就是事發十三小時之後遭到逮捕。

慈善家
philanthropist

philanthropist 為「慈善家」，為可數名詞。不可數名詞 philanthropy（慈善行為）以及形容詞 philanthropic（慈善的）為同一組字彙，可以一併學起來。

新聞這樣說

Meet one of the world's most unlikely and humble philanthropists. Over the past two decades, Ms. Chen has donated over 10 million Taiwanese dollars to the building of a school library and a hospital wing. She has also donated to a local Buddhist organization and orphanages.

陳樹菊絕對是最不可思議且最謙虛的慈善家，過去二十年間，陳女士捐款給學校圖書館以及醫院超過一千萬台幣，她還捐款給當地的佛教慈善團體以及孤兒院。

具影響力
influential

influential 意指「有影響力的」，與表示「影響、影響力」的 influence（名詞與動詞同型）密切相關。

新聞這樣說

Director Hou Hsiao Hsien, in a 1988 New York Film Festival World Critics Poll, was voted one of three directors who would most likely shape cinema in the coming decades. He has since become one of the most respected, influential directors working in cinema today.

在 1988 年紐約電影節的一項影評調查中，侯孝賢導演被選為三位最有可能影響日後電影文化的導演之一，隨後的幾年，侯導成為全球最具影響力以及最受尊敬的導演之一。

勵志 self-help

字首 self- 有「靠自身的」之意，加上 help（幫助），有「自助、自立」的意思，例如：a self-help guide/book（自助指南／手冊）。此外，self-help 也可指「（民間的）互助會」，例如 a self-help group for drug abusers（為吸毒者而設的互助會）

新聞這樣說

A stream of self-help gurus have spent time on Oprah's stage over the past decade and a half, all with the same message. You have choices in life. External conditions don't determine your life. You do. It's all inside you, in your head, in your wishes and desires.

一群自我成長大師在過去十年間，一起和歐普拉站在舞台上，告訴大眾掌握自己的人生，外在條件絕不局限自己的發展，而是你的所作所為、你的內心世界，包括你的想法、願望和渴望。

億萬富翁
billionaire

billion 為「十億」，擁有至少十億資產的人稱為 billionaire，意即「億萬富翁」。相似的用法還有「百萬」(million)，millionaire 意指「百萬富翁」。

(1 billion=1,000million= 1,000,000,000)

新聞這樣說

She is the publisher of the Oprah Magazine, owner of Oprah Radio, launched her own network called OWN: Oprah Winfrey Network and is also a producer. According to Forbes, Winfrey is worth $2.9bn, making her America's only African-American billionaire and the second richest black woman in the world.

她是歐普拉雜誌發行人、歐普拉電台經營者、OWN 歐普拉電視台老闆，也是製作人。根據富比士報導，歐普拉身價高達美金二十九億，使她成為全美唯一一位億萬非裔富翁，也是全球第二富有的黑人女性。

慈善團體
charity

charity 可指個別的慈善團體（可數名詞），也可當作慈善團體的整體（不可數名詞），give / donate money to charity 是捐錢給慈善團體，do something for charity 則是做某些事以幫助慈善團體募款。

新聞這樣說

According to GuideStar.org and federal tax filings, Winfrey runs three different charities: The Oprah Winfrey Foundation, Oprah Winfrey's Angel Network and The Oprah Winfrey Operating Foundation. The Angel Network, of course, is heavily promoted on Winfrey's show for fans to help raise money for worthy causes.

資料指出，歐普拉共經營三個慈善團體，分別是「歐普拉基金會」、「歐普拉天使網」以及「歐普拉執行基金會」。其中天使網在她的節目裡時常鼓勵觀眾小額捐款，幫助他人。

美國脫口秀

說到美國電視節目，除了台灣人熟悉的美劇之外，脫口秀更是美國電視帝國崛起的主因之一。Jay Leno、Steven Colbert、Larry King、Oprah Winfrey、Ellen Degeneres、Jimmy Kimmel、Jimmy Fallon 等知名脫口秀主持人紛紛成為當代美國文化重要的一環，這些脫口秀主持人不但肩負娛樂大眾的責任，更俱有相當的社會引響力。歐普拉「讀書會」所推薦的書，幾乎第二天就會衝上全國排行榜冠軍，在 2006 年到 2008 年，歐普拉對於歐巴馬總統的公開支持，根據統計，對於 2008 年歐巴馬民主黨初選至少影響了超過一百萬以上的票數。

示範對話　(MP3 101)

女王歐普拉

Jane: That looks like a nice ¹⁾scooter. Where'd you buy it?
這台機車看起來不錯。你在哪裡買的？

Sam: I won it on a TV show! The Taiwanese Oprah, you know?
我在一個電視節目裡贏來的！台灣的歐普拉秀呢，妳知道吧？

Jane: Ha-ha, very funny. You mean Oprah Winfrey, right?
哈哈，真有趣。你在說歐普拉溫芙蕾，對吧？

Sam: Who else? You know she ²⁾gave away like 300 cars on her show a few months ago?
還會有誰？妳知道幾個月前她在節目中送出差不多三百輛車吧？

Jane: I heard about that. I read that Pontiac spent seven million U.S. dollars on that.
我聽說了。我看到報紙寫說龐帝克為這個花了七百萬美元。

Sam: Pretty crazy, huh? I guess it was good ³⁾publicity for everyone ⁴⁾involved.
很瘋狂，對吧？我想那對大眾來說是個很好的行銷手法。

Jane: So you won your scooter on the Oprah show, too?
所以你也是在歐普拉秀上贏到這部機車？

Sam: No, I was just kidding. I bought this scooter 5)fair and square.
不是，我只是開玩笑。這機車是我自己花錢買的。

Jane: Well, could you still tell me why Oprah is so popular?
嗯，你可以多談談為什麼歐普拉這麼受歡迎嗎？

Sam: Probably because she has an amazing talent for 6)connecting with people on TV.
也許是因為她在電視上和人相處的驚人天份吧。

Jane: Sounds a bit different than Sisy Chen.
聽起來跟陳文茜有點不一樣。

Sam: Very. There's no one quite like her in Taiwan. She doesn't do politics. She talks about personal stuff with her guests.
非常不一樣。台灣沒有人跟她一樣。她不做政治議題。她都和來賓談論個人私事。

Jane: That sounds 7)refreshing. And she gives away lots of stuff, too, right.
那聽起來讓人耳目一新。而且她還送很多東西，對吧？

Sam: Yeah, sometimes. But she also has all these other businesses, too.
對，有時候。不過她還有很多其他的事業。

Jane: Like what? Does she own Pontiac?
比如說？她擁有龐帝克汽車公司？

Sam: No, but she has a magazine, a book club, a movie production company, charities, etc. She's the first African-American billionaire.
不是，不過她擁有一家雜誌出版社、一個讀書俱樂部、電影製片公司，慈善團體等等。她是美國第一位非裔的億萬富翁。

Jane: That's amazing. No wonder Pontiac would want to use her show.
真是令人訝異。難怪汽車大廠龐蒂克想要利用她的節目宣傳。

1. scooter (n.) 輕型機車
2. give away (phr.) 贈送
3. publicity (n.) 宣傳，媒體曝光
4. involve (v.) 牽涉，連累
5. fair and square （口）光明正大的
6. connect (with) (v.) 溝通，相處
7. refreshing (a.) 令人耳目一新的

好用短句 (MP3 102)

談歐普拉
你還可以說

- Talk shows in Taiwan are all mostly about politics.

  台灣的脫口秀節目都是以政治為主。

- Oprah's show is all about life issues, which is quite different than Taiwanese shows.

  歐普拉的節目都是關於生活議題，跟台灣非常不一樣。

- The Oprah Winfrey Show is America's top-rated talk show.

  《歐普拉脫口秀》是美國電視收視率最高的脫口秀。

- Oprah's influence extends from entertainment to politics.

  歐普拉從演藝到政治方面都有相當的影響力。

- Oprah helped get a child protection bill passed.

  歐普拉致力通過保護兒童的法案。

- President Clinton signed the "Oprah Bill" in 1994, establishing a new legal basis for protecting children from sexual assault.

  柯林頓總統在一九九四年簽署了《歐普拉法案》，此法案成為保護兒童免於性虐的法源基礎。

- You must be eighteen years or older to attend a taping of The Oprah Winfrey Show.

  必須是十八歲以上才可以參加《歐普拉脫口秀》的錄影。

Hustling the Box Office

華人巨星周星馳

Hit! 話題單字 (MP3 103)

box office 票房

box office 最先是指戲院的售票窗口，現在則是指一部電影的銷售狀況而言。Box office hit 票房大賣的電影；box office flop 則是指票房極差的電影。

新聞這樣說

The sci-fi thriller Lucy, starring American actress Scarlett Johansson, has taken the Taiwan box office by storm, raking in NT$185 million (US$6.17 million) within the first five days of its local release.

由史嘉蕾喬韓森主演的科幻驚悚片《露西》席捲全台票房，在全台上映五天內票房高達台幣 1.8 億元。

爆笑的 hilarious

hilarious 為「引人捧腹大笑的；滑稽的；極有趣的」之意，可與 story（故事）joke（笑話）等名詞搭配使用，find something hilarious（覺得某件事物非常好笑）。

新聞這樣說

Directed by and starring one of Hong Kong's biggest stars, Stephen Chow, Shaolin Soccer is a hectic, funny and frantic tale of redemption, romance and the creative application of martial arts skills to soccer.

由香港超級巨星周星馳自導、自演的少林功夫，是一部歡樂搞笑的鉅片，內容與贖罪、浪漫愛情、功夫和足球相關。

三部曲 trilogy

trilogy 是指（小說、音樂、電影等的）三部曲，字首 tri-有「三」的意思，類似的單字還有 trilingual（三種語言的）、triangle（三角形）。

新聞這樣說

The retrospectively titled "Father Knows Best" trilogy marked the end of a period of creative frustration for Ang Lee, who had graduated from NYU Film School in 1985 but then for years experienced difficulties setting up his first feature.

李安的「父親三部曲」為他創作瓶頸畫下句點。他 1985 年畢業於紐約大學電影學院時，曾因為無法創作出第一部長片而相當掙扎。

場面 set piece

set piece 是指經過精心策畫的演出或行動，因此也可指（電影、文學、音樂等作品中）效果強烈的片段或場面、（戰爭中）嚴密策畫的行動、（運動賽事中）精心設定的攻防戰術。

新聞這樣說

The trailer opens with a spectacular looking set piece of Ethan Hunt diving into a 70,000 gallons of pressurized water without any breathing apparatus. The spy has two and a half minutes to open a hatch of water or else he'll be dead as will his partner Benji.

預告片一開始就看到一場震撼的動作場面，伊森杭特完全沒有穿戴任何呼吸器，一口氣躍入七萬加侖的加壓水箱中，而他只有兩分半鐘的時間可以打開其中一個艙門，才能讓自己以及夥伴班吉免於一死。

俗氣的 cheesy

cheesy 的本意是「（聞或嚐起來）有起司味的」，也做「俗氣的；老套的」解釋，相近於台語所說的「俗」例如：cheesy songs（俗氣的歌曲）cheesy pick-up lines（老套的搭訕詞）。

新聞這樣說

Now, while some disaster movies give us scenes of tense and grim death, others offer cheesy plots and just enough excitement to keep us interested. What kind is *San Andreas*? Bring some crackers to go with that cheese.

有些災難電影帶給觀眾緊張又殘酷的死亡場面，而另一些則以俗氣劇情加上一點刺激場面讓觀眾感興趣，而到底《加州大地震》是哪一種呢? 帶著一些起司薯片（俗氣和起司發音相近）去電影院一探究竟吧。

喜劇演員 comedian

comedian 是指「喜劇演員」，源自 comedy（喜劇）這個字，相關的詞組有 stand-up comedian，意指單人脫口秀（stand-up comedy）的表演者。單人脫口秀類似相聲中的單口相聲，表演者獨自上台說故事或笑話，用以逗樂觀眾。

新聞這樣說

Hollywood actor and comedian Rob Schneider received the Taiwan Tourism Award for helping to promote the nation as an international travel destination. The award was granted to travel agencies and organizations both overseas and in Taiwan that contribute to growth in the number of international tourists to Taiwan.

好萊塢喜劇演員勞勃許奈德得到台灣觀光局所頒發的獎，表揚他為台灣觀光所做的宣傳，此獎項最主要是頒發給幫助台灣旅遊人數增長的海外或國內旅行社以及相關組織。

鬧劇 slapstick

slapstick 最初是指演滑稽戲時，用來毆打對方的一種道具，打人不痛卻能發出很大聲響。slapstick comedy 則是「（以打鬧表現喜感的）鬧劇」，屬於喜劇（comedy）的一種。

新聞這樣說

Inside Out, Pixar's latest animation, is a movie that heals like few others. While it's adventurous and filled with slapstick humor, few movies are able to portray a helpless character so privately and humanely as 11-year-old Riley. Her emotions run amuck in her head as characters unto themselves.

《腦筋急轉彎》是皮克斯最新療癒動畫片，雖然是一部充滿滑稽幽默的冒險電影，卻能刻畫出少數電影才有的角色：無助、內斂、富有同情心，也就是11歲的萊利。各種情緒在她的腦海中恣意橫行，造就了角色本身多變的性格。

巨片 blockbuster

blockbuster 這個字源自二次世界大戰時，一種威力強大到能將敵方陣營摧毀的巨型炸彈，後引申為「賣座電影」，也能用來表示大受歡迎的影集或小說。「熱賣大作」的用法還有：megahit（賣座電影／唱片）、smash hit（廣受歡迎的電視劇／產品）、bestseller（暢銷書／產品）。

新聞這樣說

The Hawaii Tourism Authority representative office in Taiwan has launched a series of promotional events in Taiwan to capitalize on the popularity of the blockbuster movie *Jurassic World*—shot on the Hawaiian island of Kauai.

夏威夷旅遊相關當局在台辦事處舉行一系列活動，目的是宣傳超級巨片《侏儸紀世界》在夏威夷拍攝的場景。

周星馳小紀錄

周星馳在兩岸三地已是電影經典人物，無論是《食神》、《少林足球》、《功夫》等片，皆早已深刻影響華人社會文化。其實，不止全球華人，周星馳的獨特電影喜感及美學也將中華文化以輕鬆的方式傳遞到西方。星爺首次執導的《少林足球》成為他第一部在歐洲大規模上映的電影，該片也打破當年香港華語電影票房紀錄。三年後，周星馳以第二部執導作品《功夫》打破自己記錄，不但在華語世界創下空前成功，更在西班牙、挪威等歐洲數十國創下華語片票房紀錄。

示範對話　(MP3 104)

少林功夫就是好

Beth: Are you waiting in line to see *Kung Fu Hustle*?
你是在排隊看《功夫》嗎？

Tom: No, I'm here for *Ocean's Twelve*.
不，我是來看《長驅直入》。

Beth: You should see *Kung Fu Hustle*. It's hilarious!
你應該看《功夫》。超爆笑！

Tom: How should you know? Aren't you in line to see it?
妳怎麼會知道？妳不是正排隊要看嗎？

Beth: I'm seeing it for the sixth time! It's that funny. Do you know Stephen Chow?
我這是來看第六次了！這部片就是那麼好笑。你認識周星馳嗎？

Tom: Not [1]personally. But I've seen *Shaolin Soccer*. It was pretty good.
本人不認識。不過我看過《少林足球》。還不賴。

Beth: He's the best comedian ever!
他是有史以來最棒的喜劇演員！

229

Tom: Well, he's certainly the most successful Chinese one, right?
嗯，他的確是華人最成功的喜劇演員，對吧？

Beth: He's a good [2]serious actor, too. He won a Best [3]Supporting Actor Golden Horse.
他也很會演嚴肅的角色。他得過金馬獎最佳男配角。

Tom: Wow. That's impressive. I wonder if he'll [4]break through outside of Asia.
哇。那真厲害。我很好奇他是否會在亞洲以外的地區有所突破。

Beth: I wouldn't be surprised. Asian films are popular in the West, right?
我不會感到意外。亞洲電影現在西方很受歡迎，對吧？

Tom: If it's any [5]indication, Zhang Yimou's new movies are more popular there than they are here.
如果這能夠當作一種指標的話，張藝謀新拍的電影在那裡比在這裡更受歡迎。

Beth: You mean [6]Westerners actually liked *House of Flying Daggers*? It was so cheesy!
你是說西方人很喜歡《十面埋伏》？那片很俗！

Tom: I know, I know. I guess we just have different tastes.
我知道，我知道。我想我們西方人品味不同吧。

Beth: Westerners probably don't understand the political [7]undertones of movies like *Hero*.
西方人大概都不了解像《英雄》這類電影隱含的政治意涵。

Tom: Maybe not, but the set pieces were gorgeous.
或許不了解，不過場景設計很讚。

Beth: If you like set pieces, then you should [8]definitely see Stephen Chow's new movie!
如果你喜歡場景設計，那你真的應該看周星馳的新片！

Tom: All right all right, I think you've [9]convinced me.
好啦，好啦，我想妳說服我了。

---

1. personally (adv.) 親自地　　2. serious (a.) 認真的　　3. supporting actor 男配角
4. break through (v.) 突破　　5. indication (n.) 指標，象徵
6. Westerner (n.) 西方人　　7. undertone (n.) 隱藏的意涵，潛在因素
8. definitely (adv.) 絕對，一定　　9. convince (v.) 說服

好用短句 (MP3 105)

談論周星馳
你還可以說

· How dare you give me such good food? What if I never have the chance to eat so well again?

為什麼要讓我吃到一個這麼好的菜？如果我以後吃不到怎麼辦啊？

· Cooking will get you nowhere — the rice bowl is always empty in the end.

燒菜燒得好，要飯要到老。

· Close the door and release the dogs!

關門、放狗！

· Bad students cheat but good students cheat even more — otherwise, how'd they get ahead of the bad students?

壞學生會作弊，好學生更會作弊，不然，怎麼贏過那些壞學生？

· That's not how you kick a ball.

球不是這樣踢滴！

· Go back to Mars. This world is too dangerous for you.

你快點回火星吧，地球很危險滴！

· Shaolin Kung Fu is…the bomb!

少林武功真是——神！

· Shaolin Kung Fu is…OK!

少林武功真的是——行！

· Every second of my life is worth tens of thousands of dollars.

我一秒鐘幾十萬上下！

· Wow, that is classic!

這些簡直是極品呀！

· I really know how to clean. Let me do it.

清潔我拿手滴。讓我來啊！

NOTE

NOTE

NOTE

NOTE

NOTE

NOTE

What's Up 之後說什麼？/ EZ TALK 編輯部作. -- 初版. - 臺北
　市：日月文化, 2015.08
　256 面；14.7*21公分.
　ISBN 978-986-248-485-2（平裝附光碟片）

　1. 英語 2. 會話

805.188　　　　　　　　　　　　　　　　104010699

EZ 叢書館

What's Up 之後說什麼？
學熱門關鍵字，和老外聊時事

作　　　者：EZ TALK編輯部
英文編審：Judd Piggott
執行編輯：楊光平、蔡佳勳、葉瑋玲
特約編輯：楊晴羽、楊智銓、黃書英、蔡瀚儀
視覺設計：Yon 用視覺有限公司
內頁排版：菩薩蠻數位文化有限公司
錄音員：許伯琴、Michael Tennant、Meilee Saccenti

發行人：洪祺祥
總編輯：林慧美
副總編輯：葉瑋玲
法律顧問：建大法律事務所
財務顧問：高威會計師事務所
出　　版：日月文化出版股份有限公司
製　　作：EZ叢書館
地　　址：臺北市信義路三段151號8樓
電　　話：(02)2708-5509
傳　　真：(02)2708-6157
客服信箱：service@heliopolis.com.tw
網　　址：www.heliopolis.com.tw
郵撥帳號：19716071日月文化出版股份有限公司

總經銷：聯合發行股份有限公司
電　　話：(02)2917-8022
傳　　真：(02)2915-7212
印　　刷：中原造像股份有限公司
初　　版：2015 年 08 月
定　　價：300 元
I S B N：978-986-248-485-2

日月文化集團
HELIOPOLIS
CULTURE GROUP

感謝您購買

為提供完整服務與快速資訊，請詳細填寫以下資料，傳真至02-2708-6157或免貼郵票寄回，我們將不定期提供您最新資訊及最新優惠。

1. 姓名： _____ 性別：□男　　□女

2. 生日： ____ 年 ____ 月 ____ 日　職業：

3. 電話：（請務必填寫一種聯絡方式）

　　（日）_____（夜）_____（手機）_____

4. 地址：□□□

5. 電子信箱：_____

6. 您從何處購買此書？□_____縣/市_____書店/量販超商

　　□_____網路書店　□書展　□郵購　□其他

7. 您何時購買此書？　　年　　月　　日

8. 您購買此書的原因：（可複選）

　　□對書的主題有興趣　□作者　□出版社　□工作所需　□生活所需

　　□資訊豐富　□價格合理（若不合理，您覺得合理價格應為 _____）

　　□封面/版面編排　□其他_____

9. 您從何處得知這本書的消息：　□書店　□網路／電子報　□量販超商　□報紙

　　□雜誌　□廣播　□電視　□他人推薦　□其他

10. 您對本書的評價：（1.非常滿意 2.滿意 3.普通 4.不滿意 5.非常不滿意）

　　書名_____內容_____封面設計_____版面編排_____文/譯筆_____

11. 您通常以何種方式購書？□書店　□網路　□傳真訂購　□郵政劃撥　□其他

12. 您最喜歡在何處買書？

　　□_____縣/市_____書店/量販超商　　□網路書店

13. 您希望我們未來出版何種主題的書？_____

14. 您認為本書還須改進的地方？提供我們的建議？

_____

_____

_____

_____

日月文化集團
HELIOPOLIS
CULTURE GROUP

服務專線 02-2708-5509
服務傳真 02-2708-6157
服務信箱 service@heliopolis.com.tw

廣告回函
台灣北區郵政管理局登記證
北台字第 000370 號
免貼郵票

日月文化集團 讀者服務部 收

10658 台北市信義路三段151號8樓

www.heliopolis.com.tw

對折黏貼後，即可直接郵寄

- **日月文化集團之友‧長期獨享購書 79折**

  （折扣後單筆購書金額未滿499元須加付郵資60元），並享有各項專屬活動及特殊優惠！

- **成為日月文化之友的兩個方法**

  ‧完整填寫書後的讀友回函卡，傳真至02-2708-6157或郵寄（免付郵資）至日月文化集團讀者服務部收。

  ‧登入日月文化網路書店www.heliopolis.com.tw完成加入會員。

- **直接購書的方法**

  郵局劃撥帳號：19716071　戶名：日月文化出版股份有限公司

  （請於劃撥單通訊欄註明姓名、地址、聯絡電話、電子郵件、購買明細即可）

大好書屋　寶鼎出版　山岳文化　EZ叢書館　EZ Korea　EZ TALK　EZ Japan